for **Chris** - who made it possible, and much, much better

and **for Michael D.** - who unlocked the door

one

Clare slumped down in the car, letting the breeze slide across her, window to window. The sky was a high, thin blue, bleached by a show-off sun out to celebrate summer.

She had parked in defiance of the white lines in order to catch the wind off the straits below. It kept the car from becoming unbearable.

The summer had been hot, unusually hot so far, and on this long Fourth of July weekend most people had fled the baking streets for an illusion of coolness by the sea.

Not Clare. Not this time. She loved her adopted city. The jumble of frame houses stepped carefully down the hills, their bright colours and eccentric outlines giving it a holiday look every day of the year. San Francisco was a richly painted, angular roller-coaster that bumped the eye towards the flat blue of the water. Without the clatter and hustle of crowds she could take it in at her own speed, and had been doing just that for the past hour.

She knew that by simply opening the car door she would be free to walk down the path to the park below. Heavy old trees waited there to cool her in the pools of shadow that overlapped the grass. She could stroll the paved walks and observe the little boys setting off illicit firecrackers to frighten old ladies and exasperate lovers idling on the grass.

But Clare Randell was doing penance.

She shifted on the seat, reaching up to lift the heavy drape of hair from her neck. Silky fingers of breeze passed lightly across her damp skin.

She'd finally decided *not* to marry Dan. She should be ashamed of herself, of course, because by not marrying him she was probably negating the American Ideal. Or something. The penance was necessary because she felt such a glorious sense of relief at having made her choice at last.

What girl in her right mind could reject the undeniable attractions of Delicious Dan Fowler? His tawny good looks, his promising career, his tender affection? Or his habit of faintly clearing his throat every time he was about to kiss her?

'Me, that's who,' she confided to the steering-wheel. 'Stupid me, who doesn't know a good thing when she sees it.' The steering-wheel had no reply to this.

It was then that she noticed the man. He had just climbed back up the path from the park, and looked flushed with the effort. No wonder, she thought. Wearing a heavy business suit on a day like this. *And* carrying a briefcase. Some people just can't let go, even on a holiday.

She shrugged. It was time she got back to her apartment. There was a lot to do before facing the office in the morning. Her hair to set, papers to collate, and any number of dreadful old movies to watch on television while indulging in fried chicken from a cardboard box. Dan *never* bought cardboard chicken.

But she delayed putting her key in the ignition, and her eyes followed the man as he walked across the parking lot to one of the few other cars that baked like hers on the shimmering asphalt. Where was his fat friend, she wondered? The one he'd arrived with twenty minutes ago? The man's briefcase must have been hastily fastened, because suddenly a sheaf of papers fell out and lay unnoticed behind him on the edge of the grass. She leaned her head out of the window.

'Hey!' she called out. His head jerked around at the unexpected sound of her voice. 'On the path behind you ... You dropped something.' He looked hesitant, confused, not sure of what she had said. Clare put her arm out of the car window and waved, pointing at the ground behind him. He craned his head in the right direction, but obviously did not see what she wanted him to see. Muttering in exasperation she pushed her door open, got out, and began to walk towards him. 'You dropped some *papers* out of your *case*,' she repeated, gesturing again towards the blot of white on the grass. She'd got to within ten feet of him when he suddenly caught sight of the papers. His face cleared and he raised a hand, simultaneously thanking her and waving her back. She stopped.

'Sorry,' he called apologetically, raising his voice over the screech of gulls arguing overhead. 'I c ... c ... couldn't hear what you were saying at first.' He walked back and bent to pick up the wayward papers.

Clare didn't retreat. She was in no hurry to go, nor of a particular mind to stay. He looked a nice enough man – about forty, tall, presentable. Almost familiar, the way all handsome men are, reminding one of film stars, baseball players and other national monuments. Perfect, clean, bland. While she wasn't the type to encourage a casual pick-up, she felt unthreatened by his diffident smile. Now that he'd caught his breath after the climb, she could see his face was actually a little pale for the coast at this time of the year. From outside the state, then, and half his thoughts left back at the hotel in his other suit.

He started to walk on, saw her still standing there, and paused. 'Thanks,' he said. 'They were important – I might have been in real trouble if I'd lost them.' There seemed nothing else to say.

'Sure,' smiled Clare. 'And cheer up ... it'll be a better day tomorrow.' She started back towards her own car, but the sound of his voice came again, and she slowed her steps.

'I ... Do you ... ? C ... c ... can I ... ?'

She turned to look questioningly at him. He was reaching into an inside pocket. Surely he didn't think she expected a tip? How ridiculous. She started to raise her hand in a 'please, don't' gesture when there was a roaring screech of tyres behind her. Startled, they both turned towards the sound.

An old, beaten but obviously cherished Edsel curved into the lot. It was piloted by a World War Six flying ace in a purple sweat-shirt, accompanied by his crew of happy, beer-joyed friends. Gleeful at the sight of the open expanse before them, the driver began to rev the engine and prepare for manoeuvres. Somebody hollered and collapsed on to the rear seat in a tangle of arms and legs as the car leapt forward.

Clare grinned and shrugged her shoulders at the man across the way. The car flashed between them trailing a streamer of giggles. A scowl narrowed his grey eyes and his mouth thinned to match.

'As long as they stay here they won't kill anyone,' she called in an amused tone. 'That's some compensation.'

'I suppose so,' he answered, the sound of his voice lost in another howl of protesting rubber.

'Take care now,' said Clare. She went back to her car, keeping a watchful eye on the Edsel, revving for another pass at eternity. In her rear-view mirror she saw the well-dressed man get into his white convertible and toss his case carelessly on to the back seat. If he isn't careful he'll lose the *rest* of his life's work that way, she thought. Well, it wasn't really any of her business.

It was still Sunday, after all, and she had the rest of it to herself. What price could anyone put on the luxury of being single? The right to do whatever you wanted without asking anyone's permission? Smiling, she turned the car towards the exit, clicking on the radio with one hand. She might have opted for loneliness, but the prospect did not dismay her.

Which was a pity.

two

Monday was impossible.

Nobody in Tandy-Nicholson Advertising Inc was ready to work. They'd all had too much sun, or too much food, or too much sex, or just to much. The entire morning and a good part of the afternoon went by in a meander of compared notes.

In exasperation Clare finally typed a piece of copy herself in order to present it to the account man who managed to find his way to her office only twenty-five minutes late.

And he didn't really want to read it anyway.

By four o'clock she had collapsed back into her chair and resigned from the agency for the day. Her senior art director watched with an amused smile.

'Give up?'

'Absolutely.' She began to push papers together in random stacks, sliding them into her already over-stuffed desk. 'We'll talk about what we're going to do with the Puffies Panda tomorrow.'

He told her what he intended to do with the Puffies Panda and it was not nice. It was *funny* but definitely not nice.

As she waited for the elevator the receptionist called her over to the circular desk at one end of the lobby.

'Did that man get in touch with you? About your car?'

Clare was puzzled. 'My car?'

The girl nodded. 'He came in here about eleven this morning. Said he'd backed into you in the parking lot, and wanted to get the insurance companies on to it. I rang through to your office, but you weren't in. You didn't answer the audio-page, either.'

'I was in the projection studio. He sounds very unusual, they normally can't disappear fast enough. And the funny thing is, I didn't drive today. My car's in for servicing.'

The girl raised her carefully tended eyebrows. 'Well, I took his name and phone number anyway ... Maybe you can call him and straighten it out!'

'It's odd he should come in *here*, you know,' said Clare slowly, taking the piece of paper and staring at it. 'My registration tag carries my home address, not this one. How could he have known which office to come to?'

'Maybe he saw you come into this building and just checked through them all. What he did was, he came up and asked if we had a Clare Randell who worked here.'

'And all because he hit my car? Supposedly hit my car, that is? I can't believe that.'

The girl shrugged. 'Maybe it was just an excuse. He described you as "a pretty little brunette with a good figure". And he asked if he could wait for you in your office. I said I couldn't let him do that, so he left.'

'He was probably selling insurance himself. I'm no hag, but I haven't got any illusions about being the kind of girl men follow with their tongues hanging out.'

'Don't put yourself down.' The receptionist was an ardent feminist, in between boyfriends.

Clare made an amused face of resignation. 'Sure. Thanks anyway ... I expect all will become clear sooner or later.' The elevator bell rang behind her. She got in and asked for Dan's floor.

He was sitting behind his desk, elbows straddling an open magazine. A strand or two of short, blond hair had fallen across his forehead, and his heavy-rimmed glasses had slipped halfway down the arch of his nose. It would be better, she thought fleetingly, if he weren't *so* handsome. If someone had broken his nose or dented an eyebrow somewhere along the line from kindergarten to Andover to Harvard Business. But no one had, and probably no one ever would.

He stood up and came round to kiss her lightly on the mouth. Then again, not so lightly. She smiled him off before he got to a third.

'How was your lonely weekend?' he asked. 'You really should have come with me, we had a great time.'

'I'm sure you did. I hope you explained to your parents ...'

'That you were at death's door with a virus, just the way you told me. I'm nothing if not obedient. And you?' He watched her moodily circling the room. She shrugged, and flicked off his air-conditioner.

'You'll get pneumonia one of these days,' she warned him.

'I'm looking forward to it, I'll sue TN for every penny they've got.'

She inspected the magazine he had been reading. The only centrefold it featured was of a combine harvester. Two of his accounts were heavily agricultural, but she always found it difficult to imagine him with straw in his hair.

'Have you decided, Clare?'

'Yes.'

'And?'

'Dan ... I just ...' She met his eyes reluctantly, then rushed ahead with it.

'Oh, for goodness' sake, Dan. I just don't want to get married, not at all, not to anyone. If I did *want* to get married, I'm sure I'd grab you without a second's hesitation, but ...'

'But you've hesitated.'

'Yes.' What else could she say?

'Don't make such a big thing of it, Clare. I understand you

value your independence and all that.' He kept his voice warmly sincere. 'Tell you what ... why don't we just forget the question ever came up? Go on as we have been ... that's simple enough.'

'Too simple. You'll keep trying to convince me I'm wrong.'

'Of course I will. But I promise not to push it too hard.'

She was too weary to argue. It had been a highly unsatisfactory day all round and what did it matter, anyway? Would she be proving anything by arguing? She would play the hypocrisy game with him, that's what he wanted. It was a habit. 'We're supposed to be meeting the Whites for a drink at Clancy's aren't we?'

'Yes, at six. Dinner afterwards ... then—'

'I can't make it.' She made a quick, conciliatory gesture, and he closed his mouth.' I meant, I can't make it by six. I have to go down to the Hall of Justice ... in fact, I'm going to be late there as it is.' She began to move towards the door, all bustle and earnest endeavour.

'Traffic tickets?'

'No, idiot. That San-Ex Spray thing. Someone has complained to the public prosecutor or something ... I've been elected as a suitably innocuous representative from TN for preliminary discussions on the copy claims. If I can't make Clancy's ... Where are we going for dinner?'

He told her. She managed to get out of the office without kissing him goodbye, resolving to continue their disarmament talks later. Downstairs she stopped to buy a paper, reading the headlines before she hailed a taxi. Glancing through the news didn't take long ... there had been the usual mayhem over the holiday weekend, and indignant editorial reaction was setting in – traffic deaths up, some holiday murders, a lot of political chest-thumping over the land of the spree and the home of the rave. She left the paper in the cab and entered the Hall of Justice to do battle for San-Ex without much conviction.

As it turned out, she took longer and cared more about it than she had expected. She missed the drink at Clancy's and had to catch a cab to the restaurant still seething with indignation and a sense of frustration at the obstinacy of the law.

13

In her rush to meet Dan and the Whites she didn't notice the man following her.

She wouldn't have recognized him, anyway.

He had changed considerably.

three

Tuesday was better.

Having talked over the best of the weekend the day before, the staff at TN now seemed ready to work. The long holiday and the useless Monday had brought an inevitable pile-up of work, but suddenly everyone was very enthusiastic. It was nearly six-thirty when Clare finally emerged from the building. The day had been long and sticky, even with the air-conditioning, and towards the end of the afternoon dedication had begun to look remarkably like bad temper.

The worst of the rush-hour was over. There were a few cabs free, but they all seemed to be concentrated in the centre of the street, determined to ignore possible fares on the kerb. With a sharp and not very complimentary thought for the garage where her car was still awaiting a vital replacement part to be shipped from LA, Clare began the dry-fly technique for catching cabs, moving down the kerb sideways.

Her fellow pedestrians had enough frazzle left in them to snarl at each other, and a man banged into her without even a muttered apology. She raised her arm for the tenth time and finally managed to attract a cabby's attention. He responded with a lazy wave and glanced behind him for clearance, his amber signal flicking on and off. Realizing he was going to have to pull across gradually, she resumed her walk along the kerb. As she did so she received a sudden double blow, one from a man dodging in front of her to catch another taxi, and a second from the left.

'Excuse *me*!' she shouted sarcastically after the first man, then whirled to confront the second. There was no one anywhere near her on that side – he must have been running, she decided. He'd hurt her, too. She started to rub her aching left arm, but just then the taxi managed to gain the kerb and she ran to get in before someone else could.

Crashing into the back seat, she pulled the door shut after her and let out a heartfelt 'Whew.' The cab driver grinned at her in the mirror.

'Everybody's got someplace more important to go than where they is,' he observed.

'Right ... and they don't care who they knock down on the way, either,' she agreed, adding her address. He pulled his flag and slid out into the traffic.

Now that she was sitting down she actually felt a little queasy from all the rush and fuss of the day. The heavy, warm air of the cab enclosed her, and the jerking motion through the web of traffic soon began to be unpleasant. Leaning forward to open a window, she felt the strap of her shoulderbag pull against her arm, causing a stab of pain. That damn idiot who bumped into me must have been carrying something, she thought. Something hard like a book or box. She reached up to rub the bruise.

It was more than a bruise. It was wet and sticky. She let the strap of her handbag slide down and stared incredulously at her arm.

'Oh my god,' she moaned, a wave of sweaty nausea sweeping over her as she stared down at blood welling steadily from a neat, dark hole in her flesh.

'What's the matter, forget something?'

'I've been shot,' she managed to say. 'Somebody shot me back there in the street.'

The brakes came on, hard, throwing her forward. 'What?'

'I'm sorry ... there's a hole in my arm,' she explained, feeling idiotic. 'I'm bleeding all over your cab.'

'Jesus.' He turned round in his seat then, ignoring the crescendo of horns behind them. He reached into his back pocket and brought out a handkerchief, then opened his door and hers, climbing in beside her. 'Take it easy, lady, you haven't got anything busted or you would have known about it right away. That's only what they call a flesh wound, see? right through ... whoops, put your head down on your knees, Sure is bleeding like hell. Lean forward, lemme see. Yeah, you'll be OK.' He was busy with the handkerchief, tying it very tightly around her arm. 'Now, you ain't gonna be sick all over my nice new cab, are you?'

Clare shook her head against her knees, the shedding grey pile of new carpet swimming before her eyes. The driver's heavy black shoes looked enormous next to her narrow yellow sling-backs.

'All right, what's the trouble?' It was a heavy voice, weary and not very amused. The cabby turned and looked over his shoulder.

'Man, am I glad to see *you* for once. This lady here's been shot in the arm.'

The uniformed cop leaned into the back seat of the cab, forcing the driver to press himself back into the corner.

'Lady? That true?'

'There's a hole in my arm,' Clare said again, aware of how odd it sounded. 'It's bleeding,' she added informatively.

'Goddamn, so there is.' The big cop backed out and waved to his partner in the black and white police car that had pulled in ahead of the stationary cab. The other cop opened his door and got out, moving slowly towards them. The cabby stayed beside Clare, whistling between his teeth.

'Gonna be OK now, lady. Just relax, OK?'

The two officers were conferring. The first one leaned down again. 'Where did it happen?' The cabby told him where he'd picked Clare up. 'And do you know who did it miss? Was it somebody you knew, somebody who had it in for you?'

'No ... I didn't even *realize* I'd been shot. I thought somebody bumped into me carrying a box or something ... I didn't even *hear* anything like a shot ...'

The weary expression blinked out of the cop's eyes. 'You mean nobody was near you ... you didn't see a gun, hear a backfire, anything like that?'

'She was just runnin' along the kerb, man. Wavin' for me, you know?' the cabby put in. 'Just runnin' along like anybody.'

'Christ.' The cop turned and ran towards his car, reaching in for the radio as soon as the door was open. 'This is Zebra Five Charlie, possible sniper at the corner of Cleary and Buchanan. One victim, flesh wound only. Acknowledge.'

The radio crackled in his hand. 'Thank you, Zebra Five Charlie. Acknowledge your report Code Two-one-seven, corner Cleary-Buchanan. What is your present location?'

'Cleary and Polk.'

Clare was aware of a second uniformed officer, younger than the first, replacing the cabby beside her. The seat shifted, making her feel slightly seasick.

'Can I take a look, miss?' His voice was gentle, his hands light and quick on the cabby's handkerchief, which was now sodden with blood and useless. She had straightened up and laid her head back on the seat, staring at the light in the middle of the roof. There was a chip out of the transparent plastic cover, and one of the screws was missing.

'It's not too bad, really.'

'That's what the cabby said,' she told him, her own voice sounding far away. 'But it hurts.'

'Sure it does. I guess it hurts a lot. Your being fine about it, just fine.' There was a trace of some southern state entwined in his words.

Outside the cabby was arguing with the first cop, who'd left his radio and was now trying to direct traffic around the two stationary cars. The cabby shifted from one foot to the other, kicking at a torn piece of newspaper.

The young cop's voice glided over the cabby's whine. 'You take it easy, there, Miss ... ?'

'Randell, Clare Randell.'

'Right, Miss Randell. You just relax. We'll have an ambulance here in no time. Take you ourselves, but ... if it *is* a sniper back there, they'll need every unit they can get. You understand?'

'Certainly. You mean he might kill the next person.' Clare tried to clear her vision. The young cop had removed his cap. His face was a pale peach balloon with ears that kept trying to drift up through the roof of the cab. The balloon spoke again.

'Yes, I'm afraid so. It's a bad scene for everyone ...'

In the distance there was a ragged chorus of sirens. Their whoops and moans lifted protest banners between the glass and concrete pillars of the community.

four

'Could be any one of those three.'

Malchek looked across the street and up at the buildings, neutral and anonymous, their blank eyes winking back at the dropping sun, the top windows faintly bloodshot with cloud reflections.

'Probably the twelve,' he told Gonzales. 'Bad distance, but nobody overlooks it. Depends if he was planning to kill or just scare. You're *sure* there haven't been any more reports of hits?'

Gonzales shook his head. 'Two stores called in with shattered plate-glass windows, somebody had a tyre ripped. But no other hits, no.' He glanced around the cleared intersection. They had rolled on a Code 3000 ten vital minutes ago. Now police cars blocked all four approaches and the two alleys halfway up. Further down each street cars were being rerouted. Pedestrian traffic, ditto. In the distance crowds were milling and straining against the wooden blockade saw-horses, watching, wondering, shading their eyes to see better. A few curious faces peered down through office windows. He reached for the bull horn.

'Get back from the windows. Get back from the windows. This is the police, get back from the windows. You could be in danger.' He lowered the horn, releasing the button, and his normal voice was startling in its soft contrast. 'Not that any of them will pay the least damn bit of attention.'

'Unless he starts potting them.'

'Yeah.' He dropped the horn into the back of the car. 'Want to go on up now?'

'Why not? I didn't come to watch you sing through your megaphone.'

Malchek unbuttoned his coat and started to run across the street. Suddenly he seemed to remember the rifle he was carrying, and stopped. Coming back a few steps he tossed it to Gonzales.

'Don't you want this?' Gonzales asked, surprised.

Malchek shrugged. 'From here it's like shooting up from the bottom of a well. If I fired, the bullet would probably reach its meridian, fall back and hit me in the eye. Up there the thirty-eight will be enough.'

'You're *sure* he's up there, not on the other two?' He tossed the rifle into the back seat of the car alongside the horn and joined the younger man.

Malchek shrugged again. 'Seems likely. Late afternoon, people get bored, look out of windows. If he'd been shooting from the six or nine somebody would have seen him before this.'

They were crossing the empty lobby towards the elevators. A uniformed patrolman stood beside one with its doors open. None of the other elevators was functional, their controls now locked from the panel. The building manager peered out at them from behind the suntan-oil display in the lobby drugstore window. He looked faintly ashamed.

Gonzales pushed the button marked twelve, and the doors closed over the manager's personal sense of violation. The floor pressed against their shoes, and the numbers in the panel over the door began to flicker.

'What about an office? He could be in an office, couldn't he?' Gonzales persisted.

'Sure he could. But the manager said there were no vacant offices in the building right now. And none of the johns has an outside window, they all face on to the inner shaft.'

'But it was nearly six-thirty. A lot of the offices would be completely deserted.'

'Let's just check the roofs first, OK?' Malchek seemed bored, and it was Gonzales's turn to shrug.

'You're the expert.'

'Nobody's an expert on these bastards.'

Gonzales glanced at him out of the corner of his eye. He had worked with Malchek for five years now and he still did not understand what motivated him in these situations. He knew what it said on the record – Malchek specialized in snipers and hitmen. And each time they had sniper trouble, it was usually Malchek who advised them on how to find the guy, how to pin him down, bring him down. Gonzales liked to see an expert at work. But he preferred Malchek on his ordinary days.

The elevator doors grated back as the cage jerked to a stop, and they stepped out into the hall. A uniformed patrolman was at the far end next to a door succinctly marked 'Roof'. They went towards him, their steps echoing off the glass in the doors, the linoleum, the ice-cube-tray light-fixtures overhead.

'Unlocked?' Gonzales asked when they were about twenty feet away. The patrolman nodded, his voice hesitant.

'Yes, sir. Are you going up? My orders were not to.' He had clearly yearned to go, it was written all over him. 'Unless I heard more shooting, they said.'

'That's right. My orders.' Malchek yawned. The patrolman stared at him, not sure of what he'd seen. Malchek caught the look and grinned. 'Stress reaction. Body demands an increase in oxygen to promote the production of adrenalin. Look it up. I'm not falling asleep on you.'

'No, sir.' The patrolman seemed unconvinced.

Malchek reached under his jacket, drew his .38 from the holster, and Gonzales copied. Turning the knob as slowly and soundlessly as possible, Malchek eased the door open a few inches, looking up the stairway. It was steep and it was dark. At the top a thread of light outlined the closed second door to the roof with striated clarity. The stairwell itself was empty. Just concrete steps gritty with soot.

Malchek went up first, moving fast to a halt beside the door as Gonzales waited below. Easing the second door an inch at a time, Malchek let in the light of the late sun, bathing his face and the top of the steps in a bloody glow. When nothing happened, he stepped up on to the cracked and blistered asphalt of the roof itself. After another second's hesitation he stepped round the edge of the door.

Still nothing.

Gonzales followed him up, catching the door as Malchek let it go. The roof stretched away on all sides. Immediately beside the door was the housing for the air-conditioning system and water tanks. The boxy enclosure of the elevator mechanism cast its shadow halfway to the rear parapet.

Cautiously, Malchek went forward along the wall of the structure, while Gonzales closed the door quietly and isolated himself between the top of the stairwell and the fabric of the housing itself. The massive aluminium framework of the building's TV aerial stood just beyond the end of the wall, and as Gonzales ducked under it the reaching metal fingers caught his hat and dropped it behind him. Coming carefully round the corner, he saw Malchek already standing at the forward edge of the roof, looking over. Gonzales grunted in a mixture of relief and disappointment, holstered his gun and joined him.

'Wrong building?'

Malchek glanced at him expressionlessly. 'Nope, just too slow.' A heap of brass cartridges was half-hidden under a crumpled paper bag. 'We didn't get *any* other reports of hits? Just the property damage?' he asked again, leaning forward to squint at the empty streets below and the up-tilted faces of the uniformed men watching.

'None. The minor property damage reports started coming in fast, just after the woman was hit. Only the one woman, hit in the arm while running for a cab, they said.'

'Funny. What kind of a woman?'

'Kind of a woman?'

'Yeah, old, young, fat, thin, housewife, shopper, what?'

'Youngish, good-looking, they said. Office worker.'

Malchek nodded as if coming to a decision. 'You can tell them they might as well open things up down there, he's long gone.'

'You figure?'

'I figure.' Malchek hunkered down on his heels and prised with his gun barrel at the edges of the paper bag, pulling it apart to look inside. Wax paper, a double crust of whole-wheat sandwich. He handled it gingerly. They got good prints from sweat and skin-oils on paper these days. He was reaching for the cartridges when his hand froze.

As Gonzales came back from shouting instructions down to the patrolman waiting at the foot of the stairway, he heard Malchek cursing. 'What is it?'

Malchek pointed with the gun, reaching inside his jacket at the same time. A faint series of white streaks patterned the asphalt and the bottom edge of the concrete parapet. One, thicker than the rest, still had a wet look in the shadow. He dabbed at it with the corner of a handkerchief, sniffed, wrinkled his nose. Standing up slowly, he wrapped the cloth in on itself. 'Couldn't stand the excitement of it all,' he said in disgust, and shoved the handkerchief into his jacket pocket, then holstered his gun. He turned and walked away. Gonzales stood looking down at the white marks for a moment, then followed him.

'I'll tell the lab to send someone up,' he commented as they clattered down the stairs. 'There might be some saliva on the bread, too. We know one thing, anyway. It wasn't a jealous *wife.*'

Clare was trying to flex her fingers one by one when the two men knocked and entered her spartan hospital room. She looked up warily.

'Miss Randell?' the older one asked, smiling encouragingly and holding out some identification with his picture on it and a gold badge pinned to the leather below. 'I'm Lieutenant Gonzales of the San Francisco Police Department. This is Lieutenant Malchek.' The younger one nodded without smiling. 'We've come to ask you about the shooting, if you feel up to giving us a few minutes?'

'Of course, but I don't know what I could tell you, really.'

'I thought they said you were shot in the arm?' Malchek spoke abruptly from the bottom of the bed where he stood regarding her stonily.

'I was.' She moved her arm in its sling slightly.

'What happened to your head?'

Clare started to blush, feeling suddenly defensive under his steady, unsmiling gaze. 'I'm ashamed to say I passed out downstairs after they gave me a tetanus injection. I crashed into a tray of instruments on the way down. They were going to send me home up to that point ... but now I have to stay in overnight for observation.' She reached up to touch the edge of the bandage that encircled her forehead. 'The doctor said I'll probably have a couple of black eyes too ... just to make things interesting.' She appealed to the older man, who seemed sympathetic. 'I feel like an absolute fool.'

'Perfectly understandable reaction, Miss Randell. People have fainted over far less than being shot. Nothing to be ashamed of.'

'Well, I thought I was a little more grown up than that.' The younger cop looked as though he agreed with her. 'Anyway,' she continued, ignoring his superior expression, 'I'll tell you whatever I can.'

'The first question is pretty straightforward.' Gonzales got out a notebook and pen. 'Do you know of anyone who would like to kill you?'

'No one.'

'I understand you work in the building outside which you were shot ... what do you do there? Secretary?'

'No. I'm a copy group head with Tandy-Nicholson Advertising.'

'Really? That's a pretty important job, isn't it?'

The younger one was looking out of the window, shifting from one side to the other as if trying to see something outside. Clare wondered if he was even listening. She turned her attention back to Gonzales. His face was nicer, with eyes like a grandfather spaniel's. Olive-skinned and overweight, with heavy eyebrows and dark hair cut short behind a bald semicircle.

'I don't know how you'd grade it. I have a fair amount of authority, earn a respectable salary, and I think I'm pretty good at it. They haven't fired me, anyway ... I've been with them eight years.'

'But I pick up Middle West in your accent, don't I? You haven't been out *here* eight years?'

Now the younger one ... Malchek, that was it ... was looking through the pile of copy-folders the nurse had put on top of the table, along with the newspaper Clare had been carrying. He was holding up a yellow sheet of rough copy, reading.

'I was born in Connorsville, Indiana. Went to Northwestern University, worked for TN in New York first, then transferred out here about six years ago.' She paused. 'You won't find any clues in there unless you suspect Mother Hardy and her frozen apple pies.' This last was directed at Malchek's back. He turned and looked at her. Again she felt uncomfortable, but stared steadily back. He had a high-planed face, a long, straight nose, level green eyes. Lots of light-brown hair worn just over his collar. Full lower lip, thin, arched upper one, not a smile anywhere. Just that icy arrogance.

'Advertising is a pretty cut-throat business,' he observed. His voice was light, with a metallic base. 'They can get very nasty over some of those big accounts, I hear. Piracy, isn't that what you call it?'

'Sometimes. But we have special sneak troops to take care of that. I only write the words. None of them has been worth shooting anyone over.'

His eyes narrowed at her sarcastic tone. 'Not even ... "Deep Dish Delightful" ... ?' He managed to curl the words round the edges.

'Not even that. And that wasn't mine, by the way. In case *you* feel like shooting me for it, I mean.' She tried to smile.

He shrugged and went back to the window. Really, Clare thought, it's no wonder the police get such a bad reputation if that's an example of their manners.

Lieutenant Gonzales cleared his throat beside her. 'You have a regular boyfriend, Miss Randell?'

'Is that relevant?'

'It could be. People get very uptight about things like being turned down, say. You turned anybody down lately?'

Clare stared at him. Dan? Impossible.

'I haven't ... turned anyone down, as you put it. I *have* been dating one man pretty regularly for a couple of years now ... we're more or less engaged.'

'What does "more or less" mean?' Malchek's voice came over his shoulder.

'It means we're perfectly happy to go on as we are without benefit of clergy, I suppose,' she offered.

'You live together?'

'No.'

He turned to look at her finally. 'A platonic relationship?'

'No.'

'Miss Randell.' Gonzales's voice brought her head round from the thin figure at the window.

'Sorry, Lieutenant Gonzales. But I really don't think *Dan* wants to kill me.'

'Dan ... that's your fiancé?' She could see Gonzales was the kind of man who preferred conventional categories. A nice man, round, fleshy, with a soft face and a soft manner. His chocolate-brown eyes were kind, understanding. Suddenly she began to chuckle, startling him.

'What is it?'

'You ... him ... I just realized.'

'Realized what?' This question came from Malchek. She did not look at him but concentrated on Gonzales.

'You're playing out the role-game the police are famous for ... nice cop, nasty cop. What am I supposed to confess to? Shooting myself or just scratching dirty words on the walls of the ladies' toilet?' She continued to chuckle, and Gonzales grinned.

'Is that what it seemed like? Really? How about that, Mike, the lady thinks we're manipulating her.'

'How about that?' Malchek's voice was toneless.

'Honestly, Miss Randell, we weren't.' Gonzales's smile coasted to a stop. 'And if it sounded like that, I'm sorry. Fact is, Mike can't help sounding rude, he's simply a natural-born hard-nose. Kicks old ladies in the street, you know the kind of thing. Famous for it, aren't you, kid?'

'Famous.'

Gonzales patted her hand in fatherly commendation for her insight. 'You may be right, though, you know. Some of us might just slip into it out of habit, now and again. But Mike and I don't normally work together, see? He's just along for the ride this time. Because of the sniper angle.'

'Oh, I see. Sorry.' Clare shifted in the bed. The painkiller the doctor had given her was beginning to wear off, and her arm was throbbing like a rotten tooth. 'Is there anything else you want to know?'

'Not for the moment. You told the uniformed officers that you didn't see or hear anything?'

Clare described the events leading up to the shooting. He nodded finally, and closed his notebook. 'Well, so far as I'm concerned, that's it. You don't seem like the kind of person anyone would want to kill.'

'I'm not sure how to take that. You mean I'm kind of ... neutral?'

'No, he doesn't mean that, Miss Randell.' Malchek came away from the window and round the side of the bed to stand near Gonzales. 'The fact is, we think you probably just got unlucky.'

'I see. Just ... unlucky?'

'That's right. We found quite a few empty cartridge-cases on the roof where the sniper was located. We've had no other reports of injury – just property damage. He was probably some nut shooting for fun who just happened to hit you.'

'For *fun*?'

He shrugged. 'It happens. The psychologists tell us it's a sexual thing, a power thing. A guy goes unstable, gets hold of a rifle and heads for some high spot. *Got* to be up high. He sits there, pretending to take out his hate on the unsuspecting ants below. The operative word is "pretending". Real mass killers really kill ... and we've had a few. But most of them aren't interested in reality ... they just like the feeling of being *able* to do it without actually doing it.'

'But ... what makes you think he was one of those?'

'We found a semen stain near the cartridges. He was having a really great time up there on his own, aiming the gun and ... getting his satisfaction. Then he hits you. You're young, good-looking ... I guess you gave him a little extra charge, made his trigger finger pull just a little too tight.'

'Thanks a *lot*.'

Malchek continued in a clinical voice. 'Actually wounding you was probably too real for him ... he took off right away.

26

We'll pull in some of the guys in our Creep File ... we might get lucky. But I doubt it.'

'And you think it's as simple as that?'

'Don't you? The alternative is to assume someone is trying to kill *you*, you specifically, that is, and you're not buying that. We've had cases like this before, believe me.'

She shivered in distaste. 'Ick ... it makes me feel ...'

'Shouldn't make you feel anything but glad to be alive,' Gonzales put in briskly, and stood up. 'Now you get some rest. Has anyone notified your fiancé for you?'

'I didn't ask ... I was just going to when you came.'

'Well, you do that. Get him down here to give you a little sympathy, it will do you good. We're sorry this had to happen to you ... I suppose you could say it's our fault, not protecting the public and all that.'

She shook her head. 'You can't turn off the world, lieutenant. There's too many of us and not enough of you. But as far as getting shot goes ... I'm sorry, too. It *hurts*.'

He laughed. 'I know. I've been there myself.'

Malchek was already waiting impatiently at the door. With a final smile and a wave Gonzales joined him and they went out. His smile faded fast.

'You buy all that?' he asked Malchek. 'She just got it by accident?'

'It's probably true.'

Gonzales shook his head. 'There was something ... when I asked about turning somebody down. Something behind her eyes ... she thought of her boyfriend right away, if you ask me.'

'He wouldn't do it from a distance.'

Gonzales turned to look at him as they waited for the elevator. 'What do you mean?'

'She's the kind of girl ... you'd want her to *know* you were shooting her.'

five

The tall man had been watching the emergency entrance for over two hours in the fading evening light. He looked at his watch again. There was not much time left, his flight was leaving at eleven and he still had to collect the two Vuitton suitcases from the hotel.

He had seen her walk in from the ambulance, so she was not that badly hurt. Unfortunately. If only that big, fat-faced bastard hadn't cannoned into her on the kerb just as he'd pulled the trigger, she would be out of his hair by now.

It would not matter half a damn if only he were not due in Buenos Aires tomorrow before two o'clock. The ceremony was set for four and, although he knew that he could count on the usual half-hour of delay and confusion that attended any civic ceremony, he needed time to set up. With a muttered curse he got out of the car and went across the street into the shadowy entrance and the antiseptic air beyond.

The receptionist was not as helpful as she wanted to be.

'I'm sorry, I just came on duty an hour ago. I'll see if anyone else knows. Wait here a minute.' She smiled at him and came out from behind the horse-shoe desk, giving her hips an extra hitch.

After a few minutes she returned, giving him the full benefit of her approach down the squared linoleum.

'Apparently she's being held overnight for observation. There was some complication or other. Would you like me to find out her room number?'

'I'd appreciate it.' She made the call and turned to him with her hand over the receiver.

'She's on the fourth floor, but the floor supervisor says she has some visitors at the moment. The police, apparently. Shall I say you're coming up?'

He shook his head regretfully. 'No, never mind. I have a plane to catch, unfortunately. I'll just call her tomorrow. As long as I know she's OK. Thanks for your help.'

'That's what I'm here for ... to help.' The smile was more

than polite. Some other time, lady, he thought, and left the building.

Outside he made a U-turn and chanced the speed as he raced back to the hotel. Time was short, but the girl was a problem he could not leave unsettled.

He was not sure he had enough with him, because the job he had come to do hadn't required that kind of supplies. Still, there was probably enough to do this *and* the job in Buenos Aires. He could buy more wire down there if he had to, although it would not be up to his usual standard.

If Clare Randell was going to be in hospital overnight her apartment would be empty. Looking at his watch again as he left the hotel lobby, he saw the margin was even more narrow than he had thought. It was good he'd looked over the apartment the day before. Even though he had opted for the downtown play, the things he had noticed then would be useful now.

It wasn't far to the apartment house, and he parked his car under a sapling that was struggling to establish itself in the grass between sidewalk and kerb. It only took a minute to round the corner and walk down the ramp to the parking area under her building. Looking down the line of cars he noticed that her Cougar was back in its slot. It hadn't been there yesterday. He hesitated, wondering if the car would be better.

Two things made the decision for him.

Another car came down the ramp just as the elevator doors opened in front of him.

And he suddenly realized that she would not be doing much driving with her arm in a sling.

The apartment door opened to him easily enough. The entry hall was narrow, and empty of decoration other than a line of pen and ink sketches he would have liked to linger over ... the technique looked familiar.

He continued to the living-room and glanced around. Big place. Too big, really, for what he intended. But he approved of the white walls, the bronze shag carpet, and the smoked-glass table. It sat under a big window that framed a darkening turquoise sky and silhouetted hills already scattered with chains of twinkling lights.

It only took him a few minutes to find a china bowl the right size ...

When he had finished he brushed the knees of his tweed trousers and put the plug back in. He still had enough time to make the airport if he drove fast. But he would have to watch the mirror.

The pigs had just changed shift, and fresh pairs would be patrolling the freeways. They would just love to start filling their books early, before the drunks came out to play.

six

Clare found it difficult to get to sleep that night. Her arm hurt. Her head hurt. Her ego hurt.

She had not liked the things Malchek had told her – that a pervert had shot her in a moment of sexual high. Because she was young and good-looking, he said. It made her feel dirty, as if she had actually been raped.

And *his* attitude hadn't helped, either. He'd looked at her as if it were all her fault. The old story, blame the victim. But what had she done except run for a taxi?

And then Dan had arrived, surrounding her with flowers and fuss, clucking, stroking and kissing her as if she were a two-year-old.

She shifted irritably in the bed, jerking the sheet smooth impatiently. At least one other person agreed with that assessment. That cop.

The ridiculous thing was that when we had walked into the room she'd liked the look of him. The economical way he moved, the taut way he held himself together. There had been laughter lines around his eyes, but it was fairly obvious they hadn't been reinforced lately. I wonder why he was so angry? Maybe he has an ulcer, she decided, and banished his image from the room. She slid further down in the bed, settling her strapped arm as comfortably as she could. Twenty minutes later she was asleep. No dreams of angry cops or possessive boyfriends or perverts with ejaculatory rifles disturbed her. She slept in a deep trough of reaction, consciousness only returning with the morning and the salty-sweet smell of bacon.

The doctor come in at ten, peered into her eyes with a light, prodded her forearm with a pin and told her to get the hell out of there, they needed the bed.

Dan arrived around eleven-thirty, all jolly and encouraging. His opinion was that she should go back to the office to get into the distracting hassle of work as soon as possible. Getting back on the horse, he called it.

She disagreed. Repeatedly. In the end he gave up and took her back to her apartment. She told him she needed to reinforce her identity before facing the office – after all, she had never even made it home the night before. She needed fresh underthings, didn't she? In fact, she just wanted to be left alone with a box of cardboard chicken, a trashy novel and as little reality as possible. Dan would hardly accept *that* as therapy.

Which only proves how little he really knows about me, she realized as they walked down the carpeted hall towards her apartment door.

'I'll just come in and get you settled, then,' he insisted, paying no attention to her protests.

'I never saw a sheepdog in glasses before,' she told him sharply, going into the living-room and letting her home settle around her. The noon sun still had enough slant to make a puddle on the carpet, and washed brightly up one side of the paisley-covered chesterfield. The water of the bay in the distance was a deep blue today, and a heat haze quivered over the hills beyond.

'I think you should have some lunch,' he said, rubbing his hands together purposefully, a gesture that always annoyed her. 'I'm not going to leave you alone *and* starving.'

'Really, Dan, I'm not hungry,' she lied.

'You're always hungry, and you know it. Just go and change into something luxurious. I'll show you how to handle a real role reversal and make you a salad.'

'I don't *want* a salad,' she shouted from the bedroom. She wanted a big, drippy pizza and a gallon of coffee ice-cream.

Salads were for sophisticated people who were sensible about their diets. She wanted to let something dribble down her chin.

'Well, French toast, then ... or I'm fantastically good at –'

She never found out what his other speciality was.

An obscenely brief thunderclap drove both Dan Fowler and the contents of the refrigerator across the kitchen and sieved them halfway through the wrought-iron grille-work of the breakfast-bar before it gave way and fell outwards. Protected from the full force of the blast by the framework of the bed-room door, Clare was still thrown back violently on to the bed itself, sliding off seconds later on to the shaggy white carpet.

The sound of breaking glass, falling objects and splintering wood seemed to go on for some time. Then the first lick of tentative flames curled round the edge of the sitting-room carpet, darkening the bronze fibres to black, and singeing frayed pieces of a linen and polyester jacket that had once belonged to a sheepdog in glasses. Smoke and the sweet stink of plastic explosive billowed through the apartment, obscuring the expensive view, permeating every corner, sinking deep into books, upholstery, clothing, curtains.

Through the sound of running feet, through the gasping chorale of voices from the cluster of people at the unhinged hall door, through the whooping, dragon-slayer screams of the fire engines and the police cars, Clare lay unconscious.

It was the only mercy shown her on that particular day.

seven

Gonzales did not get the report of an explosion in Clare Randell's apartment until nearly five that afternoon. He had spent the morning testifying on an existing case and the hours after his snatched lunch interviewing a few culls from the Creep File. The conversations were unproductive.

Malchek had not taken part in the interviews. He had another case on the boil and had only come along with Gonzales the previous day because of the sniper angle. His office was still empty when Gonzales finally came up from the interview rooms, damp with sweat and distaste. The glass wall between their offices at the edge of the big duty-room was nearly obscured by taped-on 'Wanted' notices, vacation schedules, charts and posters on crime prevention – as if they needed reminding. But Gonzales could see the clutter on Malchek's desk had not changed its pattern all day – which meant he'd been on the street with his men and *not* checking off reports. Like Gonzales, he preferred action to six-layer paper work. Like most cops, for that matter.

Gonzales had not had a chance to finish his cup of coffee when Grogan came in. Normally the report would have circulated through in the captain's morning read-out. Fowler's death had been tagged as a separate case initially and given to Grogan and Johnson, who had been catching at the time. Grogan was good on names.

'Isn't this the girl you and Mike talked to yesterday about that freak sniper thing?' he said, leaning in at the door and handing his preliminary report to Gonzales.

'Well, I'll be damned,' Gonzales breathed as his eyes raced over the sparse details. 'Mike was *wrong*. Was she hurt ... the Randell girl?'

'Not bad, I don't think. She's back in the hospital, though. The other one ... we're still scraping him off the walls.'

'Any make?'

'Guy name of Fowler apparently, Dan Fowler. His wallet was just lying open on the coffee table, can you beat that? Blown out of his pocket and dropped there nice as you please. Open at his membership in the Downtown Athletic. Guess *he* won't be playing any more handball.'

'Funny.' Gonzales didn't smile. 'Where's Mike today?'

'Out chasing a lead on that Dondero killing. He's convinced it's a reprisal hit, not a felony homicide. Sometimes I think he's got hitmen on the brain.'

'It is his speciality.'

'Sure, but every punk who buys out isn't necessarily a contract, is he? I mean ... remember two months ago – Funky

Donaghan was brought down by his old lady, it turns out, because he'd been screwing the butcher's wife. That was no contract hit, was it? But *he* was Organization.'

'Organization, yeah ... But not at Dondero's level.'

Grogan pursed his lips and tilted his head. 'Maybe not, but Dondero wasn't no Legs Diamond, either.'

'Well, neither is Clare Randell. But somebody is obviously trying to kill *her*.'

'Maybe *she's* been sleeping with the butcher?' Grogan offered.

'Maybe. Will you tell Mike if he comes in? About the Randell girl, I mean.' Gonzales reached for his hat and went past Grogan into the duty-room.

'So you're taking Fowler away from Johnson and me?' Grogan followed him as far as the water-cooler. Gonzales turned but kept walking, backwards, towards the hall.

'You never had it. It's part of the Randell thing. But thanks for the preliminary work, I'll do the same for you sometime.'

'Listen, you can have it. I don't like bombs.'

Gonzales raised an eyebrow. 'You feeling sensitive these days?'

Grogan scowled. 'I'm feeling Irish these days.'

Gonzales paused. 'Oh, yeah. Well, I can always send you over to Juvenile for a while.'

'For what? I already got six of my own. If I understood *them* I'd be happy. Don't give me *strangers*, for crying out loud.'

Gonzales left him at the water-cooler, a man beset by the world and a leaking paper cup.

Someone in the hospital administration staff obviously had a sense of continuity, because Clare Randell was back in the room she had occupied the night before.

'They needn't have bothered to change the sheets,' she told Gonzales in a voice husky with smoke and misery. Betrayal was in her expression as she watched him pull a chair over to her bedside.

'I guess it's obvious now that somebody *is* trying to kill you,

34

Miss Randell.' He settled down with a grunt. The hot weather was making his feet swell up.

Tears overflowed Clare's eyes, soaking into the mass of gauze that covered one cheek and her chin, masking the area where the flash heat of the blast had removed several layers of skin.

'Nobody was trying to kill Dan, though, were they?'

'No. He just got in the way.'

'But he *is* dead. They won't tell me, but I know he must be dead. They just keep saying, "Don't worry about that, now," as if I were a baby.'

Gonzales looked at her quietly. 'He's dead, all right, Miss Randell. He must have died instantly, he knew nothing about it.'

He'd been right in his assessment of her. The announcement did not bring more floods of tears, or sobs or screams. If anything, it seemed to calm her. 'Yes, I knew it had to be that. Better than to be . . .'

'It was meant for you. He saved your life, in a way.'

She looked at him, betrayal even more explicit than it had been before. 'Do you think that makes me feel better, lieutenant? I *know* it was meant for me. Dan had no choice, he didn't exactly volunteer to be slaughtered in my place, did he? But *why*? What have I done to make someone hate me so?'

'I don't know. We'll have to try and find that out together. Do you feel well enough to talk about it?'

She sighed. 'Anything is better than just lying here and thinking about . . . Dan . . .' The tears welled up and again, now as much a product of shock and exhaustion as grief. 'We really weren't even engaged. I told you that because it was easier than all the complicated explanations. He had asked me to marry him last week, and I refused him. But he just wouldn't accept that. He simply went on as before, fussing around and looking after me as if I belonged to him no matter *what* I said. The way he always had . . . just as if I still was . . .'

And that was all that the flicker in her eyes had been about the day before, Gonzales realized ruefully, handing her a Kleenex from the box on the bedside table. Her own withdrawal from the relationship apparently hadn't communicated itself to Fowler. Something else occurred to him.

'Who was your boyfriend *before* Fowler?'

'What? Oh ... nobody special. I was dating different men when I first arrived out here ... just ... nothing serious at all. But Dan sort of ... gradually took over ... the way he did everything he wanted. The others ... I lost touch.'

'And before you came out here?'

'In New York?'

'If that's where you were, yes.'

'I dated, of course. But I haven't exactly left a string of broken hearts draped from here to Flatbush.'

'You've got a sharp tongue, Miss Randell,' Gonzales observed with a faint tone of disapproval.

'Yes, I have, haven't I?' She closed her eyes and repeated it more softly. 'Yes, I have, I know. I guess it's a weapon I use too often, sometimes even before I'm attacked. Sorry.'

'Oh, I don't mind. If it makes you feel better.'

She allowed herself a half-grin, no more. 'It probably does but that's not much of an excuse, is it? Anyway, I'm just *not* the kind of girl men get wild and uncontrolled about. In any way,' she added as he was about to make a polite token protest. 'I don't mean ... I know I'm not bad-looking. No girl is these days, unless she wants to be. But ... let's just say nobody is about to fight a duel over *my* favours. I'm not exactly a rose without thorns.'

'All right, so that's not where we'll find our reason. What about your work?'

'As I said yesterday, I'm not important enough. I can imagine someone wanting to kill an account man ... I've wanted to myself, from time to time. But not *me* ... I wouldn't make any difference to anything one way or another.'

'Family, then. Stand to inherit any money?'

'No nothing. Nor do I have the secret formula for a miracle potion locked in my brain.'

He chuckled. 'Are you sure?'

'Reasonably sure.'

'Own anything somebody might want? Standing in the way of anyone or anything?'

'Really, lieutenant, I think you watch too much television.'

She ran her hand through her hair, flicking it back from her face. The gesture was faintly familiar to him but he was unable to place it for the moment. 'I own my own apartment, but nobody wants to tear it down and put up a parking lot. Yet. I don't gamble or speculate on the stock market. I own a car, but only halves with the finance company. I wear only a plain cloth coat, by the way.'

Gonzales laughed aloud at that. 'That's an area we haven't mentioned. Politics. Are you active in any political group? Been agitating for anything lately?'

'Only with the company that services my apartment building. To do something about the plumbing in the basement. It smells.'

'What about your friends? Anyone into politics, crime ... anything like that?'

'Politics, no. In advertising we steer clear of the whole scene now. TN has *always* kept well out of it. They got quite insufferably smug during Watergate. Crime? I don't know. Would anyone *tell* me if they were into it? Most of my friends are in advertising, of course. Some people call *that* a crime.' She leaned her head back on the pillow and closed her eyes.

Looking up from his notebook, Gonzales caught the lines of strain under her eyes before she blinked and erased them, readying herself for his next question. Her effort left him tired.

'Look, Miss Randell, I know you've been through a lot in the past twenty-four hours. I think we can take it as read that you're in danger, and that warrants protection in our book, even if we're a little late. We're posting a guard on your room, and I'm afraid you'll have to do without visitors for the time being. Except us, that is, until we find where the attacks are coming from.'

'Or who they're coming from.' Her voice was faint, and she had closed her eyes again.

'Exactly. So I'll leave it for the moment, and you get a good night's rest. In the morning we'll go over it again until we find what we're looking for. It's there somewhere, it has to be. Nobody goes to all this trouble to kill without a reason.'

She opened her eyes and looked into his face. 'You will be able to stop it, won't you? I won't have to go on like this ... ?'

'I'm sure we'll be able to clear it up quickly, don't worry. We've a fair amount of practice at it.' He patted her hand, and stood up. Glancing towards the small television on its stand next to the bed, he cleared his throat and said, 'I wouldn't watch too much TV if I were you. It's bound to be on the news, and there might even be pictures ... well ...'

'I'll stick to old movies, I promise.'

He nodded and said goodbye. The uniformed guard was seated between the elevators and her room, and when Gonzales went out he told him to check everyone before letting them in. That included hospital staff, even if it meant getting some backs up. 'If it gets difficult we can move her to a prison ward, although that might start a different kind of trouble. Anyway, I'll leave word they're to call me if anyhing happens. I *don't* expect to be called, though, do I?'

The guard grinned. 'No, sir. You don't.'

Gonzales nodded and left, his hard rubber heels squeaking on the tiles.

During the evening Clare watched television alone in the darkened room, the images on the small screen moving in erratic patterns before her half-closed eyes. She dozed intermittently, missing the ends of some programmes, the beginnings of others. An occasional burst of canned laughter rose above the mutter of the lowered sound, startling her into random moments of consciousness.

In one of those moments she sensed someone standing near the foot of her bed. Turning her head and expecting a nurse, she saw Malchek watching her. He stood half in a darker shadow, with only the light from the hall falling across the high cheekbones and the hard, dented line of his chin. It was in her mind to speak, but there seemed to be nothing to say. Her eyes closed again.

When morning came she was not sure if he had been there at all.

Gonzales arrived after breakfast, and she felt more able to face his questions.

He concentrated on her family first. Nothing. Then he asked whether she'd ever done jury duty. No. Been involved in any litigation? Only the San-Ex thing – she explained about the disgruntled customer.

'O-*kay*,' he sighed, making another mark in his ubiquitous notebook. 'Let's go over the things you've been doing recently. What about the holiday? What did you do over the weekend?' He had got a cup of coffee from the machine in the reception area, bringing her one as well. He sipped it slowly.

Clare shrugged, and a stab of pain reminded her that her arm still resented what had been done to it.

'I didn't really *do* anything. Dan had asked me down to his parents' place, but when the time came I didn't want to face them. I was pretty sure what my answer to Dan was going to be ... and I didn't want to complicate things any further. They're very nice people, and it didn't seem fair to ... well ...'

'I understand. What *did* you do with your time, then?'

'On Friday evening I did some shopping, food and so on for the week. Saturday I had my hair done in the morning and I went to a gallery preview in the afternoon.' She was beginning to blush for some reason, he noticed. 'I had dinner at Carlo's – early – with a girlfriend ... Barb Tennes ... do you want her to confirm that?'

'I'm not after an alibi, Miss Randell,' he reminded her with a smile, wondering why she was so embarrassed.

'Oh, of course. Well, Sunday I just slept late, then went for a drive after breakfast.'

'Where did you drive?'

'I didn't go far ... through Golden Gate Park, past Point Lobos, that kind of thing. I sort of ... meandered ... listening to a concert on the radio, stopping sometimes for the view.' She looked down at the sheet, the pale-blue knitted blanket, her left hand emerging from the unbleached muslin of the sling. 'I wanted to think about Dan. About what I really wanted to do ... getting up my courage, I guess.'

'Did it take courage?'

'A kind of courage. Guess what I was really deciding was whether I wanted to stay single for ever or not. I'm thirty now ... where I'm from that puts me into the spinster class. Oh ... I know things aren't like that today ... but it was more a decision about my attitude towards myself than it was about Dan.'

'And after your drive?'

'I went back to my apartment, had a bath, sorted some papers, sent out for some fried chicken, watched television. That's all.' The blush was even more pronounced.

'Why does all this embarrass you, Miss Randell?'

'What?' She flashed a startled look at him.

'You're blushing . . .'

She sighed. 'It's just . . .' She took a further interest in the blanket, picking at a loose thread. 'Well . . . it's so *boring*. I mean, such a *nothing* to have to tell anyone about. No swinging parties, no palpitating lovers, no . . . anything. Just a single girl drifting around like a used piece of Kleenex.'

'Could you have gone to parties, had – what was it? – palpitating lovers?'

She smiled. 'One palpitating lover, yes.' A shadow ran through her eyes on a cruel errand. She drew a sharp breath, then continued, 'A few parties, yes. There are always parties, places to go. But I sat by myself on Sutro Heights and watched the gulls instead. Very liberated, the sophisticate at play . . . What's the matter?' He had a peculiar expression on his face.

'You didn't say that before,' he challenged her.

'Say what?'

'That you went to Sutro Heights.'

'I *did*.'

'No, you didn't. You said you went through the Park and around Point Lobos. Point Lobos, you said, not Sutro Heights.'

'Well, it's nearly the same thing, isn't it?'

'Not by about two miles, it isn't. What time were you there?'

'Well, for heaven's sake . . . from about one-thirty until nearly three, I guess. I parked and stayed right in my car. I didn't actually go into the Park itself.'

'Tell me about it.'

She was perplexed. 'About *what*? I just sat there. It was hot, I opened the windows and let the wind blow through. Listened to the concert. I *enjoy* being alone like that. There were only a few cars in the lot, one or two people passing through. I could hear people in the distance, of course. Finally I got bored and came home.'

'Be more precise. *What* people passing through?'

She was getting annoyed. 'My God, *I* don't know. A family with a couple of kids, a pair of teenage girls, some men, another family . . . how can you expect me to remember *now*?'

'Did you hear anything?'

'*Hear* anything?' He nodded, trying not to press her, trying to keep the eagerness out of his eyes. She shook her head. 'I heard the gulls, the music, people laughing and talking, kids shouting and setting off firecrackers, freighters hooting, cars passing . . .'

'Fireworks are banned in this state,' he reminded her.

She gave him an impatient look. 'Sure, and people bring them in by the trunkload from Mexico all the time, you know that. Kids still blow their hands off on the Fourth if their parents are stupid enough.'

'Tell me about the men.'

'*What men?*'

'You said you saw . . .' He glanced down at his notebook. 'Your words were "some men" . . . what men?'

'Oh. Well, two men, actually. Of course, I remember the tall one because of the papers.' She saw his eyes narrow, and hastened on. 'Two men drove into the lot in a white convertible. I noticed them because they were dressed in business suits, and that seemed ridiculous on a hot Sunday. They walked down into the Park. Later, one of them came back and, as he passed me, he dropped some papers out of his briefcase.' Briefly she outlined her exchange with the tall, good-looking businessman, and the intrusion of the joy-riding kids in the Edsel.

'Would you know him if you saw him again?'

'I suppose so. He wasn't very unusual, though. Just . . . quite a handsome face, grey eyes, good teeth, good bones . . .'

'You were close enough to see the colour of his eyes?'

'Well, yes . . . about ten feet away, I guess.'

'Was he wearing a hat?'

'No. Dark hair cut quite close to his head . . .' Her expression changed, slipped, started to come apart. 'Him? He's the one who's trying to kill me?'

'I don't know. I don't know, but it could be. You say you were there until three?'

'About that.'

'Can you describe the other man?'

'The one he came with? I'm sure I'd know him. A short, fat man with long, black hair and very white skin. He had a lot of rings on, I remember, his hands just flashed with them. He didn't look a very nice person ... not like the other one. The fat man was cheap, but the tall one was very dignified ... attractive. You know.'

Gonzales just stared at her. 'I guess I know.'

She waited for him to go on, but he just continued to stare at her, a kind of pity in his eyes. 'Well? Is that what you've been looking for?'

'Maybe.' He stood up, sliding his notebook into his jacket pocket. 'They'll be bringing your lunch soon, Miss Randell. I'll be back this afternoon, and I'll be bringing an artist with me. I'd like you to try and describe the man to him, and we'll hope for a good likeness. Do you think you could do that?'

'Which man?'

He gave her a faint smile. 'The "nice" one, Miss Randell. The nice one.'

'Jesus Christ.' Malchek stared at Gonzales from behind his littered desk.

Gonzales stared back impassively, his notebook open in his hands. He had his feet up on Malchek's desk, and he scissored the toes of his shoes, open, shut, open, shut.

'You think that's it?'

Malchek rubbed the bridge of his nose, ran his hands through his hair and shook it back from his face. 'The fat one was Dondero, all right. I mean, what she said about the rings, and the long hair ...'

'And the white skin ...'

'I'll *bet* it was white. If he realized who he had with him ...'

'We'll never know that.'

'No. Ten feet away?'

'He has grey eyes, she said.'

Malchek obviously could not believe what he had found in his Christmas stocking. 'No scars, no warts, no limp, no ... ?'

42

'A nice face, she told me. Good bones. I got the feeling she thought he was really something.'

'A pretty shark? That's new.' Malchek stood up, walked over to the window, hunching and relaxing his shoulders, clenching and unclenching his hands.

'Your boy's in town.'

'I told you.'

'Yeah, you told me.' Gonzales flipped his notebook shut. 'You also told me he was a straight in and out man. Gets it all done in a day.'

'That's the way it's gone before.'

'But if it *is* him, he hung around to make a second play this time. Dondero on Sunday, but not until Tuesday for the Randell girl. Boy, he sure conned us with that phony sex-freak detail, jerking off like that.'

Malchek's mouth quirked. 'A professional right down to his fingertips.'

'And then not until Wednesday for the bomb.'

'Well, he probably planted the bomb on Tuesday, as soon as he saw he'd missed with the long shot. He knows she'll finger him, he can't risk it. He forced his own hand.'

'But he's struck out twice, now with her. I thought he was the Great White Perfecto.'

Malchek shrugged, still looking out of the window. 'Maybe she's got a fairy godmother.'

'And maybe you have, finally?'

'We'll see.' Malchek had been born in California, but his sceptical tone of voice came straight from Missouri.

eight

It was a small item on an inside page of the *Times*.

The tall man bought his copy from the news-stand in the lobby of the hotel, counting out the pesos with practised ease,

43

keeping enough back to tip the waitress in the coffee shop.

He was on his second piece of toast when he read about the death of Dan Fowler. Even the rich Mexican honey he favoured didn't sweeten his disposition that morning. The waitress went without her tip as he stormed out of the restaurant, slamming the door behind him. The glass shivered, but did not break.

Back in his room he swallowed two capsules with a tumbler of mineral water, and lay down on the bed to wait for the release. Some days it took longer than others.

He just could *not* tolerate this kind of distraction. The job here in Mexico City was one of the most important and certainly one of the most difficult he'd undertaken in the past ten years. The security alone was nearly perfect, and it had taken him three days to find a hole in it. As it was, the timing had to be split-second, or he would lose the chance.

Now *this* annoyance. It was neither fair nor just. He had his work to do.

Gradually the chemical fingers of the pills smoothed his tension, stroking along his muscles and flooding his system with a sensation of delicious isolation.

There was no reason why he need bother with it at all, if it came to that. Anyone could take care of her, dozens of them were available.

He rolled over on the dark-patterned bedcover and dragged the phone towards him. Morrie would know. He could take care of it without even leaving his office. There were always up-and-comers waiting for a chance to earn a place on Morrie's short-list. He chuckled as he dialled the first number in the chain. *He* was no longer pleading for top dollar, God knew. He could pay little men to take care of his little problems.

What was Clare Randell to him?

A notch in his Swiss bank account.

nine

Clare lay on the hospital bed and watched Malchek walking back and forth in front of the window. He took it slowly and stopped often, but it *was* back and forth. Repetitive, compulsive. It made her wish there were bars between them.

'I still don't see why this ... Edison? ... feels he has to kill me. What made him think I was dangerous in the first place? If he hadn't shot at me I'd *never* have made the connection.'

'He didn't know that. As far as he was concerned, you'd *already* fingered him.'

She glared at him in exasperation. 'How?'

'Think back. What did you tell Gonzales you did after work on Monday? You came out of your building, bought a paper, looked at it, then hailed a cab. Supposing he followed that cab. Where did you go?'

'To the public prosecutor's office.'

'Uh-huh.' He shook his head like a displeased tutor. 'To the *Hall of Justice*. It's a big place. Sure, the PP's office is there, along with a hundred others. *And so are we.* Your life doesn't mean anything to him, Miss Randell. If there was the slightest chance you'd identified him to the police, that's reason enough to kill so far as he's concerned. All he'd need is the off-chance. Remember, he kills for a living. Killing comes as easily as breathing to him.'

'Oh God,' she moaned, rocking slightly in the bed. 'How about my taking a big ad in the *Examiner* saying "Dear Mr Edison, your secret is safe with me"?'

He looked at her in disgust. 'You think this is some kind of game, I suppose ... that it has some kind of *rules*? Wake up, Miss Randell. I'm sorry, you're sorry, he's sorry. But he'll try to kill you all the same.'

'But you'll protect me ... you *said* you'd protect me ...' Panic made her voice lose about twenty years, and the cry of 'Daddy' was only an echo, but it was there. Gonzales reached for her hand and squeezed it gently.

'Of course we'll protect you, Clare. You know we will.'

'Is he ... ? when ... ?'

Malchek dropped a hip on to the edge of the table under the window. 'We don't think he's in the city at the moment. There was a major hit in Buenos Aires late on Wednesday that had his signature all over it. Even if he flew back this morning it would take him a while to get a line to you here. And we'll have moved you out of the hospital by then.'

'Why? Isn't this a safe place either?'

'There's no such place as a safe place so far as he's concerned. Don't you understand that?'

'Mike.' Gonzales's tone hardened, but Malchek ignored the unspoken comment.

'She might as well know what she's up against. It'll make her more careful.'

'Being careful is *our* job,' Gonzales said.

Malchek shook his head sharply. 'Hers too. If I tell her to hit the floor and she hesitates, that's all it takes. I can give orders until I'm blue in the face, but she has to follow them if she wants to live.'

'For how long?' Clare asked the lump under the blankets that were her knees, pressed together hard to stop the shaking.

'What?'

She raised her head and looked into Malchek's eyes. They were as cold as a glacial pool, and about as inviting. 'How long do I have to go on taking your orders? How long will it be before you catch him? How long will you be in charge of my life?'

'If I'm not in charge of it, it's going to be a very short life.'

'That doesn't answer my question, though, does it?'

Something shifted in the grey-green depths of his eyes. Something hungry. 'As long as it takes. With the description you've given us, we've got a real chance at last.'

'At last?'

Beside her, Gonzales cleared his throat. 'Mike has been after Edison for a long time, Clare.'

'Then why hasn't he caught him yet?' She spoke to Gonzales, but her eyes were still locked with Malchek's.

'We've never had a reliable description of him before. He's famous for his disguises. Works through a jobber, uses cut-outs even with him. And I couldn't *make* him kill in San Francisco, I had to wait for it,' Malchek answered.

'I don't understand. Jobber? Cut-out?'

'It doesn't matter.' He looked away, then back, and his tone was sharp again. 'All you really have to understand is that when I say jump, you jump. OK?'

'No.' She turned to Gonzales. 'Why aren't *you* doing it?'

He looked embarrassed. 'It's Mike's case, Clare. You came into it from a funny angle, but it centres around the Dondero homicide, and that's his. You couldn't be in better hands.'

'I could be in kinder ones, though.'

Gonzales's face creased into a roadmap, all roads leading to his smile. He winked at her, then looked across at Malchek. 'She's right, Mike. Where're your manners? Didn't your mother teach you "please" and "thank you"? Clare's on *your* side, not his.' Malchek glared at them both, but said nothing. Gonzales went on in a deceptively soft voice, 'Come on, hardnose. This is a lady, a nice lady, and she's in trouble. What the hell's the matter with you?' This last had a sharper edge.

Malchek removed his hip from the table and bowed, his voice slow with irony. 'Thank you, Miss Randell. I will protect you for as long as it takes, Miss Randell, to the best of my ability. And now, if you'll excuse me, I shall away to build you an ivory tower.' He straightened with contempt in his face and went out through the door without looking at her again.

Clare winced. 'What is it? Is it *me*?'

Gonzales was staring at the empty doorway. 'I don't know. He's always been a little peculiar about Edison ... and the rest of the contract killers. But I've never seen him this bad. I'm sorry. I wish I could tell you why his hate seems to be getting splattered all over you as well. But I just don't know.'

Malchek stood very still in the searing afternoon light, waiting for the worst of the heat to ooze out of his open car door. He looked back at the hospital building, its painfully white stone bandaging a square of the sky.

He could have told Gonzales about his problem, if telling had been in his nature. It was not.

His route to the police department had been a circuitous

one. Like some freak talents, his had grown from many seeds, working into his structure without showing on the surface until the fatal flower opened in Vietnam.

In the inexorable way of the military, the army ground Malchek exceedingly fine, discovered his abilities, exploited them. He had been prepared to do just about anything – general combat, mechanics, office work, peeling potatoes, whatever. He didn't mind, he told them. So they watched him and weighed him and tasted him and tested him. Then they told him what they expected him to do, and he found he *did* mind. Not at first. But ultimately.

Malchek became a sniper.

So far as the captain of his 'unlisted' unit was concerned, Malchek was simply a weapon. The same as a rocket-launcher or a bazooka. He was deployed accordingly, where and when he could do the most damage.

And it was not up a tree.

They called it 'tactical take-out'. Or 'selected elimination'. Or 'palliative removal'. A hundred names and words to avoid using the real one.

Murder.

He slid behind the wheel and started the engine, bracketing sunglasses over his aching eyes. It had been too long since he slept. Too much hunting, too much waiting and watching.

He drove towards the house he had selected, drifting with the outgoing tide of lunch-hour traffic. How safe is a safe house? he asked himself. How safe do I really *want* it to be? 'What the hell's the matter with you?' Gonzales had asked What's the matter with me? I'll tell you, Gonzo old buddy. I want to take that nice lady, that pretty lady with the big eyes and rich handful of boobs under her hospital gown, and hang her up high in the sun. I want to say, 'Look, Edison, look what I've got for you.'

And then, when he tries for her, I want to shoot his throat out.

The trouble being that the little lady might get it first, and I'm not in that business any more. Not since that old man in the garden.

He parked in the drive and let himself in through the front

door of the long, single-storey house. It suited. The more he went over it, the happier he felt with the choice. He especially liked the raked gravel in the garden, instead of cat-footing grass. The ten-foot hedge was old, clinging with knotted fingers to the edge of the yard, complete and unbroken except where the drive cut through at the front.

The whole neighbourhood was cloistered with quiet money. Normally used by the city for visiting dignitaries, this particular house was vaguely oriental in décor. Big rooms. Simple, elegant furniture placed in islands on a vast sea of moss-green carpet. Light and shadow used instead of wallpaper. No clutter anywhere. Beauty in itself. And, practically speaking, it was an open beauty that could conceal no obscenity, no trap, no machine for death. Of course, it also meant they had very little to hide behind should Edison opt for assault tactics, but on the whole that was unlikely. Edison liked to work alone.

Malchek had always preferred it too.

The doctor at the hospital had told him they could move the Randell girl at any time. The problem would be getting her past Edison's certain surveillance. He obviously knew she had been injured, he might even know the extent of those injuries. Although he was doing this one for himself, he'd earned enough over the past years to buy just about anyone. A quick glimpse of her chart would probably run him no more than fifty dollars, if that. The hole in the arm, two cracked ribs, a sprained knee.

How do you bundle all that up to look like something else? Malchek had an idea, but it was ludicrously theatrical and it would not be easy for her. She'd have to walk a long way on that knee, and never once could she limp. Edison would be watching for the limp. Edison would be watching for *everything*.

When Malchek finally returned to the hospital the worst heat of the day was over. An evening breeze was sending torn newspapers and dust devils skittering across the street in haphazard patterns. There was moisture gathering in the air, but the sun was still above the horizon. It had the look of a slow-dying thing positioned for a long goodbye.

The guard told him Gonzales had left about an hour before, and that she hadn't wanted her dinner. She was watching a newscast on the little TV.

'Hello.'

She seemed surprised to see him. 'Hello.' No smile, just a wary watchfulness in her dark eyes.

He pulled the chair Gonzales had used back beside the bed and turned it round, straddling the seat and resting his arms across the back. She had given her attention back to the television commentator, obviously preferring his company to Malchek's.

'Look,' he began awkwardly. She turned towards him, her eyes lagging behind for the weather map. 'I'm sorry I was so ... abrupt this afternoon. There wasn't any need for it, you're not to blame for all this.'

'No. I'm not.'

He gave her a rueful grin that seemed to startle her even more than his rudeness, as if she had expected another snarl. He couldn't blame her for that.

'Like Gonzo said, I've got a ... crusade going on Edison. I've been chasing him for a long time. He poisons everything he touches ... well, to me he does. If I ...' For some reason he wanted her to understand his attitude. 'He chokes me ... they all do, the professional killers. They're real filth.'

'Lieutenant Gonzales said you were an expert on these men. That you were a sniper yourself, for the army. You know how they work, how they think, he said.' His narrow face tightened again, muscle by muscle, paled slightly, although her tone was merely curious. 'Is that why you hate them so?'

'Maybe.'

Something in her could not resist the obvious corollary. 'Does that mean you hate yourself?'

He stood up abruptly and addressed the ceiling. 'That's *all* I need, another two-bit, amateur psychiatrist who's read the first chapter of all the right books.'

She was sorry to see his face closing, and could have kicked herself. He'd looked human for almost a full minute. 'Sometimes I even read the *second* chapter,' she told him, in an effort to apologize. 'If it looks sexy, that is.'

He wasn't buying it, her tone hadn't been right. He put the chair back against the wall and faced her across the rail at the foot of the bed, his fingers wrapped tightly round the metal on either side.

'You're going out of here soon. I've arranged for the doctor to bandage your knee for support and inject it with enough pain-killer to let you walk naturally. You are *not* to *limp*, do you understand?'

An hour later Clare said, 'I'm not worried about limping. But not laughing right out loud when I look at *you – that's* going to be difficult.'

'Don't look at me, then. Keep your eyes down and think about someone having a rifle on you every step of the way. Think about everyone you pass in the hall and in the street having a six-inch switchblade up a sleeve that could cut through your gut like butter, or lay your throat open like a calf on a hook.'

'My, he *is* a silver-tongued devil, isn't he?' The policewoman was pinning Clare's sleeve to the front of her habit, hiding the safety-pins within the voluminous grey folds.

Malchek had already put on his robes, and stood beside the window as usual, looking at the street through the venetian blinds. Fortunately the hospital stood back from the street, surrounded by a wide moat of trees that washed together in the breeze. Their glossy leaves turned back to show silvery undersides, the vague shadows sliding over the cars below them in the parking lot.

When the two nuns had rustled into her room, Clare thought at first there had been some mistake. She was not Catholic, she started to say, but had been interrupted by the taller of the two.

'Boy, these goddamn outfits are hot. How do they stand it?' And she had turned to close the door behind her.

Malchek had laughed out loud at Clare's dumbfounded expression. The 'nuns' – two policewomen, in fact – had disrobed quickly. One, dark and about Clare's build, was her replacement. The other, a taller blonde, would wait in the room for a while after Clare and Malchek had left, then filter out through the hospital visitors in the normal way.

Malchek's explanation had been terse. 'The Sisters of Matthew move in and out of this hospital all the time. They're mainly an order of social workers. That's what gave me the idea. I went to their Mother Superior this afternoon and explained our problem. Since I'm a nice Catholic boy, she was happy to help.' He gestured towards the habits. 'Nuns walk with their hands together, anyway, so we can immobilize your left arm easily enough. The rib strapping won't show under all that cloth. The wimple and coif change the shape and emphasis of the face – and anyway, most people never look directly into the face of a nun. But I'll need to borrow some of your make-up for my upper lip and chin, just in case.'

When she had finally got the habit on, Clare gazed in fascination at her reflection in the mirror. Only a triangle of her face showed, bound on all sides by the brilliantly white linen. Swooping stiff wings curled out around her face, and the grey layers draped down over her shoulders, just reaching the floor. Only the tips of her shoes showed. Around the general area of her waist a black-beaded rosary hung heavily. When she locked her right hand in the suspended fingers of the left, only her knuckles showed. 'It's really incredibly complex, isn't it? So many layers, so many bits and pieces.'

'Enough to put off the most insistent medieval monk, I imagine. These habits haven't changed much in the past five hundred years,' Malchek commented from the window. For some reason the habit suited him far more than it did Clare. The flat planes of his face emerged from the coif undistorted by the tight linen bands. With his thick hair hidden, the emphasis was stronger on the narrow nose, the unyielding mouth. She could imagine him burning books and addled young virgins without a smile.

'A lot of the habits have,' she argued automatically. 'In fact, some modern nuns don't wear habits at all – they wear Bermuda shorts on hot days, and put their hair up in rollers.'

'Fortunately for you, the Sisters of Matthew are still conservative in that area.' He looped his heavy rosary through his fingers, covering his obviously masculine hands with the generous sleeves.

The injections that the doctor had put in her swollen knee had virtually erased any pain, and she was able to walk quite naturally. He had warned her it would not last long, it was the kind of thing they slipped football players if no one was looking.

'OK,' said Malchek abruptly from the depths of his winged headpiece. 'Let's get moving.'

'So quickly?' she protested, suddenly afraid of emerging from the familiar womb of the hospital room.

'Unless you wanted to wait to see how Dr Welby gets out of this one?' he said sarcastically, referring to the TV programme her replacement was watching. The girl was already bandaged around the face, and had climbed under the bedclothes wearing Clare's nightgown.

'Listen,' she called to them cheerfully from the high bed, 'I think he's going to have a baby.'

'That ought to push his ratings up,' Malchek muttered. 'Right, now keep your eyes down and your face expressionless. Walk as smoothly and evenly as you can.'

'Nuns aren't expressionless, nuns smile,' she told him. The linen bands constricted her, forcing her to speak without moving her jaw.

'*These* nuns are crabby,' he growled, and they glided out into the hall, elbow to elbow.

They made it through the halls and lobby of the hospital easily enough. But within minutes of leaving the hospital it was obvious to him that she was in trouble. Apparently it was her ribs, something he hadn't considered. The walking was easy enough, the injection in the knee was holding. And Malchek had stifled his urgent impulse to walk quickly in the interests of maintaining the disguise. Gradually, however, he had to slow his steps even more to accommodate her. Although she didn't complain, he could sense her keeping her inhalations to a minimum, and heard a faint whistling in her throat every time the pain stabbed.

'You could try prayer,' he told her in a soft tone as she struggled along.

'I'd be struck down for blasphemy,' she gasped.

Under the habit his skin crawled with a sensation of being

watched, but there was nothing he could do about it. He finally stopped, tugging her sleeve, and they pretended to inspect a shop window full of clocks. It could have been worse, he decided. We might have inadvertently stopped in front of a porn shop. He used the window to make a quick con of the street behind them. There was nothing to see but passing cars and walking people. Was Edison one of them?

'Can't we hail a cab?' Clare pleaded.

'Nuns walk. It's good for the soul. We're not far from the mother house now. You can rest there for a few hours. We're going to move you out after dark in a linen truck. Hang on, only another six blocks or so to go.'

'Jesu,' she breathed.

'Say, that's very *good*,' he told her in mock approval. 'Stanislavsky would be proud of you.'

Her reply was badly out of character.

ten

Malchek set up a twelve on twelve watch to cut down on the traffic in and out of the safe house. He posted four unmarked cars to watch from the streets, two on two, organized the food deliveries (Dave's Supermarket and Deli ... owned by an ex-Captain of Detectives) and the entertainment (a cardboard box of assorted paperbacks, a colour TV and six packs of cards). Two detectives and a policewoman sat each watch in the house, two more in each car.

He intended to concentrate on Edison, outside.

The newspapers were full of the death of the American ambassador in Mexico City, supposedly shot by one of the anarchists who had been mobbing the front of the embassy when he left for the airport by a rear entrance. At least, the papers put it down to anarchists, and conjectured who the ambassador's party would put up for president now that he was out of the way.

Malchek teletyped the Mexico City police for a courtesy copy of the ballistics report. (As the murder had taken pace outside the embassy grounds it was in the laps of the MCPD rather than the Secret Service. Officially.)

Their reports confirmed his opinion. The bands and grooves on the bullets matched two in his personal files, both from hits attributed to Edison, one and three years ago respectively. One in Denver, one in Palo Alto. He had a possible eleven guns down for Edison so far.

'We needn't have gone through that damn charade after all,' he complained to Gonzales. 'He wasn't even in the city.'

'You didn't know that. You did the right thing.'

'Yeah. Sure.' He yanked a file drawer open. 'Anyway, she's safe enough for the moment.'

'I'm surprised you didn't take a watch yourself.'

'That's what inspectors and sergeants are for,' Malchek commented, filing the Mexico City flimsy along with the rest. 'Brilliant administrators like you and me have to stay here and read reports.'

'You've never been much of a report man before.'

'The quickest way to get Clare Randell out from under is to nail Edison before he makes another try, right? Now that we've got the artist's impression circulated, we can probably get him *if* we coordinate right. I'm coordinating.'

'The FBI were very interested.'

'I just bet they were.' Malchek stopped to glance out of the window. The weather had turned cool and cloudy, the sun sulking unseen ever since they had closed Clare Randell into the safe house.

'Well, hell, we aren't the only state that wants him. He's not proud, he'll kill anywhere. Lots of wants out on him. The Feds say they want him for the Strinder assassination five years back.'

'He *won't* kill anywhere, Gonzo, nothing in the east at all. And the Feds also want him for the attempt on Senator Santos, I think.'

'I didn't know that was him. They never said.' Doubt was in Gonzales's tone.

'*I* say it was him. It had his dirty fingerprints all over it; the "tall woman" who left the package, the stainless-steel wire, the box of the very best cigars, the knots in the string – double reefs – he always uses them. Edison all right.'

Gonzales watched him at the window, thin and rigid with anger. 'Boy, you've got him taped, haven't you? Every little detail. You should be watching the Randell girl, Mike, not sitting here stewing. He couldn't get any cigar-boxes past *you* out there.'

Malchek did not answer him. His eyes followed a gull that was dipping and gliding in the updraughts between the buildings, cutting white circles against the dirty sky. He couldn't explain his own hesitancy to close himself in the safe house with Clare Randell. It was certainly the most logical place for him to be, the only place his specialized knowledge might make a difference. Anybody could sift reports. Hell, he could sift them out there as well as in here.

But Clare Randell rubbed him the wrong way, and it made him uneasy. She seemed to delight in getting his back up, and always chose exactly the right thing to set him off. It was uncanny. Every time he made some effort to be human, she parried it with that mouth of hers, keeping him at tongue's length. He felt anger would only impair his efficiency, and she kept him angry ninety per cent of the time.

Gonzales watched him as he stared out of the window, and waited for him to work himself into it. It was logical, and so was Malchek. Most of the time.

Gonzales had seen Mike work his way up through the Division stage by stage. At one time he'd been one of his own inspectors. Malchek was now accepted in the Department as being icy-cold, somewhat lacking in humour, super-competent, and scrupulously fair with all his people. Good men who had worked with him on his way up to lieutenant usually ended up liking him and never quite understood why. Weak or dishonest men always ended up hating his guts, and also never quite understood why. It was not that he acted like a righteous judge, but it was hard to look away when he fixed you in his sights.

'I suppose *you* could coordinate from here,' came Malchek's reluctant voice.

'You know I could.'

'I'll have to change the schedules all around, for crying out loud. I had it worked out perfectly.'

'Uh-huh.' Gonzales stared at the ceiling. His stomach growled.

'Oh, shit, you're right,' grudged Malchek, turning round. 'But do you have any idea how *boring* it will be out there?'

'Not if Edison shows up. Can your inspectors and sergeants handle that?' Gonzales brought his eyes down from the light fixture and he grinned into Malchek's glare.

When Malchek and Grogan arrived at the safe house just before nine that night, they walked unannounced into the living-room. The outside unit had passed them, but just out of curiosity Malchek picked the lock on the front door. The chains hadn't been on. The blare of the television set masked their steps, and he walked over and turned the sound off angrily.

'This is supposed to be a *safe* house, not a goddamed circus. What if I'd been Edison? You'd all be dead by now, you half-assed clowns.' He turned on the two detectives in accusation as they lounged in easy chairs with their shoes off. *That* was bad enough to earn them a reprimand at the very least if he'd wanted to push it. But the anger stuck in his throat.

Clare Randell was staring at him, curled into a corner of the brocade lounge. It seemed to him she had shrunk since he had last seen her, become smaller in every way, except for her eyes. They were enormous, deeply shadowed, terrified.

She'd been lost in the television programme, a mindless situation comedy, and his abrupt and unexpected entrance had broken the spell. Her frozen position reminded him of a lemur on a branch caught by a flash of light. Something in him made a strange turn, like an animal settling, and then his anger slipped its leash.

'Get the hell out, you two,' he spat at the startled detectives. 'And don't come back here in the morning. You'll find new assignments on the board. If you've got any questions I'll be in around ten, tell me your troubles then.'

They got into their shoes and disappeared, exchanging a glance as they went. He walked over and looked down at Clare. 'Have you seen a doctor since you came here? You look like hell.'

'Ever the flatterer,' she managed to say, without much attack.

He turned to the policewoman who emerged from the kitchen with a dishcloth in her hands. 'Call headquarters and get Bannerman over here right away.' He looked back at Clare. 'You, go to bed.'

'I don't *want* to go to bed.'

'If I tell you to go to bed, you will go to your goddamned bed,' he ground out between his teeth. 'Move it. Go with her,' he added to the policewoman. 'I'll call Bannerman myself.'

The policewoman nodded and went over to the sofa. Defiance flared briefly in Clare's eyes, then died. Her shoulders slumped, and she rose and followed the other woman like an automaton, avoiding Malchek's eyes.

He aimed himself at Grogan. 'I thought you were a family man. I thought you were a good *cop*, for Christ's sake. Why didn't you report her condition to me? All I've been getting every day in your reports is "Situation unchanged, subject comfortable." Balls. She looked better than *that* after walking a mile and a half from the damn hospital. Haven't you got eyes?'

Grogan spoke defensively. 'She hasn't been sleeping too good, that's all.'

'*Or* eating. Has she been eating? She sure as hell doesn't look like it.' He went over to the telephone and began to dial without waiting for Grogan's reply. 'She's not a prisoner, Dave,' he continued. 'We're supposed to be looking after her, not ... Give me the ME's office, this is Lieutenant Malchek.' He reached out to straighten a sloppy stack of magazines that were sliding towards the telephone. 'This is Malchek, is Bannerman there?' Behind him, Grogan changed the TV channel. The random, monosyllabic shouts of a fight crowd filled the room. After a moment, the phone murmured in his ear.

'Bannerman? This is Mike Malchek. I've got a problem, I need you to see someone. Can you come right now?' He gave him the address, then listened impatiently to a short lecture delivered in soft, reproachful tones. 'I *know* that, but Naudo is an asshole, and this is a lady who needs a light hand at the moment.' He listened again, then smiled. 'Yeah, I heard you'd quit doing private abortions for the plainclothes division. Listen, get over here, will you? I'll bury your wife's next speeding ticket.' The voice in his ear murmured on.

By the time Malchek had hung up he felt a little less like kicking in the television set. If Bannerman had the same effect on Clare Randell, he would feel even better.

Clare heard the thousand busy footsteps of the rain before she opened her eyes the next morning. It had the steady sound of a downpour that would last the day out, curtaining the house with silver, bringing an evening chill into the rooms well before lunch.

She did not like the continuous whisper outside the window. It reminded her again how trapped she was, with even the weather conspiring to enclose her. Raising her arm to look at her watch she was surprised to find it was only seven o'clock. With all the pills the doctor had given her last night she'd expected to sleep through half the day. But she felt better, definitely better. Even her arm didn't hurt so much – she'd lifted it without even thinking. In fact, it was the first complete night's sleep she'd had since arriving.

There was no one in the living-room, and the curtains were still drawn. It looked different from the night before, neater somehow. The lamps were still on, but the television set was a silent blind eye in the corner, reflecting her slippers and the hem of her robe as she passed. She pushed open the kitchen door.

Malchek was there, wearing only his trousers and cursing in exasperation at the percolator. A gold medal hung on a long, thin chain around his neck. His body was not skinny as she had thought, only narrow and compactly muscled, the sinews taut under lightly tanned skin. His feet were bare and his long, thick hair was wildly rumpled, half into his eyes.

He came around fast at the sound of the door, automatically reaching across to his left hip and the gun that was holstered there. Then, glaring, he said, 'I suggest loud whistling if you're going to creep around here early in the morning.'

'Sorry.'

He dropped his hand from the butt of the gun, then raised it again to run it awkwardly through his hair. His glare gentled. 'You know how to work that damn thing?' He jabbed a finger towards the percolator.

She let the door swing shut behind her. The percolator came into instant order under her touch.

'Now why wouldn't it do that for me?'

'Oh, I used to work on the Sunbeam account,' she explained, as if that clarified matters. 'The coffee is in the cupboard behind you.'

He turned and reached upwards. As he did so she saw a scar on his shoulder-blade with unexpected clarity. It was jagged and new enough to still show pink across the skin. Another, older scar streaked silver along the back of his ribs just above the waist. He handed her the coffee and she measured some into the percolator basket. 'Where are Sergeant Grogan and Nancy?'

'Asleep. Nancy only needs to be awake when you are. Grogan gave me three hours last night, I gave him the same this morning. It will take me a couple of watches to adjust to nights.'

'Oh.' She turned on the burner under the coffee.

'You look better this morning,' he observed, leaning against the counter and folding his arms.

'Yes, I feel better. Thanks for getting that Dr Bannerman over here.' The tone was polite and careful and it felt strange between them.

'He's a good man. You should have asked to see someone sooner.'

'I suppose so.' She got the bread wrapper open after a struggle. 'I didn't like to ... make a fuss.'

'That was stupid.' The tone was still polite, but losing. 'He said you were undernourished, exhausted, and had started a low-grade blood infection. What the hell is the point of our protecting you from Edison if you're going to drop dead on us anyway?'

'I *can* see how that would look bad on your record,' she snapped, turning around to confront him. There was a long moment when they locked eyes, and then his dropped to the front of her robe which had come partly open. Her hands clutched involuntarily around the belt and she tightened it, suddenly aware of her own nakedness under the light flannel. He raised his eyes again, but they were as impersonal as an intern's. Then they both smiled.

'Pax?' he asked softly.

She nodded and turned away. 'Pax. Until I get my strength back anyway.'

They ate their toast and coffee side by side from the counter-top, staring out through the latticed blind at the shifting curtain of rain. When Clare got up to make more toast, he pivoted on his stool.

'Still hungry?'

'Yes, starving. Would you like some eggs?'

'Sure, if you're going to fix some.' He watched her moving from refrigerator to skillet. 'Did he give you something for your appetite last night?'

She shrugged and spoke to the melting butter. 'Aren't I allowed a little early-morning hunger?'

'If your apparently massive sense of guilt says it's OK, I certainly have no objection.'

The eggs hissed an opinion from the pan. 'I thought we'd signed a disarmament treaty.'

'I said pax, not silence. I'm interested.'

She glanced over her shoulder briefly, glossy brown hair swinging across her cheek. 'In my guilt?'

'If you like.'

'Do you like them hard or soft?'

'Soft. You haven't got any *reason* to feel guilty. It was only chance that made him open the refrigerator, after all. It could have just as easily been you.'

'It was *intended* to be me, that's the whole point. He was only there because he . . .' She faltered.

'Because he cared about you and was looking after you, right?' He made it sound very reasonable, very normal.

'Right. But I . . .' Her voice broke, and she took a deep breath, getting control. 'I didn't *want* him to be there.'

'Oh?' He drank the last of his coffee and went slowly past her to the percolator. 'I thought you were engaged.'

'How about pax *and* silence?' she finally asked, tilting her head back and sniffing.

He poured coffee and added cream. 'OK. But before we close down communications, do you want more coffee?' She nodded, and he carried the percolator with him back to the counter.

Above the clatter of their knives only the rain whispered in the room. When she had finished, she made patterns on the plate, drawing her fork through streaks of egg-yolk. 'Is that a bullet scar on your shoulder?'

'Switch blade.'

'It looks recent.'

'Six months.' He stirred cream into his third cup of coffee.

'And the other one?'

'What other one?' He sounded genuinely puzzled.

'On your side. There.' Her fingers grazed his skin as she gestured, and he flinched. 'Sorry, you're ticklish.' She was embarrassed at having accidentally touched him. His side had been as warm as a cat's.

'Oh. That's old. Rifle, in Nam. I didn't know it still showed.'

'You're lucky, aren't you? A lucky man.'

'What makes you say that?' He turned fully towards her, and the sudden sharpness in his voice made heat rise under her skin. Sliding off her stool, she picked up the plates and fled to the sink.

'You survive. Two small scars out of how much violence? How many attacks?'

His shoulders were hunched over his coffee, the steam curling up beyond him. 'Not lucky, just careful. Twice, not careful enough. That's all.' Abruptly he pushed his cup away and stood up. 'The melodramatic thing would be to say that the real scars don't show.'

She went on washing the dishes, swishing the cloth under the foam. Knives and forks clinked invisibly against one another. '*Are* you saying that?'

'Hell, no. I'm getting dressed.' He went out. She continued washing, doing the same dish over and over again. The door opened and he stuck his head through.

'Thanks for breakfast, by the way.'

She caught herself nodding her acknowlegement long after the door had swung to a standstill behind him.

In the bedroom he had slept in earlier, Malchek looked at himself backwards in the mirror, touched lightly the silvering scar across his ribs. His own fingers brought no defensive convulsion, only memory and a wry smile.

He had always been called lucky. Lucky to have the mind for straight As. Lucky to have the coordination for cross-country and tennis letters. Lucky to have all those expectations of easy success.

Other people's expectations. That was what finally drove him to consider dropping out of university. Everybody else wanted to make plans for him. He became moody, dissatisfied, wild.

But none of his own ideas had been much good, either.

The old man's voice had been harsh as he laid it down to his youngest son, his brightest hope, his bitterest disappointment.

'Go on the way you're going, Mike, and you'll be in jail this time next year. What the hell use is that? You don't want to go back to school? OK. OK. I give you a choice. You go into some branch of the military and learn some discipline, or you walk out of this house and you don't come back. Hurts me to say it, boy. But I'm saying it.'

The old-world solution to the problem of the wayward son. Laughable if it had not sounded so natural in his father's voice, the words undercut with an echo of the accent his grandfather had brought over on the boat. He did not doubt his father's pain. He could see it, hear it. The old man had gone on talking for what seemed like a century, each word falling like an axe-blow, cutting off Malchek's retreat. He had watched his father in silence; the white mouth, the white hair, the blazing eyes, the old, old hands gripped together.

He had tried out the guns, the petty crime, the drugs, all the other trappings of aggressive adolescent defiance. But he could not take that last step. He could not stop loving his father, nor deny his awe of the iron will that kept the old man's tears from falling, the voice from breaking.

And, God help him, he had chosen the military. Jail would have been better. He might not have learned the art of murder in jail.

When he came back on duty that night, Malchek was annoyed to see that the place had grown messy again since morning. The two new detectives assigned to the day-watch were, if anything, worse than the previous two.

He was not obsessively neat by nature, far from it, but for some reason the vista of sliding piles of magazines, swamped ashtrays, furniture pushed out of line and curtains tangled in their pullcords got under his skin. He had spent much of the previous night clearing up, partly to stay awake, partly because he could not stop himself doing it. Now it was out of control again.

Grogan came in, shaking the moisture from his coat. 'The fog is going to get worse, you can smell it coming in.'

'Beautiful,' Malchek said heavily, going past the two police-women chattering in the hall, one arriving, one leaving.

He knocked lightly on the bedroom door, then opened it. The bedside lamp was on, and she put down her open book.

'Everything all right?' He glanced at her, letting his eyes slide past to the window, making sure it was shut and the cur-tain completely drawn. She was wearing some kind of old-fashioned nightgown, long-sleeved, high at the neck, with buttons and a foam of lace under her chin. Her hair was shin-ing in the light from the lamp, several strands flying away against the headboard like dark cobwebs. She looked about twelve years old.

'Yes, thanks. I've taken one of the pills the doctor gave me. I'm getting my strength back so I can start arguing with you tomorrow. You get your way far too much around here. Dr Bannerman and I had a long talk, and you were torn limb from limb.'

'I never felt a thing,' he grinned.

'That was mentioned too.' She fixed him with a bright eye, and his grin faded.

'I liked you better when you were sick,' he said briefly, and shut the door before she could answer.

By midnight they could hear the foghorn moaning from the Golden Gate. Grogan and Nancy were engrossed in an old Bogart movie, but Malchek was restless.

He went into the hall that ran straight from the front door to the back and intersected the rear hall to the bedrooms dead centre. He shrugged his raincoat on as he opened the Yale lock without letting the tumblers snap, and went out into the night.

The fog clung in gauzy curtains around the house, pushed fitfully by a breeze that was too weak to do more than ripple it across the gravel. The raked patterns in the stones were like pale waves in a pale sea.

The area in front of the house was dominated by a single rock that crouched like an enormous black toad, its blind face towards the drive. Staying on the path, he crunched along the gravel past the rock, clouds of droplets swirling around the flying edges of his open coat. The fog made excellent cover, and he didn't like it. *I could have dropped a hundred men a night if I'd had fog like this in Nam*, he reflected.

He emerged between the wings of hedge into the street, and started a slow circuit of the house, stopping to talk to the men in the dark, unmarked sedan that was parked twenty yards from the entrance.

One of the men in the car acknowledged him. 'Mike. How's it going?'

Malchek shrugged. 'I guess it's better in there than out here. Seen anyone?'

Both men shook their heads, the farther one ducking his a little to see Malchek's face better. 'Regulars only. Guy who walks his dog, lady who needs exercise for her varicose veins, that's all.'

'Yeah, well, you get some exercise too. Take some circuits on foot, get rid of that gut. If he's looking for his chance, this fog is a gift.'

He walked on without waiting for their reply. It would do them good to get off their asses, he thought. Standing a surveillance watch in a neighbourhood like Highshore was damned boring. That made it better for Edison, worse for them. There wasn't much to keep a man awake except an occasional cat crossing the wide, well-kept lawns. Mostly he knew, from experience, that the men in the cars would not stay all that awake, but would depend on their subconscious to bring them up at the first unusual sound. In an area that quiet, noises stood out.

The fog, however, interfered with hearing as much as vision. The heavy moisture in the air helped to carry sound, but also distorted it. His own footsteps seemed both to follow and run ahead of him. More than once he whirled before realizing he was following himself.

The hedge gave him a point of reference, and he stayed close to it, appreciating its dark bulk, old and impenetrable. Occasional glints from condensation on the leaves gave it a jewelled appearance, and he struck at it lightly on impulse, loosing a shower of spray over himself. Suspended between the faint, opalescent pools of the street-lights, surrounded by the hanging mist, his steps echoed strangely, eerily.

He reached the end of the safe house boundary and turned between it and the next property – a new house, sitting front-of-central on its plot, surrounded by soft, freshly turned earth. There was a musky, pleasant smell of peat in the heavy air – the owner was obviously after the best lawn in the neighbourhood. He edged along between the soft earth and the prickly wall of hedge, nearly losing his balance twice in his efforts to respect the neighbour's horticultural ambitions. The second time his hand went right through the hedge itself, twisted branches dragging back his coat sleeve and scratching his forearm in two places. Cursing under his breath, he raised the arm and sucked at the welt where beads of blood were pearling up. Standing still for that moment, he noticed a flood of fog pouring across his feet. A broad, grey stream, flowing over the ground like liquid.

That's wrong, he thought to himself. That's very wrong.

Forgetting the neighbour's sensitivities, he sprinted over the soft earth and went round to the front, pounding in along the drive. Something was open in the safe house. A door, a window, something. The warm air from within was pushing the fog outwards.

He could barely make out the house, seeing it only as a long, low darkness within the pale draperies of the fog. He went past the living-room windows, past the kitchen windows, and round the rear corner to find the kitchen door standing ajar. Reaching under his coat, he pulled his .38 out of its holster and clicked off the safety. As he did so, a figure came towards him out of the mist. His finger began to tighten on the trigger before he recognized the broad, round-shouldered shape of Grogan, also moving with drawn gun. He froze for an instant on sighting Malchek, then relaxed in recognition.

'What the hell, Grogan?' Malchek hissed. Grogan came up to him, standing close in the damp shadows.

'I heard a noise. It was too soon to be you coming back, so I came out.'

'And left the goddamn door open?' Malchek gestured towards the open kitchen door.

'Nancy's in there . . . the only exit from the kitchen is through the living-room,' Grogan pointed out.

'And if three guys came in, how fast is she?'

'I thought Edison always worked alone.'

' "Always" is a word you *never* use with guys like Edison. You find anything in the back?'

Grogan shook his head and started to holster his gun.

'What kind of a sound was it?' Malchek made no move to put his own gun away.

'Kind of a thump . . . like something falling. But all the windows are tight, no marks, no breaks in the gravel, nothing.'

'OK, we'll go in, wait ten minutes, then make another circuit.' He herded Grogan into the dark kitchen and shut the door, locking it. When he joined Grogan at the door to the living-room he said, 'Go straight through, out the front, and circle around again.'

'You said to wait ten minutes.'

'Did you hear me say that?'

'Sure ... you said—'

'Then if anyone else was out there, they heard it, too. Move.'

Malchek called out their identity, and they went through the swinging door together. Nancy was holding her gun on the door, resting it against the back of the sofa, steadying it with her left hand over her right wrist. She looked frightened, but the muzzle did not waver.

Relief softened the lines in her face, and she put the gun down as they came towards her. Grogan did not pause but went straight out into the front hall.

'Check on her,' Malchek told Nancy, then followed Grogan. They opened the front door noiselessly and split, taking alternate sides of the house. Two minutes later they met at the kitchen door.

'I think it must have been a cat or something,' Grogan said. 'Sorry.'

'You'd be sorrier if it was a two-legged animal.' He tried the kitchen door, and the lock was firm. 'Cross around, meet you at the front door. Let's check the perimeter this time.' They crunched across the gravel to a mid-point inside the rear of the hedge, separated, and were curtained alone in the fog in seconds. Malchek kept his head down, using his pocket flash as he had along the house, shielding the glow with his cupped fingers, looking for ... something. Anything.

They came back with nothing, re-entered the house through the front door. Malchek double-locked the Yale, re-throwing the bars of the two bolts that held the door top and bottom.

'Nothing like a little fresh air.'

Grogan coughed. 'You're right. That was nothing like it.' He coughed again.

Five minutes after they had settled themselves in the living-room again, there was a sound. A definite thump, just as Grogan had described it.

'There it is again.'

They listened. It was repeated, and then there was another

sound, like something sliding or slipping heavily, reluctantly, down the roof above them.

'Hey, look at that screen.' Nancy indicated the TV, which had begun to striate and waver, the colours separating erratically. 'It's the TV aerial, for crying out loud. The guy must not have fastened it right.'

'What guy?' asked Malchek in a deceptively quiet voice. Her face froze and she spoke stiffly.

'M-M-Mary said they had trouble with the TV aerial this morning. Headquarters sent somebody over to fix it. He was up there this afternoon, and it was fine after that. You saw it.'

'*Jesus Christ!*' Malchek exploded. 'Why didn't you tell me? Why didn't Fiddler or Dunn tell me? How the fucking hell am I supposed to *do* this job . . . ?'

Nancy was defensive. 'But he was sent by Headquarters,' she protested. 'I *thought* of that – but Mary said he had all the right ID, he never came *in* the house at all, and he was *black*. Edison isn't—'

'I don't give a damn if he was *purple* and stood in the drive with his pants down singing the Australian national anthem. *I want to know everything that happens here.*' His face was white with rage, and he was reaching for his gun again. Grogan started to rise hesitantly, and Malchek barked at him, 'That's right, that's *right*, you fat bastard, get *up* . . . let's go . . .'

He was halfway to the front hall when there was another, heavier and more final thump from above, followed by a flash beyond the front windows. Even filtered through the heavy curtains it was a brilliant silver-blue, and accompanied by a ragged, vicious crackle. Almost immediately the light changed to a dull red and began to flicker.

'Goddamn it, god*damn* it,' Malchek shouted. 'Incendiary on a timer, the sneaking bastard.' He ran into the hall, Grogan at his heels. Nancy was at the phone, dialling frantically.

Grogan threw the bars on the front door, struggling with the Yale and his gun at the same time. Through the glass on either side of the door they could see a drip of flame cascading down from the overhang of the roof and splashing up from the gravel.

Malchek went straight to Clare's room.

I should have thought of the roof, I should have checked it when I arrived, it was still light enough. You stupid son of a bitch, he cursed himself.

Edison knew the people inside would be bored enough to watch TV constantly. A silenced rifle and a good sight, easy to find an empty house during the morning and pot the supports of the aerial until it fell. *Easy.* They'd call for repairs right away.

He burst through her door and stared in disbelief at the empty bed. Then, from behind him, he heard the toilet flush and glanced down the hall. A line of light on the carpet was widening in a wedge from the bathroom door. He whirled and went along to it, pushing a sleepy and astonished Clare back into the tiled room and switching off the light. She staggered against the side of the tub and sat down abruptly on the rim, a hand clutching the shower curtain. Then he closed the door and there was only blackness.

After a moment her voice, softened by the pills, said, 'We'll have to stop meeting like this, darling, the plumber is beginning to suspect.'

'Shut up.'

Slowly he turned the handle and pulled the door back against himself, leaving about a half-inch of clearance through which he could see down the rear hall. Her bedroom door was still open, and so was the door to the front hall.

'Is it—?' she began again, her voice sharper as reality filtered through the barbiturate haze.

'Shut *up*,' he hissed.

A smell of scorching paint was beginning to seep from the front of the house, along with a thin pall of smoke. The mayor is going to love *that,* Malchek thought wryly, as the first distant sirens lifted above the sound of the flames. He was amazed, as usual, at the sheer speed of the FD boys. But this time there would be an extra yellow slicker in the milling crowd of hose-tenders, axe-wielders and crowd-controllers. A slicker that covered . . . I bet he's out there waiting for them to pull up and run in, he thought. Come on, baby I'm waiting too.

If Clare had not already been in the bathroom he would

have dragged her there. It was an ideal hole-up, no windows, one door, solid.

'Get into the tub,' he whispered. 'Throw in a couple of towels if you have to, but get in and lie face down.' She did it instantly, without arguing, without even stopping for the towels. He heard her catch her breath, sharply, and remembered she only had that nightgown on, and the bathtub was probably cold as hell. He reached out blindly in the dark and touched thick terry-cloth. Pulling towels off the rack he tossed them in the general direction of the tub. As he did so there was a movement in the entrance to the front hall.

He'd been wrong. Edison had not been waiting to play volunteer fireman. A motorcycle cop stood there, the white helmet gleaming under the overhead light. Everying about him was right. Grogan had probably walked right past him in the excitement, and no doubt a good departmental cycle stood on its kickstand in the drive, still hot and steaming in the mist. But it took no complex chain of reasoning to tell Malchek this was no cop.

The six-inch switchblade that the figure flicked open as he came down the hall towards the bedroom door said it all. Malchek raised his gun through the crack of the bathroom door. 'Drop it, Edison.'

The ant-like, helmeted head did not even turn towards the sound of Malchek's voice. One instant he was there, a black, faceless stick-insect, the next moment diving through the open bedroom door. Malchek's gun fired even as the figure started forward, and he cursed himself again for bothering to shout his obligatory warning. I should have put one in him and *then* yelled. Who the hell was going to tell me off? Her?

He was across the hall while the echoes from his shot were still bouncing painfully off the tiles in the bathroom. They mingled with echoes of the involuntary, half-stifled scream Clare had made when he fired.

As he neared the bedroom doorway a shot came through. He flattened himself alongside the frame, thinking, 'Shit, he's got out his piece ... that makes life interesting.' He looked around the hall but saw nothing he could use. Stepping back slightly he stretched out his arm and flicked off the hall light. 'I like the dark, Edison. Do you?'

Edison must have, because almost immediately the light in the bedroom went out too. The only illumination now emanated from the front hall, a combination of the fire's glow and the light from the living-room. The red glow dominated, and he heard the fire department pulling into the drive, their heavy engines sending a dull, rhythmic throb right through the fabric of the house. There was an obbligato of shouts and a clatter of equipment being rolled out. Within, there was carpeted silence, and Malchek could almost hear his own sweat popping out of his skin.

He knew even the dim, reddish glow from the open door could outline him for Edison as he waited in the darkened bedroom. Edison himself had two choices: out of the door or through the window. If he takes the window he has to open the curtains, and that puts *him* up as a target, Malchek decided. But I've got to cover myself too. He slipped off a shoe, and lobbed it into the room at a shallow angle. As it hit on the far wall with a crunch of breaking glass, followed by the inevitable shot, he was across the gap and down the hall, closing the betraying light out with one sweep of his arm. The door slammed and latched, the hall was as pitch black as the bedroom, and the odds were coming down.

He slipped off his other shoe and went down full length on the carpet, bellying forward on his elbows, gun in one hand and shoe in the other, approaching the bedroom door from the opposite side this time. He was expected, of course, and the same trick too. Unfortunately it was the only thing he had going for him at the moment, and he knew what Edison was thinking. He threw the shoe. Sure enough, the gun inside the room barked again. This time, however, the bullet came out through the door and into the hall, followed by another, lower, and a third, higher. They thudded into the wall opposite. It was enough. He didn't *want* to enter the room, he only wanted to place that flash, and did.

He returned three shots himself, close-grouped and centred vertically on the flash pattern that still flared on his retina. There was an animal grunt in the darkness, a moment's silence, and then the sound of ripping cloth. Malchek watched the long, heavy curtains torn away from their rail over the bedroom window by the clutching hand of a body, going down. He saw a darker shadow beneath the folds of cloth convulse, sprawl forward, convulse again, and then lie still.

Lowering his forehead on to the pile of the carpet under him, he waited, breathing as shallowly as he could. The only sounds he could hear were from outside. They could be masking Edison's breathing too, he thought, he could have faked it.

Maybe he's lying in there just like I am out here. Listening.

But the minutes stretched, and he knew he would eventually have to make a move for or against his instinct. Rolling over to the wall, he braced himself and slid slowly upward. With a deep breath he extended his gun and followed it, tight in, ready to drop at the first faint movement from inside the room.

There was none.

He levered himself around the doorframe and stood against it inside the dark room, still waiting. Nothing. He felt the light-switch pressing into his back, dropped below it and pressed upwards with his shoulder, still holding his gun with both hands aimed at the heap of shadow beneath the paler rectangle of window.

The light clicked on and, blinking in the sudden brightness, he saw that the leathered figure was still, the head twisted and the mouth hanging slackly open under the blank visor. The circle of the overhead light made a cyclops eye in the centre of the plastic, bright, empty. Finish. He had him at last.

The expected surge of triumph did not come. Instead there was only a half-nauseated relief that it wasn't himself lying there, followed by the hollow gut-ache that accompanied any kill he made now, however it was achieved.

He went round the bed and pushed the body with one foot. Dead, certainly. Pinched in by the helmet, distorted through the smoky plastic of the visor, the face was lax and empty, the eyes half-open.

Going across to the door he called, 'Clare? It's all right, you can come out now. Clare!' Inclining his head, he could hear her moving, getting out of the tub. Outside the shouting and noise were as loud as ever, loud enough to have covered the shots. Grogan probably figured he'd gotten Clare out by the back way.

There was a click as she switched on the bathroom light, a pause, and then she opened the door. He should have become angry at that. It could just as easily have been Edison calling out her name.

'It's all right,' he said quietly. 'He's dead.'

A residue of adrenalin still pulsed through his veins, and he felt a chattering high beginning in his body. Because of it, he involuntarily took in the outline of her body under the thin cotton of the old-fashioned nightgown. He felt his body rise to the unconscious invitation it was offered. He wondered wildly if that was why rape so often went with war, because the least thing could have set him off, across the hall, bringing her down beneath him, speading her and taking her. The least thing. The impulse shamed him, but it was there. Jesus, he thought, get the hell out of that light, woman. Please.

She was poised to retreat, frightened, vulnerable, but the betraying glare from the room behind her outlined her pose – legs apart, breasts rising and falling with her panic-short breathing.

'It's over,' he said, short of breath himself.

She came slowly down the hall and he remembered that she must be wrapped in a sleeping-pill cocoon, everything would be moving fast and slow, all at once.

He took a step towards her, then stopped himself, letting her come to him on her own, watching his face without wavering. The light behind her still showed her body, but with diminishing clarity. Slowly, with each step, the generous curve of her hips, the long, tapered thighs, the narrow ribs and the swell of her breasts were lost within the folds of soft white cloth. He pressed his hands hard against his sides.

'You killed him?' she asked in a small, dazed voice. There was a patch of dampness over one shoulder, and her shiny hair was wet against one side of her head. The taps in the bath had tickled icy water over her as she lay in the dark, listening to the shots, terrified into rigid immobility on the hard porcelain. She had been obsessed with the thought that the bathtub was the same shape as a coffin.

When she was next to him he took her elbow abruptly and moved her with unnecessary force into the room and over to the body of her hunter. It lay empty and inert, staining the carpet with crimson. The mayor wouldn't like *that*, either.

He glanced at her and was startled to see puzzlement on her face.

But she was shaking her head with maddening and insistent regularity, arguing with him soundlessly.

He bent over the body and pulled off the helmet, suddenly filled with a terrible suspicion. Thick, curly, blond hair spilled out from under the rim of the white plastic. Released from the constriction of strap and shell, the face assumed a wider, flatter shape.

'That's not the man from the park,' she told him softly, her eyes fixed on the death-mask beside his foot. 'That's not the man I saw.'

But he'd known it before she spoke. He knew this face, knew it of old from juvie show-ups, then more recent arrests.

It was worse than he'd thought.

Edison had sub-let his own contract.

eleven

Malchek had never been in the commissioner's office. He was impressed. Not because of the wood panelling, the heavy, shot-silk drapes, the deeply comfortable, mustard leather chairs, the obviously well-used lawbooks. But because of the man himself. The contrast.

He knew Clyde Reddesdale by reputation, every cop in the city did. For once somebody had used a modicum of intelligence and chosen the right man for the job. Although independently wealthy, Reddesdale had been a working cop for eighteen years, going into the force straight out of law school. A man of exceptional ability, he could have chosen from any one of a dozen offers extended by established law practices, politics, the FBI – whatever he wanted.

What he had wanted was to be a cop in the streets. To work his way up through the ranks to the office he now held, and do the things he thought had to be done. During his two years in the top office he had set a lot of old heads rolling, and a lot of others right on their ears. Reddesdale had started out with his own ideas of how a police department should work. Although he had learned enough during his working life to somewhat modify his methods, those basic ideas had not changed.

One of them had been that the rule-book was *essential*. You could prop doors open with it. You could keep your notes in it. You could throw it through a window to let out smoke or leaking gas. And, if you were really strapped, the end pages made serviceable toilet paper.

Otherwise, it was only there to stand on while you tried to find the human, common-sense, fair way of dealing with the situations you were handed, day in and day out. Too often he'd found this was simply a choice between the right way and a way that would work. Invariably he chose the latter, and worried about criticism later. Malchek agreed with him. In a big city with enough ethnic and religious threads to re-weave Joseph's coat, with money and politics and social pressures from top and bottom, with tourists, terrorists and organized crime walking side by side into the best restaurants with ordinary citizens, your *only* hope was flexibility.

Reddesdale must have had to stand on a couple of rule books to make the height requirement, Malchek decided. Either that or the years had pounded him a few inches into the ground, because he was dwarfed by his massive desk. He watched Malchek and the others and listened to the problems, crouching in his chair like a child.

The fact that it was two o'clock in the morning, and that he and Captain Halliwell had been dragged from their beds for this conference, seemed to bother the commissioner not at all. He was interested.

'So what you're saying is that you want us to lie all down the line, is that it?'

'More or less,' Malchek admitted.

'Halliwell?' Reddesdale's pale-blue eyes held on the captain's heavy-boned face while the older man thought it out.

'Hell of a lot of corners to pin down,' Halliwell finally gravelled out reluctantly.

'But we could do it?'

Halliwell looked across at Malchek, glanced past him to Gonzales who was slumped on the base of his spine in the next chair. The silence lengthened, nobody moved.

'It could be tried,' he finally said, his tone indicating a conviction of early defeat. 'It needs pressure from the top to hold it down, though.'

'Which is why, presumably, Lieutenant Malchek asked to see *me* in the middle of the night?'

Malchek nodded. It had been a wild, chancy thing to do, and he was still sweating over it. The commissioner's oft-repeated statement that any cop could come straight to him at any time might have been merely a political mouthing.

Reddesdale was staring at Malchek, looking through his skin to his bones, gauging his blood-pressure, heart-rate, digestion, and how he liked his women. At least, that's how it felt.

'Tell me why again,' he demanded.

Malchek took a breath, let it out, scuffed a toe against the carpet. 'Edison works on his reputation. Until we got Miss Randell's description, he just didn't *have* a face. He takes all his assignments through a jobber, Morrie Wallack, and he even uses a phone cut-out for him, apparently, because the word is Wallack's never seen him either. We knew he was tall and white, some said good-looking, some not.'

'Miss Randell says yes?'

'To him being good-looking? Yes.'

'Why doesn't he just have plastic surgery, then? She's only seen his face once, even though she's very clear about it. All he has to do is change his face.'

'I don't think he can.'

'Why not?'

'Over the years there's been a definite pattern in his work. Two or three months go by – nothing. Then a series of killings. Then another gap. Then more hits. And so it goes on. He schedules them for some reason. I think he's got another life,

77

one where his face is well known. Where he can only get away at certain times. Maybe a family even. He *can't* change himself.'

'He could stage an accident.'

'Sure. But he'd find it easier, quicker, and less complicated to simply kill Miss Randell. I think he's a vain man too. Anyway, arranging an accident takes time.'

'Why vain?'

'Well, he's very big on disguises, of course, but he's also very high on pride. He likes it known that *he* did a job, and so there are a lot of trademarks he leaves behind. Advertising, I guess. Useful, if the job goes well. Sometimes he flubs, but not often. Like when Senator Santos's cigars didn't blow up in *his* face but took his assistant's head off instead, because the assistant was in charge of filling the senator's humidor.'

'That was Edison, was it?'

'I think so, yes.' He gave the reasons he'd given Gonzales.

'That why I've been getting so much flap from the FBI about this Randell girl? They want her, you know.'

Malchek went rigid. 'It's *our* case, not theirs.'

'For the moment, yes.' Reddesdale's tone was even.

Malchek's face and voice sharpened. 'We still have to ask them, don't we? They can't tell us what to do, as long as it stays in the state, isn't that right?'

Reddesdale smiled suddenly, dropping ten years off his face. The Princeton-cut grey hair fitted his skull like a cap, and the tanned skin whitened around his even, rather over-large teeth. 'They seem to have got the idea that Edison's work *could* be designated as inter-state commerce.' He stood up, went over to the percolator, and busied himself pouring out steaming cups. He had not lost a cop's taste for constant coffee, but he laced all the mugs with generous slugs from a bottle with a label that raised Malchek's eyebrows slightly.

'They can't be serious?' Halliwell asked the little commissioner when he had returned to his big, clear-swept desk. It was highly polished, except for a mottled patch of intersecting white rings that scarred the surface by Reddesdale's right elbow. He put his mug on top of it without looking down.

'They're *always* serious, Tom. They have plastic surgery

done their first week with the Bureau. Cuts right through their smiling muscles. That's why I didn't join – hated to lose my boyish grin.' He demonstrated. Malchek decided he'd been right, it was probably worth hanging on to.

Reddesdale dropped the grin and turned to Malchek. 'So you think you can decoy Edison by hitting him in his reputation and vanity?'

'Yes, sir, I do.' Malchek took another sip of his coffee. 'In my opinion, Edison is a conceited man. It would hurt like hell to have it look like he'd been sloppy. Even if he got the word circulated fast, it would still mean he was *connected* with sloppy work. They'd wonder about him. He'd hate that.'

'So when he goes for the Randell girl – and you're sure that he will . . .'

'I'm sure.'

'Then he'll not only want to kill her, but he'll want to do it in some impressive, splashy way. Pull out all the stops and try to make us look like horses' asses, right?'

'Probably.'

Reddesdale swivelled in his chair, full circle, like a kid on a merry-go-round. His face came into view, then disappeared around for a second time. None of them smiled, although he was obviously enjoying the ride. He threw himself into a stop.

'Tell me Mike's good enough, Tom,' he snapped at Halliwell. The captain paled a little, not wanting to commit himself.

'He's good,' he finally ground out.

'I didn't ask if he was good. I *know* he's good. I wouldn't have got out of a warm wife to come all the way down here if I didn't know *that* much about him. I asked you if he was good *enough*.'

Halliwell licked his lips nervously.

'He's good enough,' came Gonzales's laconic voice from Malchek's other side, the first time he'd spoken since the talking began.

Reddesdale's eyes flicked to him instantly. 'You're his friend.' It was a mild accusation.

Gonzales didn't rise to it. 'I'll stand next to him anywhere you say,' he told Reddesdale quietly. 'And I'll leave my gun in my desk.'

It was an incredible thing to say. The commissioner took it at full worth, because he knew Gonzales had never seen Malchek's confidential personnel file. He had. Quite unknown to the department in general, Reddesdale kept copies of the *complete* personnel files of all men above the rank of sergeant in a special room he'd built into his basement a week after taking office.

Malchek hardly knew what think about Gonzales's mildly voiced statement. He decided not to think about it until some other time.

'You realize you'll have to get her to agree to this in writing. She's a member of the public, there's no reason she has to risk her neck this way,' Reddesdale mused.

Malchek sighed. 'What are her options? We go on holding her a prisoner in protective custody for how long? Weeks? Months? Or we let her go back out there and hope we can block out the entire population of San Francisco plus one? Or do we give her a gun and hope she has time to shoot straight?'

'Whereas you're offering a combination of all three in one bright, shiny package, right?' Reddesdale grinned.

'It has the virtue of concentration, I'll admit that,' Malchek smiled back.

Halliwell grunted. 'I still say she's better off right here where we can keep an eye on her, instead of traipsing off across half the state with only you for company.'

'Me and six others,' Malchek corrected him. 'And not ordinary others ... I already explained ...'

Halliwell waved a weary hand. 'Yeah, yeah ... super-nuts like you. Single, marksmen, experienced in undercover, familiar with the parks, bike riders if possible, camping experience, and ... blue eyes, was it?'

'One blue, one brown,' Gonzales put in.

'Yeah, right,' muttered Halliwell, sinking his opinion in his coffee cup.

'I just think if we set this up right, we'll keep the danger to other people down to a minimum. He's quite capable of blowing up her whole goddamn advertising agency just to get her. You want to lie awake nights thinking about *that*? He doesn't give a fuck who goes down, as long as she does. If we're out there with her, the risk is eight people, maximum. Cheap.'

'Hardly cheap,' Reddesdale observed, counting on his fingers. 'Extra cars, expenses for eight, salaries of men we could use here . . .'

'Malchek likes to spend money,' Halliwell muttered.

'Things are cheaper than people,' Malchek said.

'You didn't always think so, snap-shot,' Halliwell returned.

Only Reddesdale saw Malchek's hands clench and then relax, finger by finger. Gonzales was staring at his own empty cup, Halliwell was locked eye to eye with his subordinate.

'Maybe I've learned better,' Malchek finally said, his voice level. 'Maybe there's always a lot of things you learn about as you go along, including your own mistakes.'

Halliwell snorted. 'Tell it to the Pope.'

Reddesdale waited, but Malchek said nothing. Nothing at all.

'OK, Mike, go ahead with your plan. I'll sign the orders for you,' the little commissioner said suddenly. He'd seen enough.

Halliwell stared. 'Just like that?'

'How else?'

Reddesdale was still sitting behind the big desk when the knock came. He had decided not to bother going home, but to wait until Dempster and the secretaries came in at eight-thirty. He could catch an hour or two on the leather couch against the inner wall. He'd done it often enough in the past.

Of course, he would have to face Dempster's not quite concealed air of disapproval in the morning when he found the commissioner shaving in his private bathroom. Dempster had been aide to the previous office-holder, and that had been very much a tight ship sailing high on political waters. When his previous boss had opted for the full political life, Dempster had been left behind. His was not the kind of face that fitted in with the glad-handers. Since he had only five years to go until retirement and pension, Reddesdale kept him on. Reddesdale's ideal was efficiency, and Dempster *was* efficient. So he ignored his personal feelings towards his protocol-bound and prissy assistant because Dempster knew everything and everyone – the systems, the way things were done. He kept the office going, and that left Reddesdale free to operate in his own way.

If the price was a constant atmosphere of disapproval, then that was the price he had to pay. There were more important things to spend his energy on, more important people.

'All right,' he answered when the knock was repeated.

They exchanged a look after Malchek closed the door behind him, and the commissioner nodded. 'I thought there was more.'

'Yeah, I thought you thought so,' Malchek murmured, dropping wearily into the chair he had vacated twenty minutes before. He rubbed his eyes with stiff fingers and ran his hands through his hair uselessly and repeatedly, only looking up when he heard Reddesdale's chair creak. There seemed no need to comment on the rapport that had manifested itself between them when they'd first shaken hands a few hours before. It was so complex and complete that words would have been a waste of time.

The pale-blue eyes looked into him. 'Which one don't you trust?'

'It's not that simple. I wish it was,' Malchek said.

'If it was simple my mother would be running this place, not me.'

Malchek gave a wan smile. 'The house alone I could buy. Or the schedule. But the place has *six* bedrooms. There were three doors open in that back hall and the bastard went straight to hers, no hesitation.'

Reddesdale gave him a glance of disapproval. 'You could have moved her around if there were six, couldn't you?'

'She's had a lot ... It seemed a rotten thing to do to her, so I just kept the lights going on and off in the others, and let her keep to the one bed. She's ...'

'OK, you've got nice manners and you nearly lost her. I'm Lutheran, I don't hear confessions. Spit it out.'

'Leak.'

'Obviously. What's the field?'

'Maybe fifty. If anyone talked in the locker-room, maybe more. But the guy got on to the roof with *good* papers, and the call for the television repair was sent to headquarters. He was sent out from *here*.'

'That's very loose, Malchek. Very, very loose.'

'What can I tell you?'

Reddesdale shrugged. 'I'd be glad to do your legwork for you, but it would look a little funny, me hanging around the duty room. I haven't been doing it much lately. Pick somebody.'

'Gonzales.'

'Not Halliwell?' He could see Malchek hesistate, thinking politics. 'Forget the goddamn power structure.'

'He's too old. He wavers, he worries.'

'And Gonzales doesn't?'

'He's always been straight as far as I know, and he hasn't got a lot to lose. Divorced, no living kids, halfway to pension, he could survive outside. He works hard. He cares.'

'I know. I've used him twice on special work myself. He also keeps his mouth shut.' He smiled at Malchek's expression. 'If he didn't, you wouldn't be looking so surprised, right?'

Malchek nodded and drank some coffee while Reddesdale took a few slow spins in his chair. It was obviously a habit he'd developed and he didn't give a goddamn what anyone thought of it.

'Of course, we've got the Internal Affairs Division to handle things like this. It's what they're here for,' he pointed out after a few minutes' silence. Malchek said nothing, and it was Reddesdale's turn to nod. 'Yeah, me too. But you've got to have vacuum cleaners if you want to pick the crap up off the floor.'

'I guess.'

Reddesdale banged his mug on the desk. 'OK, Mike, I'll talk to Gonzales for you, and we can start exposing your location bit by bit from back here. But in return, you've got to bring Edison down without killing him. That's my deal.'

Malchek was dumbfounded. '*Why*, for Christ's sake?'

'We can use him. Once he's nailed and he knows he won't get out, he'll buy as many cushies as he can, with whatever he's got to sell. Even in twenty minutes he could flush a lot of the big guys down the drain.'

'Sure. So even if I let him live, his former employers won't.'

'But I *want* those twenty minutes. More, if possible.'

'I can't promise. How the hell ... ?'

'You can promise to try. I accept the problems, but you *can* try. If he dies and you had no control over the situation, I'll

83

know it. But if you could let him live and don't, I'll cut you into stewing steak. Deal?'

Malchek sighed. He wanted Edison dead, but he had no leverage, not on this man, anyway. 'Deal.'

'What about the girl?' Reddesdale wanted to know.

'I haven't asked her yet. No point.'

'Can she hack it?'

'Only one way to find out, isn't there?'

'She's your weak point. You can't shoot and mollycoddle at the same time, it knocks hell out of your aim.'

'I know that. I don't think she likes me much, but she trusts me.'

'You like her?'

'Yeah, I do.' He was surprised to hear himself say it. But it was true, he did like her. She didn't bleat, she bit. And *that* he could handle.

'Rather you than me,' Reddesdale said, standing up. 'But good luck, Mike.'

'I'll need it.'

'If this falls apart? You're so right.'

twelve

The tall man collected the papers that had accumulated during his absence. He never cancelled them. He liked to catch up with the world at his leisure once he got home.

He put his suitcases aside to unpack later. He was hungry and wanted breakfast, even though it was nearly two in the afternoon.

When the bacon, sausages, eggs, fried potatoes and sliced tomatoes were artistically arranged on his plate, he took it through to his study and sat back to read as he ate.

Having methodically arranged the papers in chronological

order, he was able to finish one egg, two strips of bacon, half a tomato and a sausage before he lost his appetite.

'Police triumph in California shoot-out' the headline ran on the second front page of the *Times*. Underneath was a blurred death-mask that might have been anyone's, and a picture of Clare Randell with a cop, smiling into the camera.

With fury rising in his throat on a tide of half-digested food, he read of his own death. That was bad enough, but it could be handled. What really sent him to the telephone in a blind haze was the cop in the picture, one Lieutenant M. Malchek:

'I'm not really surprised we were finally able to bring this man down. He's been in the game a long time, and it was obvious that his work was getting more and more careless lately. This particular operation was really sloppy, and it was just a matter of time before some police officer put an end to him. It happened to be me, but it could have been any rookie.'

He skipped the cut-outs and got Wallack himself on the phone, bending his ear under the earpiece in his rage.

'You get the word out that I'm *not* dead, that it wasn't me in C ... C ... California, that I had nothing to do with it.'

'You arranged it.'

'No, Wallack, I paid for it, but *you* arranged it. You gave it to one of your little protégés and he blew it. The egg is on your face, not mine. But when you're getting the word out, you c ... c ... can tell them that I'm not due for pasture yet. Tell them to watch the papers, and they'll see something worth while on the Randell girl *and* that big-mouthed pig.'

He slammed the phone down and went back to the papers. He was so angry it took him nearly twenty minutes to focus on the words. The picture over Mary Byatt's syndicated column stopped him. Ordinarily he did not linger over the women's page, but the sight of Clare Randell and that cop together again made it mandatory.

They make an arresting couple, if you'll pardon the pun. She is small, dark and pretty, with a bubbling laugh and a quick wit. He is handsome and watchful, his smile slow to start and slow to fade. It is, in the very best sense, a romantic story. After all, how many dragons are there these days for a knight to slay? But that is exactly what Lt Michael Malchek was able to do for his lady love, Clare Randell.

Assigned to protect her from the professional hit-man known only as 'Edison', he killed him, saved her life, and proposed within twenty-four hours.

'You really get to know someone when you're thrown together under that kind of stress. I know it seems quick to outsiders, but really, I feel as if I've known Mike for years instead of days,' Clare Randell told me happily.

He keeps her close to him, as if the habit of protection has become part of their relationship. I asked if it had been love at first sight, but he shook his head.

'I wouldn't say that. In fact, I couldn't really say *when* it happened. I just suddenly realized she was the one, and that was that.'

And it's obvious that as far as this man of action is concerned, that *is* that. He has rescued his princess and she is his. I asked if they had set a date for the wedding.

'No, but it will probably be fairly soon after the honeymoon,' she began with a laugh, then caught his eye and stopped. There's no doubt who will rule this relationship.

'We've both been under a strain over the past ten days or so,' Lt Malchek told me quietly. 'We'll be taking some time off together, that's all.' And that *was* all.

I was outside his office before I realized the interview was over. Handsome Clare Randell's dragon-slayer might be, but that kind of domination isn't for me. I've never felt able to look at a man with eyes that glowed blindly like hers. On the other hand, I've never had my life saved by a shining knight, either.

Could I be missing something?

When he'd finished the story, Edison knew he'd been had.

'You bastard,' he breathed, looking at the picture of Malchek smiling calmly at the girl. 'You cunning bastard.'

thirteen

It really hit Clare about forty minutes over the bridge.

She had been covertly watching Malchek. He'd started the run clenching his jaw, as if he had someone between his teeth. His eyes were on the rear-view mirror almost as often as he watched the road ahead. Dark glasses hooded his face, and his hands were tight on the wheel. Gradually, as the miles slipped back under the car, the lines of tension between mouth and eyes disappeared. He looked less often at the mirror, glanced less often at the glove compartment.

The morning was already hot, and they had the front windows open. The contingency budget of the SFPD did not run to air-conditioning. They passed a lot of cars with families. As the broad road began to climb into the hills, more and more cars with trailers hugged the edge of the concrete like a chromium-plated dinosaurs.

'School's out,' he commented, as a pair of shiny-faced kids stuck their tongues out, safe behind the rear window of the car ahead. Clare astonished them by sticking out her own in return. They grinned and said something to their parents. When Malchek flicked the signal and pulled past the car, the parents looked over and smiled.

We look perfectly ordinary to them, Clare thought. Just like any normal couple. She smiled back. The smile stayed. When she wanted to let it go, she couldn't. It was as if they were leaving fear behind them in the city. In a moving car she did not feel the sense of entrapment that had filled the safe house. If nothing else, his plan had the advantage of making her feel less of a victim and more of an aggressor. As the road lifted, so did her spirits.

Finally, unable to unlock her idiot grin, she took a deep breath and yelled, stretching her arms out ahead of her and opening her throat with a vengeance.

Malchek nearly went off the road.

Staring wildly across at her, he shouted, 'Sweet Jesus,

woman, what the hell's the matter with you? You nearly made us Traffic Statistic No. 873.'

'Did I? Did I, Mike Malchek, Champion of the People and Protector of Helpless Women? Would they have uncovered us a thousand years from now as part of the floor of that canyon down there, and wondered at us? Found us amazing strange, this lady and man in the metal box?'

He couldn't believe his ears, she had snapped already. His foot lifted from the accelerator automatically, and he began to slow down. Then he caught the wayward glint in her eye as she gazed at him in defiance. She looked so pleased with herself, so mad and idiotic, that he began to laugh. And like her smile, he found that, once started, it was hard to stop.

'You're out of your mind,' he finally managed to say.

She had never seen him do much more than smile, and that only politely. If he had laughed at all, it had been brief and thin, stretched over some dark silence within himself. Now she was delighted with the result of her imbecility. Whether it was the release from the two previous days of intense preparation, or the lushness of the morning and the road that stretched ahead, she couldn't say. All she saw was that under the cop, inside the cold dominance of his expertise, there was a man.

'You're beautiful, Mike Malchek,' she told him.

'You left out Champion of the People,' he reproached her, still amused.

'And Protector of Helpless Women, so I did. What else are you?'

'Oh, poet, lover, philosopher. All them good things.'

'Especially poet.'

'Oh, especially. I read and write good.'

'Like a cigarette should.'

This adolescent inanity set them off again. Malchek felt as if something were snapping apart thread by thread from across his chest. The more he laughed, the deeper he breathed. And the deeper he breathed, the better it got.

But hearing your own name on the radio when you don't expect it is an unnerving experience. During the news, a voice slapped the smiles off them with painful abruptness.

The saga of Clare Randell and Police Detective Mike Malchek doesn't seem to have reached a conclusion as yet. It's only days since Lieutenant Malchek killed the gunman who had been threatening Miss Randell's life. They subsequently announced their engagement, and the romance caught public imagination. However, an hour ago bomb blasts ripped their respective apartments to rubble. Both were out at the time. Damage was extensive. A police spokesman said the bombs were probably the work of vandals or cranks attracted by the newspaper stories. Neither Miss Randell nor Lieutenant Malchek was available for comment.

The announcer's final words were drowned out by a burst of the most dreadful curses Clare had ever heard. The fact that half of them were in Russian did not help. (These were the only heirlooms passed down from Malchek's immigrant grand-father.) When he had cooled down and fallen silent once more, she ventured to speak.

'I'm sorry, Mike. About your place, I mean.'

He shrugged. 'It was only a place to sleep. I'm insured, any-way.' Glancing across, he actually smiled. 'The insurance company isn't going to appreciate such an expensive message, though.'

He seemed indecently cheerful to her, now that he had vented his initial anger. She felt sick, not only at the final destruction of her possessions, but because reality had come back so quickly. That will teach me to feel safe, she thought, twisting her hands tightly together to stop the trembling. She was still being hunted, she still might die. Desperately she looked at the cars around them, the road ahead.

'Are you sure they're out there? Near us?'

'Who? My men? Very, very sure. Don't worry, Clare, we're ready for him.'

'Oh God, Mike ...' She could hardly speak. The shaking moved up to her wrists for some reason. Then, like snakes, it slithered through her body and she could do nothing to stop it. The fluttering muscles, the hollow bones, the feeling that her flesh was melting, running out from under the sheath of skin that held her together, a thin, vulnerable envelope. Not enough. Not nearly enough.

Without saying anything he flicked on the turn signal, cut between a Chevy convertible and a Cadillac, and pulled over on to the dusty shoulder of the road. When he turned off the engine the only sound was the swish of the traffic that slapped impersonally past them.

'Let it out, Clare. This is the last chance I'll give you.'

'Can I change my mind? Can I go back?'

He sighed, stared out at the rough rock wall that thrust up out of sight only inches beyond her window.

'You can do anything you like.'

Clare could not stop staring at him, even though she knew tears were close to betraying her. He's a small man, she wondered to herself. Thin and fine-boned, not tall, not bulky, not anything like a bodyguard should be. Edison was big, she remembered him clearly. Tall and long-armed and deep across the chest.

A panel-truck slowed, going past them, and Malchek reached up to adjust the visor, throwing some shade against the hot sun that flooded in, heating the car like an oven without the cooling wind of forward movement.

Clare watched him, still unable to look away. What am I doing out here with this little man? In the next minute Edison could walk up behind the car and shoot me. Now the sunlight, then the dark. The shaking intensified, loosening everything within her. Her bones jangled.

Malchek's voice cut across her thoughts, his tone reflective. 'He thinks the destruction of home will make us feel isolated and vulnerable, like having no cave to run back to when the storm hits. It shows he's angry, and that's good. His anger is more dangerous to him than isolation is to us. We can always buy new furniture, but he can't buy back the mistakes anger will make for him. He hasn't really touched us, Clare. Nothing has changed.'

He sensed her shaking, and turned. The dark eyes swallowed him, and he saw her doubt. She's shrinking again, he thought. Strange the way she seems to grow smaller and smaller in her fear, condensing to something rather like a bird, tiny bones and no wings to fly. He slid over on the seat

and put his arms around her in an instinctive impulse to comfort a frightened child.

Pulled in against him, she was more aware than ever of his
slight build, compared with Edison. But his bones were hard
and unyielding. His arms were unyielding too, and gradually
she trembled no more, forced to stillness within them. I am
perfectly safe right here and right now, she told herself in
astonishment. Nothing can touch me except this man. Why
am I so sure of that? Something of what he had just said
played itself back in her head.

'How do you know what he's thinking?'

His quiet voice vibrated through the bones of her skull, and
she knew his face was against her hair. 'I don't know how, but
I *do* know.'

'Does that mean he knows what you're thinking too?'

'Probably.'

So it was not his body that she had to trust, after all. She
relaxed against him suddenly, and he felt her do it. The moment
had passed, she was building again. He waited. Eventually she
straightened and he let his arms slide away from her.

'OK?'

She nodded, not lifting her face to look at him.

Well, that's probably better, he thought, watching the shin-
ing curtain of her hair. I have no idea what I look like at the
moment, but I don't think it's very inspiring. Her body had
been so warm, he hadn't wanted to stop holding her. His hands
had itched to move, explore, unlock and surprise her. There,
in the middle of the day, with a hundred cars passing and a
killer coming along from any direction. He spoke sharply.

' I don't want that to happen again, Clare. I haven't got time
for it, do you understand?' He echoed Reddesdale's words like
a shibboleth. 'I can't mollycoddle and aim a gun at the same
time.'

'I understand perfectly. It won't happen again.' She folded
her hands in her lap.

He let it go at that. Pushing himself back under the wheel,
he started the engine and pulled out into the stream of traffic
as a gap appeared. Smoothly he fed gas, changed down for the

grade, checked the mirror for the Yamaha, the road ahead for the Impala convertible.

They had lost about ten minutes. And maybe something more.

He pushed the sun-visor back up into position, and the cycle dropped back a couple of cars. Not that he blamed her for breaking down. He'd been there himself, that empty place, that desert of isolation where the ground moved and you could not.

The old man in the garden had turned, suddenly, but the bullet was already flying. The fragile bones of flesh flew apart and shattered in an expanding balloon of destruction, a mouth that screamed without a jaw, eyes gone, nose gone, but a throat that still convulsed around a howl of death, slow death, too-slow death.

A light-stepping insect of sweat crossed his stomach, and his shirt was suddenly glued to his shoulders.

He opened the rear window on his side, holding the wheel with one hand and reaching back over the top of the seat to struggle with the winder on the rear door.

They'd have to stop for lunch soon.

They started hitting motels early in the afternoon, and finally got into the third one, just on the edge of Richardson Grove. Malchek was pleased. This location had been the first alternative on the list. Garner and Martin would be able to pitch their tent near enough, after all.

When they drove into town to find a restaurant, he saw the convertible parked in front of the next motel. It would not always be so easy, and he wished they'd saved some of their luck for later on. They might need it more as time went by.

He had elected distance, although he knew it would make no real difference in the end. Edison had contacts everywhere *if* he wanted to use them.

He had elected mobility, but not too much. They would stay here tomorrow, and give Edison his first chance. In the morning they would wander, drop-jawed and wide-eyed with the rest of the tourists, in among the towering redwoods. With the tourists, but slightly apart from them, in typical honeymooners' tender mutual absorption. Isolation was what he was after, narrowing the threat and keeping it to themselves.

After that the great northern semicircle of National Parks and Forests lay before them, beautiful under blue skies and the drifting hazes of summer. He and his six were familiar with most of the areas they would be visiting, some with one more than another. Together they made possible a fairly clear coverage. He only had to keep in touch with one a day, anyway.

And Gonzo, of course.

Gonzo would be exposing them from behind, widening the circle of their vulnerability day by day, until the right ripple shimmered over the right stone, and Edison got the word.

He waited at their table until he saw the convertible pull into the parking lot. Once Terson and Gambini were seated about ten feet away from Clare, behind and to her right, facing front and back, he got up and found the public phone near the kitchen.

Gonzales sounded harassed. 'You're an hour late,' he snapped.

'Hey, I'm on *vacation*, man,' Malchek protested good humouredly.

'I got some bad news for you.'

'If you mean the apartments, we heard it on the radio.'

'Oh. She OK?'

'You've got a father complex. She's fine.' He glanced over at their table. Clare was reading the menu, a little pale but otherwise looking good. She had changed into a white jersey dress that clung to her breasts and swirled away from her hips, a red belt around the small waist.

'How's the cover working?' Gonzales asked, bringing his attention back abruptly.

'So far, so good. Garner and Martin on the cycle, Terson and Gambini in the convertible. They're here now, doing meal duty. They'll drive on tomorrow, and Van will close up on us before they leave. He's alternating with Davis, in the trucks.'

'When do you catch up with Gambini and Terson again?'

'Day after tomorrow, they're switching to a station-wagon somewhere around Forest Glen, then a Buick convertible the day after.'

'You got a nice cross-pattern going.'

He didn't need Gonzo's approval, he knew it would work. If anything would work. 'You getting any closer back there?' He glanced around the restaurant again, the doors, the windows, the faces, the dusty cars outside in the lot cooling as the sun dropped. Plastic violins fluttered from a speaker overhead, and drifted with the smell of frying ham and onions.

'I dropped Richardson Grove to the first ten this afternoon in the duty room. We're A-OK and counting, as they say. You're still sure this is how you want to go?'

'Yes. As long as you've been keeping them off their asses and looking to catch the bastard before he moves on us. What are you picking up from the street?'

'Not a goddamn thing. The lid is on.'

'That's funny.' It was not, in point of fact, funny at all. He wasn't amused in the slightest. 'Is he spending?'

'I guess he must be. Or somebody's got his thumbs in. Whatever it is, nobody knows from nothing, and isn't it a nice day? You know the kind of crap they give you. All smiles.'

'Yeah, I know. Keep on it, OK?'

'Hey ... *I'm* not on vacation,' Gonzales mocked him. '*I'm* not tooling around the countryside with some good-looking broad, taking in the sights, eating that fine, expense-paid food, sleeping on all those crisp, clean sheets.'

'I'm glad to hear it,' he said drily. 'You can get to me through Terson if you have to.'

'Until when?'

'He'll let you know before he leaves.'

When he got back to the table, Clare was looking uneasy.

'That man keeps looking at me, the one in the corner.'

He picked up his menu, flipped it open too fast and let the purple-mimeographed à la carte sheet slide out on to the floor. When he sat back up again he had the man in his horizon. Good-looking, blond, slope-shouldered. He was reading his own menu with unnatural concentration.

'He still watching you?' Malchek asked, inserting the loose paper under the clip at the top of the menu-card. She glanced across.

'Not since you came back, no. Is he one of yours?'

'No,' he grinned. 'He's one of yours.'

'What's that supposed to mean?'

'It's supposed to mean that, as Gonzales just reminded me, you're a good-looking broad. The guy was wondering if you were alone, that's all. Now he knows you're not. End of story.'

'He isn't one of your . . .'

'Oh, he could be one of mine, sure. But that's a good demonstration of the reason I haven't introduced you to them. If you know he's been watching you, it means you've been watching him. You're not used to this, and I don't want my men shown up. OK?'

She looked at him in exasperation. He had changed into a dark-blue denim shirt open at the throat, jeans and a chamois jacket that hung loosely over his belt, covering the .38.

'What would I do if he shot you first? How would I know who to run to, who to ask for help?'

'If I go down, you just go down too.' He smiled as if they were discussing which of the six kinds of pie to have. 'Lie still. They'll run to you. Don't worry about it. What are you going to have?'

'Ulcers.'

'Want a salad with them, or french fries?' His face and voice were bland, and she realized it was one of the reasons she kept trying to bait him. He could simply shut her out with no effort at all. On the few occasions he lost control and hit back at her, she felt a sense of triumph. Suddenly it seemed a very cheap way to pass the time. He was trying to keep her alive, wasn't he?

'I'll have the lamb chops,' she apologized.

Sleeping next to someone you hate is easy.

Sleeping next to someone you like is not. Particularly if you've decided you're not going to like them any more than you do already.

Before they'd left the city that morning he had slipped a wedding-band on to her finger and muttered, 'With this ring I thee disguise.' There was a matching band on his hand. She had said nothing, merely resumed brushing her hair. Perhaps a little more vigorously.

The situation could have been simple. They were both

healthy and attractive, neither was a prude. It would have been easy to say 'Look, since we're here ...' and made the most of it. But though on the surface the situation was simple, they were not.

And so the double-bed in the first motel was a problem. To toss a coin and stick one of them with a chair or the floor seemed juvenile. In the end they both got ready for bed, went to bed, and lay on the bed, wrapped in more than blankets.

He was very aware of her nakedness under the white jersey pyjamas she had chosen in an effort to appear sexless. In fact, all they did was outline her body even more emphatically than a nightgown would have done.

Normally he simply slept in his skin, but had borrowed some pyjamas for the trip. They constricted him and he felt strange, finally tossing the top back into the suitcase.

Later, when her hand inadvertently touched his naked back, Clare felt the velvety warmth of his skin and had to turn away. The urge to stroke the curve of his spine and the scar on his shoulder-blade was so strong it almost made her hand feel like a separate and uncontrollable entity. She was afraid of what it might do. It was an animal that wanted to crawl softly towards him, seeking his warmth now that the sun was gone and the night was cool.

Eventually they slept.

For the first time in days Malchek was able to sleep deeply, knowing that Garner and Martin were somewhere outside in the dark, taking alternate watches from a shared sleeping-bag.

The nightmare caught him unawares.

He hadn't had it for over three years. Maybe it was the shrimp salad, maybe it was the war movie they had watched on the motel TV, maybe it was simply weariness.

Whatever the reason, coming up from the blank trough of his initial unconsciousness, his eyelids began to flutter. He twisted, clutched the sheet, muttered more and more insistently. He groaned, not very loudly.

Clare sat up, terrified, not knowing what had awakened her. Then, when he moved convulsively once more, she turned and saw a second cry starting to rise in his throat. He was going to scream, she could see the taut muscles in his neck, the lips parting over clenched teeth, the teeth parting. Faint light from the street outside threw his face into a mask of inhuman fear, the scream was bubbling up out of him like vomit.

Instinctively she moved to him, holding him, shaking him, calling his name.

'No. It's all right, Mike, it's all right, you're all right.' She clung to him, calling over his terror until he shuddered and came up and awake in one violent movement, the scream choked off, his eyes wide in the darkness.

She was still pressed against his side, arms around him, her hair drifting across his mouth. He didn't even know she was there.

'Jesus,' he said in a strangely calm voice. Then, again, 'Jesus,' and he began to shake. She let her arm drop, slowly, not knowing whether he wanted her to touch him or not. After a while he threw off the covers and stood beside the bed in the darkness, a darker shadow, faceless.

'Sorry,' he said briefly, and went into the bathroom.

She turned on the light and listened to the bath water running. Finally there was silence behind the closed door. After a long, long time, she got worried and went over to knock on the door, her bare feet curling up at the cold touch of the floor.

'Mike? Are you OK?'

'I'm fine. Go back to sleep.' His voice sounded strong, level, normal. Producing it took a great deal of effort.

He lay in the warm water as he had been taught to do, and heard her get back into bed. His head lay back on the edge of the tub, and he turned his face periodically to allow the cold porcelain to drain away the heat of his skin.

It would be a while before the shaking stopped. Before the bright reality of the hard-edged bathroom tiles and mirror would empty his mind of the darkness and the shame. Before he could get out, dry himself, put the pyjamas back on and return to lie beside Clare.

It was bad enough that he'd had the nightmare. Worse that she'd been there.

When he finally returned to bed, he knew she was not asleep.

He could feel her alertness across the space between them. When he lit the match for an unaccustomed cigarette the flare reflected in her open eyes.

After a while she took a breath. He'd hoped she wouldn't speak at all, but he should have known better. No doubt she'd have some snide remark to make, he decided, and braced himself.

'Does it happen often?'

There was no aggression in her voice. Relieved, he let his muscles relax. 'It hasn't happened for years. I thought it was over.'

'Was it the war? Something in the war?'

'Yes. I'd rather not talk about it. It's gone now.'

'Sure. Sorry.'

It surprised him that she would let the golden opportunity for sarcasm or glib amateur psychology go by. Gradually he accepted the comfort of her silent presence. He stubbed the cigarette out in the ashtray, and slid down under the covers.

She still did not speak. But, beneath the sheets, he felt her hand slide into his and stay there. He closed his fingers over hers and interlocked them.

He stared up at the patterns of light and shadow on the ceiling, listening to random cars hum past on the blacktop, going from one anonymous point to another. Faceless passengers on their nameless journeys.

After a while he realized that her breathing had grown shallow and slow. The long sighs of her sleep filled his head and he drifted with them.

Small Clare, smaller every minute in your own fear, how can I explain? I can't, any more than I was able to tell my own father. He sent me off with the simple conviction that the army would do what he had somehow missed doing. That it would make me into a man. Instead . . . He sighed, closed his eyes.

Instead, one dirty night after another, one dirty bullet after another, the knife, the garrotte. His father had died just before he'd left Nam. Because his grief was mixed with a shameful relief that his father would never be able to demand the truth about his war, he had never allowed himself to cry over his father's death. Not then, not since.

How could Clare or his father understand the filthy thing he had become over there? Understand how he had done it, gone *on* doing it, and doing it well, until ... no. No! That was the way back to the nightmare.

The hard-packed earth under bare feet, the fronds of willow and fern, the gun heavy in his hand ...

He turned his head on the pillow and kept his eyes on Clare's profile until a cleaner sleep claimed him.

When he awoke in the morning he found she had turned away from him in sleep. But her hand was still curled within his, small and warm.

fourteen

By the ninth day it seemed to Clare that she had been a tourist all her life. That she and Malchek had gaped at every redwood in the forests, leaned backwards to take in every mountain, pored down or across every canyon, gulch or valley the National Parks Department had to offer.

It might have been enjoyable if, while she was doing the ooh-ing and aah-ing, he had joined in. He always looked everywhere *but* at the scenery. In a broader, looser sense, he continued the same pattern he had maintained in the city. The same way of going before her into every bar, restaurant or motel room, the same rituals of search and suspicion.

She came in from the bath that night to find him looking out of the window at the rear of the unit. He had put her case on the rack and, as she crossed to it in the dark, she was aware of him turning first to one side and then the other, as if searching for something outside. He was humming under his breath.

'Let me guess,' she said. 'We overlook a nudist colony.'

'No,' he said idly. 'Just lining up possible trajectories.'

He crouched down on his heels to look up the slopes that rose behind the motel. It was nearly pitch-dark outside, but he could see the top edge of the hill behind them, and decided the angle was too steep to worry about. The woods were more dangerous than the heights. He closed the curtains, switched on the lights, and turned to find her regarding him in rigid dismay.

'What's the matter?' There was a glimmer of deep fear behind her eyes, the first he had seen for some time. He felt compelled to apologize, although he wasn't sure what for. 'Sorry ... it's just force of habit. I never come into any new place without doing that. Even if I'm alone ... not working.'

'But *why*?'

He felt suddenly embarrassed. 'It's why I'm here, isn't it?'

'Yes ... but you said you do it all the time ...'

'It's just a habit.' He tried an unsuccessful laugh. 'You know, dogs walk around and pee over any new territory they come into ... maybe that's what I'm doing. I just can't settle until I've checked out all the weak points. Accessibility, ways out, that kind of thing. I have to know the way out, wherever I am.' She kept looking at him. He went across to the door passing close behind her. 'Of course, *you* don't have any stupid habits, do you?' he growled, and went out.

She stood by the suitcase looking after him. It was the first irritability he'd shown since the night of the bad dream. Although he had looked drawn and weary the next day, he'd been more relaxed and affable than at any time since she'd met him. As if the dream had purged some poison from his system. She didn't think it was worth it. And, apparently, the relief had been only temporary. In the intervening period she had allowed herself to like him more and more. He was a man who knelt down to feed squirrels, who tipped tired waitresses higher than he tipped pretty ones. It had begun to be very nice, being shepherded and looked after by that Malchek.

Now the other one was back. The stranger.

She sighed and sorted through the case to find the white jersey dress. It needed washing. As she pulled it out, a brown glass medicine bottle came with it and fell on to the carpet. She remembered collecting it with her own things from the bathroom shelf of the last motel. She looked curiously at the label. 'M. Malchek. Paludrine. As needed. Dr K. Stammel.' The label was from a drugstore in Malchek's home neighbourhood.

She put it back in his case, tucking it into a side pocket. Probably it was a freezing agent, to keep him as chilled and remote as he'd been in the beginning.

How infantile to think the old Malchek had ever been far away. There were always the rituals, the watchfulness, the sometimes sharp orders to move back or away or to stand still. Smiles had made them easier, but they had been orders, and she'd obeyed. She knew that, in some mysterious way she couldn't fathom, he constantly wove around them a web of other watchers. Small notes would appear on the floor of the car. She would turn and find him just dropping his hand after making some surreptitious signal to someone, somewhere. She'd given up trying to guess how it worked.

She almost wished that Edison would try. At least it would be a kind of resolution to this ridiculous situation.

When Malchek came back to the room he heard the hiss of the shower and Clare's voice raised in defiant and peripherally dissonant song. Sing away, babe, he thought. You've earned it.

Restlessly he searched in his suitcase for the pack of cigarettes. He lit one and blinked at the flare of the dry tobacco. His cigarettes were invariably stale, he only smoked about two a week.

'Hi,' she said, patting her face and hair with the loose sleeve of her terrycloth robe as she came out of the bathroom. 'I'll be ready in a few minutes.'

'No hurry.'

'I thought you said you were so hungry?' She was gathering up her things from the case, a cascade of lace and nylon dripped from her hand as she stared at him.

'It's over, Clare. You're off the hook.'

'Gonzales has caught him?' She knew he'd been calling headquarters. He nodded.

'Not Gonzo himself, but some sheriff in a town called Spider Meadows.'

She couldn't believe it. 'Are they *sure*?'

He smiled briefly, her question an echo of his own to Gonzo. From the other end of the line Gonzo's voice had been elated and unnaturally high.

'On a *rape* charge, would you believe it?' he had shouted gleefully into Malchek's ear. 'This sheriff is either a hotshot or he hasn't much else to do but sit around on his ass and read our flyers. Anyway, he said he thought this guy looked familiar, so he pulled the sheet and had a second look. He says it's Edison, all right.'

'Hell, I'm not buying *that*,' he had protested.

Gonzales had chuckled down the line. 'That's what *I* said. So I had him send me prints, and I compared them with the one on your files.'

'That's only a partial.'

'Yeah, I know. Even so, I picked up seven points of similarity – that's not bad.'

'Not proof, either.'

'What do you want from me, blood type and his mother's maiden name?'

'Have you got them?'

'Not yet, but I will.'

'Where did you say he was?'

'Little two-bit town not far from you, called Spider Meadows, like I said. On Route Thirty-two. You're there to-morrow – right?'

'They've got a *teleprinter* in a place called Spider Meadows? That sheriff must be some kind of hotshot, all right.'

'No, for crying out loud. He drove into Paradise and sent them from the police station there.'

'Oh. So Edison's in Paradise, then?' That sounded desirable, but unlikely.

'Ah. Well ... no ... *he's* still in Spider Meadows.'

'Why?'

Gonzales was apologetic. 'Well ... This Sheriff Hoskins ... he's a little worried about taking him into the Paradise jail-house ...'

'What?' Malchek was wearying of the whole thing.

'Well ... The little girl involved in the rape—'

'*Little girl? I've* no pervert info on—'

'No, no ... she's fifteen, the sheriff says, and big with it. Well ... She's his niece, it seems. Small town, see ... and—'

'And he's kicked the shit out of Edison, is that what you're telling me? Beautiful.' He thought for a moment. 'Route Thirty-two, you said. My side of Paradise, or yours?'

'Yours.'

Malchek sighed. 'OK, we'll bring him back with us. This Hoskins ... he's not going to press for a prior, is he?'

'Shit, no. I think he wants to get the hell out of it. The fact that it's Edison scares him ... and he's not so sure about the rape charge anymore, either.'

Malchek grinned and shook his head, running his free hand through his hair. Still need it cut, he thought. 'What's this so-called sheriff do the *rest* of the time?'

'Yeah ... he's the local feed and grain merchant.'

'God save the amateur cop.'

'He *got* him, didn't he?' Gonzales sounded hurt at Malchek's lack of enthusiasm.

'Yes, OK, he lucked into it, and you and me and the big city pros never got near. I got the message. We'll pick him up tomorrow. I've got everyone here as it happens – we were making a cross-over tomorrow. I guess six are enough to handle even Edison?'

'There's seven of you.'

'*I've* still got the girl ... or had you forgotten that?'

'Oh, yeah. She won't exactly want to ride home next to him, will she?'

Malchek chuckled. 'No, somehow I don't think she will.'

When they finally returned to their motel after dinner with the other six cops, Clare felt relaxed and light-headed. Malchek had not taken much to drink, but she had. He was bending over to tune the TV when she came up behind him and ran her hands along his back to his shoulders, and ruffled his hair. For a minute he continued to lighten the commentator's face to a paler hue, then straightened slowly and turned to her, expressionless.

'I just ...' She faltered a little under his cold green eyes, but went on, driven by a need she only vaguely understood. 'I just wanted to say thanks for ... for everything ... you've done ... I mean ... I know ... the danger ... he could have ...'

'And you'd like to say thanks in bed, is that it?' His light, metallic voice cut sharply across her stammer. She actually fell back a step under the sound.

'Well ... that's ...'

He tilted his head to one side. 'It's a nice gesture. I don't mind. It's not easy sleeping next to a good-looking broad night after night without doing anything about it. Sure. Why not?' He looked her over from head to toe, grinned, and reached for her. She fell back another step.

'Don't ... You make it sound so ... just a ... physical thing ...'

His eyes narrowed. 'Why ... what else would it be? A nice gesture, like I said. People do it all the time ... perfectly normal ...'

'I didn't mean to make a *nice gesture*.' She struggled in her confusion and shock at his unexpected brusqueness. 'I ... I *like* you, Mike. You're someone special ... I feel I ...'

'Well, that's nice. I like you too,' he said impatiently. Somehow it sounded different in his mouth than in hers, and he was destroying something every time he spoke. She's getting small again, he thought despairingly as he retreated behind his face.

'No ...' She turned away finally. 'I'm sorry ... I guess I just had too much to drink.'

He clenched his fists behind him, and put all the ice in. 'You want to screw or not?'

Her head came up and her shoulders stiffened. 'No. No, thank you, I do not ... want ... to screw. Just ... forget it, I guess. Sorry.'

'Whatever you say. I'm not big on rape, myself.' He watched her grab blindly at her night-things and slam the door of the bathroom behind her. He closed his eyes.

You bastard, he told himself, turning to stare at the TV. Correction. A real bastard would have smiled and said the easy words. It's only cop-worship, anyway. Only relief and gratitude and a bottle of wine. I don't want to screw you either, Clare. I want to make love to you, and that would screw both of us. But if there's a patron saint for cops out there, listen, will you? Don't let her look at me like that again. Please.

His eyes cleared on a talk-show host who was talking to a

chimpanzee with earnest attention. The chimp continued to eat a banana, staring out at the audience. The host then ate a banana.

He changed the channel and watched some lone-star hero punch a drunken cowboy through a bar window in an explosion of sugar-glass.

There's only room in here for me, he tried to explain to the guy in the white hat. I can't let anyone get inside me. I'm not going to hurt any more. Not going to *be* hurt any more. When I killed my first one in cold blood, I locked the door. She deserves more than that.

The population of Spider Meadows only exceeded a thousand when it took the overflow of the near-by ski resorts in winter. Now, in August, there was a hot emptiness under the trees, and the houses sat behind their long lawns with drawn shades. Following the directions Gonzales had given them, they turned left before the actual town centre and went about half a mile down an unpaved side road. When Malchek stepped out of the car, the stillness startled him. No shrieks of children, no barking dogs, nothing. Behind him, the convertible bumped its tyres against the broken edge of the kerb, and in the distance he saw double dust trails flowing up behind Van Schaaten's pick-up and Davis's panel-truck. Garner and Martin had arrived ahead of them, and were sitting under a pine tree next to their bike. Heat shimmered up from the engine and dissipated among the heavy branches overhead. Garner called that he'd checked out the rear – one car, unmarked. Nobody around.

'Wait here until I call you,' Malchek said, leaning down to speak to her through the open window. Clare nodded, and he turned to approach the house.

He wondered if it had been money or a sense of humour that had marooned the canary-yellow Nob Hill frame house out here under the pines. It had a fair piece of ground around it, but the grass had grown wild, and a briar rose had a stranglehold on the gingerbread around the porch roof and gables. The trim had originally been red, but it, like the yellow, had faded under time and rain. The fire was out. Creaking porch stairs announced his arrival better than any doorbell, and the front door opened before he had reached the top step. A big figure in tans stood behind the screen watching him.

'You Malchek?' rasped the voice, harsh with bitter times gone by.

'Hoskins?' Malchek flipped open his leather identity fold and held the gold badge towards the screen-door. The big man hardly glanced at it, being more interested in the approach of Terson and Gambini from the convertible. His bullet-hole eyes flicked past their casual figures to Van Schaaten and Davis coming from further down the street, swivelled again past Malchek to Garner and Martin under the tree, then to Clare in the sedan.

'You always travel by wagon train?'

'Coincidence,' Malchek answered. 'Where's the prisoner?'

'I got him in here.' A lazy hand snapped the hook out of its ring and swung the screen door back with a whine from the spring at the top.

Seen without the filter of the rusty screening, Hoskins was a big, florid man with thinning grey hair and a body running to fat in the belly. He had a black eye and a strip of adhesive running along the bulge of one cheek. It did not completely mask the scabbing graze that cut an angry line from ear to nose.

'He gave you trouble, I see,' Malchek observed, coming into a hall that stretched long and dark to the rear of the house. A steep stairway rose along the right-hand wall, just beyond a pair of double doors. Another pair were across the hall.

'He's a big old boy, all right,' Hoskins grunted, letting the screen door snap shut just as Gambini came up to the porch. Terson reached past him and opened it again, and they leaned against the jamb with their jackets unbuttoned, looking in.

'And you're sure it's Edison?' Malchek persisted, assessing the narrow hall with its rag rugs floating on the old, unpolished floor-boards. At the rear there was a swing door hanging slightly ajar on tired hinges, its pushplate black with age. The house had an air of no woman in it, a house where a man lived alone and begrudged every minute he had to spend looking after himself. A house for coming and going, neat through absence rather than habit. Like his own place had been.

Hoskins eyed him truculently. 'He don't look a hell of a lot like your picture now, but he *did*. And I got them prints off him, too ... *he* said it was a match.'

'Who said?'

'Your man ... Gonzales, is it? He told me when he phoned back to say you'd be along to take the bastard off me.'

'And that's OK with you?' It was only a courtesy. He knew he could take Edison without Hoskins's say-so, and worry about the paperwork later.

'Shee-yut, *I* don't want him. I got work to do, my business to run. Damn nuisance, taken from the start of it.' He turned and started up the long stairway, lifting his bulk reluctantly.

'Your niece, Gonzales said.'

'Sherrill Anne? Yeah. Trouble from the minute her tits began to show. Walks with a busy ass, just like her mother. Still, no reason to do what he done, you know? She's only just a k ... kid.'

'Sure.' Malchek could visualize her, they all seemed to grow up too fast these days.

Hoskins turned left at the top of the stairs and crossed to an open doorway, stepping just inside and stopping. Malchek stayed in the hall and looked in at the heavy furniture crowded between dusty walls. Taking up most of the space in the centre of the room was a dark, carved oak double-bed, and taking up most of the bed was a man.

Hoskins was right, he didn't look much like the Edison Clare had described as 'attractive'. He was tall and well built, true enough. But the face was a day-old battlefield in purple and green, scabs on cuts that hadn't been washed, eyes puffed shut and a jaw that looked strangely askew below the ears.

'You broke his jaw,' Malchek said quietly.

'He fell down the goddamn stairs.'

'Clumsy bastard.' Malchek played it out. He approached the bed, looked at the shape of the skull, the ears, the close-cropped dark hair, the swollen hands captive in too-tight cuffs. He pulled back one lid but the eyes were rolled up. The rim of iris showing looked grey, all right. 'Nice to see a prisoner so well cared for. You're sure a credit to law enforcement, Hoskins.'

'You want to hear Sherrill Anne tell you about it?'

'No thanks.' He lifted one of the manacled hands and turned it over. The fingertips were still amateurishly smeared with black ink, and there were matching smears on the sheet. He paused as he let the hands drop back on to the prisoner's stomach. There was something peculiar about the right leg. 'Saving money on leg irons too?'

'I told you, he fell down the goddamn stairs.'

Malchek turned and looked at the big man leaning against the carved oak bureau just inside the door. 'You should have told Gonzales to send an ambulance. I'm no fucking doctor,' his anger hissed out. Enough temper to break in a face he could accept, under the circumstances, but not enough to break a leg as well and let the whole result lie there like a side of beef. 'That's a badge you've got on your shirt, not a goddamn licence to torture, Hoskins.'

'Do tell?' Hoskins regarded him malevolently. 'I'll mention that professional philosophy to Sherrill Anne when she gets back from the hospital in Paradise. She'd sure appreciate it.'

'He put her in the hospital?' Malchek was surprised. That did not gibe with his files, either.

'Like I said, he's a big old boy. Likes to push hard, likes to hit. Ripped her up some top *and* bottom. You're right, Malchek, he didn't fall down the stairs, I threw him down. You want to make a complaint about the prisoner's condition, go ahead. I don't give a sweet damn, I'm fed up wearing this badge anyways.'

Malchek looked again towards the bed, and nodded. Fifteen years old and bleeding, maybe he'd throw a man down the stairs too. He'd had similar cases and experienced similar rages, but there are a lot of eyes in the city. Out here Hoskins was on his own. Edison had picked a bad place to make a mistake.

He went to the doorway and called down to Terson. 'Get Clare in here, but warn her he's in bad shape.' He saw Terson's glasses wink as he turned back towards the sun and left Gambini alone in the doorway. 'We'll need something to carry him on, Gambini. Some kind of stretcher ... see what you can put together. Van's got some junk in his pick-up that might be useful.' He could see Gambini's black eyebrows lift, but he let the screen door slam shut without comment.

Clare came hesitantly into the room and froze at the sight of the man on the bed. Malchek went to her and stood quietly as she stared and stared. 'Is it Edison?' he asked her after a full minute. 'I know it's hard to tell from the face. Look at the shape of the head, ears, so on. Things that aren't touched.'

She tried. 'I think it could be,' she finally decided. 'The hair is the same, the way it grows on to the forehead, I mean. Is that the kind of thing ...?'

'Good.' The faint warmth of his approval was short-lived. 'OK, Hoskins, we'll take him in.' The big man's eyes were on Clare, and there was something in his expression Malchek didn't like. He moved with her as she passed the sheriff and went into the hall.

'You go on down and wait,' he instructed. 'I'll be down in a few minutes.'

She looked pale and would not meet his eyes. He watched her go slowly down the stairway, moving to one side as Gambini and Van Schaaten came up with their improvised stretcher. Not much longer, Clare, he told her silently. I'll drive you home and that will be the end of it. In a few months I'll see you in court, and I'll nod and smile. I won't feel a thing. Not a thing, I'll make sure of it.

Shifting the prisoner on to the stretcher took all of them working together. Hoskins never left the bureau, watching without much interest as they struggled. The prisoner was unconscious, and Malchek wondered about concussion. He muttered something to Gambini about radio-ing ahead for an ambulance and a doctor to meet them, or maybe stopping at Sacramento.

Somehow they got him down the stairs and into the back of Davis's panel-truck. Martin and Terson would ride inside with him, Garner and Gambini would function as outriders fore and aft, with Van Schaaten coming up as drag. The pick-up didn't have much power and wouldn't be able to keep up once they hit the flat of the valley and the speeds of Interstate 5 and 80.

Malchek watched them go from the porch, knowing Clare was still inside the house. He wondered if it was habit that made him uneasy about going any further away. Or was it just the look in Hoskins's eyes as they ran over her body in the white jersey dress?

She's not my worry any more, he cautioned himself. But, once Van Schaaten's pick-up was out of sight, he went back inside quickly. She was sitting beside the door, on the seat of and old-fashioned coat-rack. Elaborate iron hooks sprouted around the mirrored wooden backrest above her head. She looked exhausted, a forlorn figure in the gloom.

Hoskins was standing on the short stretch of landing behind the stair-rail. He was staring down at Clare, and Malchek sensed he'd spoken to her and not had a response. The black eyes were re-aimed at him as he let the screen-door drop shut behind him. Hoskins repeated the question.

'Your lady looks a little beat, lieutenant. Would she like some c ... coffee before settin' out again? I got some on the stove, ought to be real prime by now.'

'Clare?' Her head came up slowly at the sound of Malchek's voice, as if she had been in another room, another house, and heard him call to her from the garden. 'Would you like some coffee? The sheriff has offered us some.'

'Oh. Yes ... yes, I would.' She turned to look up at the big man leaning on the railing overhead. 'Thank you, yes.' She stood up slowly, and turned to look out at the car through the screen-door.

Hoskins nodded and came down the stairs, smiling as if she'd told him he resembled John Wayne, which he did not. 'Nothin' like c ... c ... coffee to give you a boost. I take mine black, but I got some real nice heavy c ... cream for the lady. You folks make yourselves at home in the parlour there ... I'll be through directly ...'

He ambled down the hall, talking over his shoulder, and disappeared through the swing-door. They heard a clatter of cups after a moment, and Malchek turned to Clare.

A finger of ice trailed down his spine.

She was staring into the mirror. She met his eyes there. Her lips were parted and he could not tell where the white of her dress left off and she herself began, the blood seemed to have drained from every visible inch of her.

'He ... Mike ...' She was struggling, struggling terribly, and he didn't know how to help, what to do or say to break the lock on her voice. He took a step towards her, held out his hand. She turned. '*That's* him *That's* him ... *he* stammered ... *his* ears, *his* back ... I saw him in my rear-view mirror ...' The words were flooding now. She couldn't get them out fast enough, but he didn't need any more.

He pulled her round by the elbows. 'Out,' he commanded, his voice low. 'Get out, get to the car ...' She was as stiff as a wooden doll. 'Go, Clare ... *go* ...' He pushed her with one hand, reaching for his .38 with the other. He never made it.

The double doors on their right suddenly slid apart, and Edison/Hoskins was there.

'Don't rush off. The c ... coffee's ready. In here.'

Malchek's hand froze in mid-reach, his eyes going first to Edison's face, then to the silenced automatic in the tall man's grip. The light within the parlour was stronger than in the hall. A shaft of sun fell on the face in the doorway, and Malchek could see that the 'black eye' had smudged a little, and the 'graze' had partially disappeared. In the gloom of the hall skilful make-up had sufficed, but not now. To complete the picture, Edison reached up with his free hand and pulled off the lank, grey wig. Underneath, his own hair was short and dark, fitting closely to the well-shaped skull. Working with his tongue and the back of his left hand, he spat out the pads that had filled his cheeks and muffled his voice into an old man's husk.

'Just so you'll know me this time, Miss Randell,' he smiled.

Next to Malchek, Clare whimpered faintly, deep in her throat. The sound tore at him, but he dared not move. He could see Edison was on a knife-edge, tense and high. Dangerous beyond belief, but holding off, delaying, enjoying something. What? What was he waiting for? Whatever it was, would it give them a chance?

'I offered you c ... c ... coffee and you'll drink it. In here.' The automatic gestured, and the voice drew them in like thin wire. They went into the parlour. Edison stopped Malchek long enough to strip the .38 from his belt, then pushed him quite gently after Clare.

There was, indeed, a tray of coffee on the round table in the centre of the room.

At another gesture of the automatic in Edison's hand, Clare and Malchek sat on a dusty, old, horsehair settee that crouched bow-legged in the bay-window. He stood and looked down at them from beside the table, dropping the wig like a dead bat behind the silver tray, the .38 beside it.

'I've been reading up on you, Malchek,' he said conversationally, lifting the heavy silver coffeepot and filling the three cups. 'I like knowing about the people I go up against. You've got *quite* a history.'

Malchek could feel Clare trembling beside him, and he reached over to take her hand. Edison noted the gesture and his gaze sharpened.

'You know what you're sitting next to, my dear? A man with more victims to his credit than even *I* have. How many was it, Malchek? Eighty-seven or eighty-nine?'

Malchek waited for Clare's hand to leave his, but felt her grip tighten instead. 'Forget it, Edison,' he croaked, his voice shaking with an old and tired rage. 'Let her go. I'll take her away, make another life, make sure she never identifies you. She'll never be a threat to you, never. I promise you.'

'Ah, too late, of course. But you mean it, don't you, Malchek? You really mean it,' Edison said in an amazed tone.

'Yes, I do. You know I do.'

'I can see that.' He turned insolently, taking his time with the cream and sugar cubes, knowing Malchek would not make a move until he had his answer. He turned to look at them again, the gun level and motionless in his hand. 'So the newspaper story wasn't a plant? You do love her? My, my. What a pity it will never c ... come to anything.'

'We'll see.'

'No, *I'll* see. You'll be too dead to see anything, I'm afraid. Unless you believe in ghosts. I don't.'

'You couldn't afford to, could you?'

'You can save your bitter c ... comments. I was just interested in having a look at you before blowing you away. I'm not very impressed.'

'Neither am I.'

'Let's call it stalemate, then. A dull party. Pity, really, one always hopes for a little drama now and again.'

'Uh-huh.'

'Still . . . since we're here we might as well be polite.'

Edison came towards Clare with her cup of coffee. Malchek waited until he got close, then kicked up and knocked it out of his hand, moving forward to follow through. He got no further than the mouth of the silencer against his breastbone.

'Sit down, pig,' Edison snarled. Malchek sat. His hands dropped between his knees as the coffee spread outwards from the shards of china on the worn Turkey carpet, the stain nearly reaching the toe of his shoe.

'Just as I figured – you've lost a little speed, haven't you?' Edison observed. 'Too much desk time. I don't let that happen, myself. I work out twice a week, gym and target. If you're doing a job, you might as well do it right. Looks like you've forgotten.'

Malchek said nothing. He watched Edison warily from behind his attitude of surrender. The hand and the gun were steady, and the breathing was perfectly even, perfectly slow, despite what he had thought was a fairly fast, if predictable, attack. Maybe Edison was right, he had lost his edge. So it had to come from something other than speed. He wondered if Edison's vanity was still an open door.

'Nothing like grandstanding to give you that extra polish,' he offered. 'You like to get applause, don't you? I'd rather play it quiet, myself.'

'Like you did in Nam? What was it General Becker told me they named you? Oh, yes. The Iceman. The Iceman c . . . cometh, they used to say, every time you did a job. No flair, Malchek, no flair at all.'

'My God, is it some kind of competition between you? Is that it?' Clare's voice cracked in disbelief.

Malchek had to ignore the pain in her voice. 'Not really. It's just that Edison here thinks in terms of looking good. I did what I did—'

'Eighty-seven times,' Edison interrupted.

'—eighty-four times because when I did it I thought it was necessary. It was only later . . . that I saw how unnecessary it was. How pointless, and wrong. Obviously wherever our friend here learned the trade, he got to like the rather cheap shine some people think goes with it.'

'Not cheap. I've never come cheap,' Edison bit out.

'Stop it!' Clare shouted. 'You've made your point. We're here because you want to kill *me*. All right, if I frighten you so much, kill me. But don't try to make Mike look bad to me, because you can't. Filth like you can't come near him, can't even begin to see him as he really is.' She stood up suddenly, and Edison's gun jerked as he stepped back, startled. Malchek's eyes narrowed and he measured the new gap between them without lifting his head. Clare's voice raged on. 'Go on, do it. *Do it*.'

Edison stared at her, smiled, then began to laugh. It was a hard, ugly sound, and did not last long.

'And you love *him*,' he managed to get out. 'Isn't that incredible, Malchek?' He laughed again, briefly. 'Really, Clare, you have lousy taste in men. You think he's so wonderful because he's been acting out a little game of brave protector? It *is a game*. Accept it. Underneath that lovely legal badge he's still just like me. A killer. No more, and probably a great deal less. *Sit down*.'

Malchek reached up and took her hand, pulling her back. 'Sit down, Clare,' he said wearily, and she dropped down beside him.

Her physical defiance was finished, but her anger remained, unrelieved. She couldn't bear the sound of defeat in his voice. 'I don't care if it was seven, or seventy, or seven hundred,' she told Edison. 'That was there and this is here. He was a soldier, he was doing what he was told.'

'That doesn't make it right, Clare,' Malchek said softly.

'No, but it makes it *over*. Finished and done with. What are *your* reasons?' she hissed at Edison. 'Money? There's *nobility*, I suppose?'

Edison nodded agreeably. 'The money is good, yes. *And* it's tax-free, remember. But it's funny you should want my reasons.

You see, you're in a unique position to realize why I do it, Clare. *Very* unique. Let me tell you about a man we know.'

Malchek sat very still. There was something more here. Clare was getting through to Edison, making him strut. His knuckles were no longer white where they gripped the butt of the automatic, his legs were not locked, and Edison's weight was shifting very, very slowly back on to his heels. Yes, Clare, yes, Malchek silently cheered. And waited.

'This man we know,' Edison purred on. 'He's the kind of man everybody looks at but nobody sees. A dull man. A plodder. Good at his job, but uninspired. He's there when you need him, and out of the way when you've got better things to do. And in advertising, as you know so well, my sweet Clare, there are a *lot* of people like that. Behind the glamour-boys and the wheeler-dealers there are the hacks, the dependables, the unspecial ones. New York is full of them, and Chicago, and Detroit, and all the rest. They shuffle in, they shuffle out. They have their uses, and they are used. God, how they are *used*.'

Malchek felt Clare stiffen suddenly. What? What? What had Edison said or done? He didn't understand. It was taking a turn somewhere, and he'd lost it. He let his head hang loose, let his hair hide his eyes, let it all go on, watching for his chance. Edison was so locked into Clare that maybe, just maybe, he'd forgotten Malchek for the moment. And Malchek began to prepare, taking deep, long, slow and silent breaths.

'Click, click, Clare. Let's hear from you. A good idea doesn't c . . . c . . . care who has it.' Edison's voice was hard, almost coy. What did he want from her?

Suddenly Clare's breath stopped, hissed, went out like dying, for ever. Malchek wanted to look at her, but couldn't risk it.

'Alva?' she asked incredulously. '*Alva?*'

'Yes. *Yes!*' Edison's childish triumph was complete, gleeful, and Malchek's skin crawled. 'Ah, we were never introduced, were we? But you must have seen me, and I must have seen you. I knew your name when I found it in your apartment. I'm still there in New York, you know. Oh, yes. I know what they think of me at TN and all the other agencies. Useful hack. Here's a dull job, let's give it to old Tom, and we'll get on with the big stuff. At first it was money to eat, but never enough.

x

And it was boring, it was dull, it was empty. Other men who get bored take up golf, drink, women. But I had another alternative. I had another trade, and I had learned it well. I might be a nobody in your world, Clare, but I'm *the best killer in the country*. Maybe in the *world*. Dumb, dull Tom Alva, that's right. Oh, it makes me laugh when I take their little art assignments and look grateful. How I'd love to tell them the truth. How I'd *love* that. What would they say if the dog stood up and bit them? Hey? What do *you* say? You're the only one who will ever know, Clare. What do you say to me *now*?'

Malchek felt Edison straining, compelling Clare to respond, to be astonished, to give him what he craved.

'I ... it's ...' Clare stammered.

Malchek came up off the floor, driving straight from his spread feet, throwing his body between Clare and the gun that pointed its accusing finger while Edison sucked at her for nourishment. But even as he moved, he knew it was wrong. He should have waited, should have remembered he wasn't working alone any more, hadn't worked alone since Nam. All he'd cared about was Clare, and now, from outside, came the sound he should have waited just a minute longer to hear. A motorcycle engine, revving, screaming, sliding.

Garner.

As he was suspended between Edison and Clare in that split-second of misjudgement he knew despair, and then the gun exploded in his face, and he knew nothing.

Edison reached for Clare and jerked her to her feet while Malchek fell to the floor, sprawling as if thrown, his face a mass of blood. Clare screamed and struggled against Edison's manic strength, digging her heels into the carpet. It ripped dustily under her feet, and she had a glimpse of Garner coming across the lawn outside, jumping, already on the run from the motorcycle that dropped to the kerb behind him, the wheels still driving as the engine choked itself off. Edison's gun thumped again, so close to her body that she felt the heat, and the lower bay-window disintegrated in a shower of crystal. She flailed at Edison with her free hand, but he leaned away without losing his grasp on her arm. Slowly the gun was reversed towards her, inexorably, steadily.

Her turn now.

Garner must have heard her screams even before the window had exploded. He had his gun drawn as he leapt up the steps, and then he disappeared behind the wall. There was a shout that came over the whine of the screen-door, and Edison was forced to turn towards the greater danger. As his balance altered, Clare gave a last, frenzied pull and fell away from him, crashing back into the table. For a moment he seemed uncertain where to point the gun next, and then Garner fired from the shadows of the hall. The noise was deafening, in contrast to the eerie, half-swallowed spit of Edison's silenced automatic. Edison cursed and ran to the opposite side of the room to get a better angle into the hall. As he did so, Clare crawled crab-like behind the table and pulled it over towards her. The coffeepot crashed past her head, splashing hot liquid that stained the skirt of her dress. Cream and sugar spewed out over the dark-red carpet, and something else fell too.

Mike's .38.

She reached for it, grasped it, stared at it as it lay black and heavy in her hand. The round top of the table was shielding her from Edison, and she didn't know if he realized she had Mike's gun. The thud and clatter of the table had caused a momentary stillness, apparently startling both Edison and Garner.

'Lieutenant, you in there?' came Garner's voice from the hall. Edison's gun spat soft again as Clare shouted.

'There's only me . . .' But her weak voice was lost in the convoluted echoes of Garner's return shot. She looked round the edge of the table as something moved in the room, and saw Edison scuttling through the dining-room towards the kitchen. 'He's going out the back,' she screamed, and raised Mike's gun in two unsteady hands.

She used both fingers to pull the trigger and the gun went off. It threw her hands back against the wrists painfully and made a tremendous noise. Edison staggered but continued to move. She was sobbing now, in rage and terror, and pulled the trigger again, even though she could see nothing clearly. And again.

She heard footsteps in the hall, caught a glimpse of Garner's helmeted figure moving past the open doorway and beyond to the kitchen door. At the same time there was another sound from the rear of the house; a heavy door closing. A table was skidded across linoleum. The door was slammed open again. Then silence. Nothing but her own panting breath stitched with sobs, and the stink of firecrackers filling the room. There was even a faint skein of smoke in the air, turning and swimming like a semi-transparent eel, over and over on itself.

Suddenly, from the rear of the house, a car engine roared and tyres sprayed gravel. She heard the sound of the engine moving past the house on the side away from her, then increasing in volume as it burst past the corner of the porch and roared towards the street.

She staggered towards the bay-window, grabbing the carved edge of the settee to prevent herself falling through the glass. A car *was* swerving from the drive into the gravel road, and the back end fishtailed wildly. Edison. Getting away.

Garner ran out from the side of the house towards his motor-cycle. As he did so, Edison shot back at him from the open side window of the car. Garner went down, legs wide, still running as he fell, arms out, flailing, and then terribly, terribly still. The sound of the car engine faded, like a jet beyond the reach of its own thunder, leaving only dust hanging in the street, falling gently on to the car parked there, and the Yamaha, and Garner on the grass.

As suddenly as the noise, there came silence again. No birds, no shouts, no shots, no engines, no sound at all. A faint wind stirred the pines beyond the lace of the curtains, and Clare even held her breath. Had Edison stopped, or was he simply beyond hearing? Driving away, or turning back?

And what was the other sound? That steady whisper behind her?

She turned and looked down at Mike, lying where he had fallen only moments ago. Her breath came back with her voice inside it, moaning out of her throat at the sight of him. The left side of his face was a mask of blood, blood running into his hair, into his open mouth, dripping on to the carpet to deepen the red underneath him.

But as she stumbled round the settee to kneel beside him, she realized what the sound was.

He was breathing.

He was alive.

fifteen

There was no phone in the house.

Frantically Clare ran from room to room, searching. Most of them contained only the hunched shapes of dust-sheeted furniture, stationary ghosts waiting to resume their whispered conference as soon as she closed the door.

She went to the kitchen. Through the open back door the neglected weeds of the backyard were topped with the nodding umbrellas of Queen Anne's lace. Dust still hung in the sunlight where Edison's car had skidded away.

Clare knew she should go out to see if she could help Garner, but she was filled with a desperate urgency to get the blood off Mike's face, to see how badly he was hurt, to know at once how near or far from death he lay. She found a cracked mixing-bowl in a cupboard and filled it with water, adding a handful of salt from the plastic shaker on the table.

Grabbing a roll of paper towels that stood upended on top of the stove, she stumbled back into the parlour, leaving a scattered trail of blotches to soak into the floor.

He had not moved.

Tearing a handful of sheets from the roll, she dipped them in the bowl of salt water and began to wipe the mess from his face. Every stroke revealed only whole skin as she worked gently back from his jaw towards his hairline. She finally found the wound itself running in an angry, dirty furrow straight along his cheekbone. The tip of his ear was gone too, simply taken away by the bullet. For a moment she wondered wildly whether she should crawl around on the carpet looking for it. It seemed very important, somehow, to put Humpty Dumpty back together again.

She worked steadily, and just as steadily the blood flooded back across his face. Gradually, after changing the bowl of water twice, she began to win. The flow of blood eventually gave way to a trickle, and then only dots of seepage from the gouge.

All the while she was guiltily aware of Garner lying out on the grass, although she could not see him from where she crouched on the floor. If only Mike would wake up, if only he would speak or moan or twitch or *anything*. But he still had not moved in any way.

Why hadn't anyone come? Surely someone must have heard the shots? No, of course not. All but one had been within the house. It was an old house, well built, and the windows had been closed. Edison's gun was silenced, and his outside shot had been covered by the sound of the car. The car had gone wildly down the road, but nobody would come out for that, they were probably used to the local sheriff taking off suddenly.

What sheriff?

Hoskins was Edison, was Alva, was still out there, was perhaps even now coming back for her.

How long did they have?

She returned her attention to Malchek and was startled to see his eyes were open, looking at her.

'Darling ... Mike ... oh, Mike ...' She leaned towards him, an earnest supplicant for any response.

Comprehension rose into his eyes like someone being pulled into the sunlight from a deep, deep well. 'Where ... is he ... ?' His voice was faint, a soft wind blowing.

'Gone ... he's gone ... Garner came back,' she began, and her voice caught. 'Garner's out on the lawn ... I think he's dead. Edison shot him as he drove away. Oh Mike ... are you all right?'

She pressed a fresh pad of paper towelling against his cheek and pushed the thick hair away from his forehead awkwardly.

He struggled to sit up. She saw the wave of nausea and dizziness hit him and tried to push him back down, but he was still stronger than she, despite the wound and loss of blood. And he was angry.

'Are *you* all right?' he demanded roughly. 'What happened after ... how long ... ?'

'I'm fine. I'm all right. Garner came up just as he ... as he ... shot you. Didn't you hear the motorcycle? Oh darling, please ...'

He drew back slowly, and looked into her face. It was as if he had reached into her body and squeezed her heart, hard.

Then he was standing up, moving so quickly she nearly went over backwards.

'Where's my gun?' he demanded, grabbing at the edge of the settee as his legs betrayed him. She pointed to where it had dropped from her hands under the window. He went over and scooped it up, a puzzled expression crossing his face.

'It's been fired,' he said, lifting it to sniff the barrel.

'I ... I fired it ...' she stammered. He stared at her, and for some reason she felt almost embarrassed to tell him. 'I thought he'd killed you ... I ... it was on the table ...'

His eyes went to the fallen tray, the scattered array of coffee-pot, cream-pitcher and sugar bowl within a sticky splash of white. The table lay on its side with its legs out like a dead animal. A twitching fly was already busy on the spilt mess.

'You fired at him?'

She nodded dumbly, and then was relieved to see a smile start to lift the corner of his mouth.

'Did you hit him?'

'I think so ... I thought he was hit ... but I couldn't see. The gun flashed at me,' she added, complaining to the owner about the behaviour of his pet. The smile on his face grew.

'Where was he? When you fired?'

'Going towards the kitchen.' She still sat where he had left her, where they had knelt together for an instant, next to the darkened bowl of water, surrounded by drifts of pale-blue paper towels. She was too weary to move, suddenly.

He went into the dining-room, looking at the floor, holding a hand against the wall for support. 'You hit him, all right. Not badly, though – there's not much blood ...' He turned round, grinning, and as he did so his eyes went to the window behind her. To where Garner lay on the grass.

'Jesus ... Garner ...' he grunted, the grin dropping like another discarded paper towel. Pulling away from the wall, he stumbled out and banged through the screen-door.

Malchek could hardly see through the haze in his eyes. The flash of the gun going off virtually point-blank next to his face had stunned him, the impact of the shot transmitted directly to his optic nerve by the bony vault around his eyes. He supposed there was some concussion. It certainly felt like a hundred hammers were still falling in there. The side of his face throbbed, and his ear felt as if it were in flames.

The closer he got to Garner, the worse it looked. He could see blood everywhere. He fell to his knees next to the boy and started to turn him over. Edison had gutted him with a belly shot.

By the time Clare came out of the house Malchek was at the motorcycle's radio. As he called Gambini, he saw Clare come slowly across the lawn to stand looking down at Garner. The radio crackled faintly, and he heard Gambini's voice like a tiny insect trapped inside, the buzz incomprehensible. Too late, he remembered that Garner's speaker was embedded in his helmet, and the helmet was nowhere to be seen. Garner's long hair was wrapped round his face like a shroud.

'Listen, Gambini, I can't hear you. I can only send. This is Mike. Garner's been stiffed. Edison was here. I don't know who you've got in that van but it *isn't* Edison. He got away from me in a ...' He turned to Clare. 'Did you see the car?'

She stared at him for a moment. 'It was dark-green. A Cougar, like mine, I think ...'

'You didn't get any numbers?' She shook her head, and he went back to the radio. 'Edison's in a dark-green Cougar, no numbers, maybe heading towards you, and he's wounded. Not bad, but bleeding some. Might still have a bullet in him, I hope. Get the hell back here.'

He dropped the radio and went over to stand beside Clare. 'Come on. We're leaving.'

She stared at him, dumbfounded. 'Leaving? Leaving him here?'

'There's nothing we can do. The others will be here soon.'

'But—'

'Come *on*.' He took her hand, swaying a little but hanging on. 'When Edison stops to think for a minute, he'll be back. He knows you're still alive. That puts him right back where he was. You drive.'

He was pulling her towards the car. She came reluctantly, looking back at Garner on the grass. Malchek fished the keys out of his jeans and gave them to her, going round to get into the passenger seat. He slammed the door shut as she started the engine.

'Turn it around and go back. Towards Lassen.'

'Go *back*?'

He nodded, reloading his gun on his lap. The blood had begun to run down his cheek again, but it was a fine trickle and he wiped it away absent-mindedly with his sleeve, as if it were sweat. The ear was hardly bleeding at all now. What blood there was soaked into his still uncut hair, matting it against the side of his head.

'Come on, babe, move it,' he growled. She obeyed, rocking the car in her haste, but managing the turn. She started back on the gravel road along which they had come ... what? An hour ago? It seemed days, but it couldn't have been more than an hour.

The anger that filled Malchek suppressed for the moment the feelings he had for Clare. He couldn't consider that now. He would sort that out later. The anger came first.

If Gonzales had materialized at the side of the road, he would have shot him between the eyes without hesitation.

He wanted to do it. God, how he wanted to do it.

Instead, he said. 'Tell me about Alva.'

They left the main road an hour later, when the throbbing in his head began to beat in a counter-rhythm to the pulse of the engine, setting his teeth on edge. He wanted the car off the highway, anyway.

They stopped briefly at a drugstore, and then drove through the business section. The town was called Fraser's Grove, and it lay in a cup of the hills at the end of the secondary road. Like many others in the area, it's population swelled during the ski season. Too far off the main routes to catch casual summer tourists, it still had two good-sized motels to choose from. He took the second one, and sent Clare in to make the arrangements. With his blood-soaked hair, slashed cheek and short temper, he'd have been turned away instantly.

She emerged from the office and held up nine fingers. He swung the car around, pleased she had chosen a unit that was hidden from the road by the big neon motel sign in the forecourt. He backed into the slot, because their front licence-plate hung at a less readable angle. She waited by the boot, and took her own suitcase from him.

'There's nothing wrong with my arms,' he snapped.

'Mine either. Isn't life wonderful? All our arms work.'

He glared at her, the old habit of anger coming back along with his preoccupation over their betrayal. But her grin was crooked, and he couldn't hold the irritation long.

'How are your knees?' he countered, slamming down the boot lid.

'Not *nearly* so hairy as yours.'

'Shut up.'

'No.'

He shook his head, almost smiled, and waited while she unlocked the door. Dropping the cases, he headed for the bathroom and turned on the bath water. He began to peel his blood-soaked shirt off, leaving rusty marks on his pale skin. Picking up the bottle of shampoo she'd bought, he started the water running in the basin, too.

Twenty minutes later, clean and shaking, fighting all the way, he passed out on the bed. It was fortunate, perhaps. He was spared the sound of Clare's exhausted sobs as she bandaged the angry wound on his face.

When he finally came to it was dark in the room. He sat up in alarm and the hammer came down on his face again, pain crashing through his skull.

'Jesus.'

He waited a moment, letting the worst of it pass. The light was on in the bathroom, the door half-open. It illuminated the room just enough to let him find Clare, still dressed, curled up on top of the other bed. He reached for the bedside lamp and turned on the half that arched towards him like a dying tulip. His gun lay next to it. He remembered being so groggy that he'd left it on the floor of the steamy bathroom, under the puddle of his discarded jeans. Now the jeans hung wet over the back of the chair, and the gun was wiped clean, with even a light film of oil on the surface. She must have taken his cleaning kit out of his suitcase. He glanced across the gap between the beds at her sleeping face, turned towards him on the pillow.

'Clare?' he whispered. She didn't stir, but a dreamer's faint smile shadowed her lips briefly. Next to the gun she had put the plastic container of aspirin, a glass of water, cigarettes, matches, and his Paludrine bottle. Damn. What was he going to do about *that*? Take the chance? There was nothing else *to* do. It would be OK, he'd done it before. And it wouldn't be much longer now. He took four of the aspirin, lit a cigarette, and leaned back against the headboard. His watch showed nearly midnight.

Clare still hadn't moved, but lay breathing, dreaming, smiling.

How did you get past me, Clare? he asked her silently. How did you get inside? Why did you want to? Edison told you the truth about me. I *am* a killer. Why didn't you believe it?'

His throat closed. He stubbed out the cigarette until it shredded into the tray.

He pulled on a pair of slacks, took a dark pullover from his open case. All the while watching Clare. Wanting her to wake wanting to be distracted. He stood beside the other bed and looked down at her. She's *not* beautiful, he decided. Her nose is too short, her mouth too wide. Lines are beginning to star her eyes. Why is she so beautiful? And why can I still only really look at her when she's asleep?

He turned abruptly and went out, locking the door behind him. There'd been a phone-booth at the side of the road just before the motel. The number he wanted was very clear in his mind. Taking up a stone from the edge of the motel drive, he walked to the booth and smashed the overhead light before closing the door.

Reddesdale answered on the second ring. Malchek identified himself, and exploded his grievance.

'Gonzo ripped me off, Reddesdale, he put me right in it, smiling all the while.' He felt anger rising again. She was lying back there, alone. *Alone* except for him.

'He didn't.' Reddesdale was maddeningly calm.

'He *did*, goddamnit The bastard just led me by the nose and I went, singing. It was a trap, a stinking trap.'

'It was a mistake.'

'Mistake, hell. Is there a Sheriff Hoskins in Spider Meadows?'

'No.'

'No. *Big* surprise. And who have you got in the hospital with a broken jaw?' He realized he was shouting, and made sure the door of the booth was closed.

'We don't know yet. But it isn't Edison.'

'I *know* it isn't Edison, for Christ's sake. Edison nearly blew my head off.'

'Where are you?'

'I'm in South America. Olé. What are you going to do about Gonzo?'

'Nothing.'

'Nothing? Jesus, he sold me *out*. *He* told me about Hoskins, *he* said it was OK, *he* sent me right into it. *He's* the goddamn leak we told him to go looking for. What a gift. Isn't that beautiful?' The aspirin was useless, his head pounded when he raised his voice.

'It was a *mistake*, Mike. Why can't you accept that? We all wanted to believe it was Edison so badly, we just *made* a *mistake*. We didn't check. You probably wouldn't have checked, either. Do we usually check on every cop who calls in on a police line, and who sends us prints through the police teletype, for God's sake? Do we ask when he left the Academy?'

'Edison bought into that station.'

'Of course he bought into that station, the chief at Paradise is doing his nut over it. But Edison had to have your itinerary first, before he set it up. Long before.'

'Gonzales sold it to him.'

'*No.*' Reddesdale was losing his cool. 'It was Gonzales who sent Garner back to find out why you hadn't caught up with the rest. It wasn't me, I was at a goddamn Civic Committee meeting. It was Gonzo.'

'Oh yeah?'

'Yeah. *Yeah.* When Gambini called ahead from a payphone because of the prisoner's condition, Gonzo wanted to talk to you. They told him you were still back here. So Gonzo ordered Garner back stat to get his ass next to yours, just in case. When the rest of them got back to the house and found you and the girl gone, he nearly went up the goddamn wall. We all did. Why the hell did you leave?'

Malchek leaned against the wall of the booth and put his face against the cool glass. Outside the night was warm and heavy with the resinous scent of pines. A lone car came out of the distance. He slid down instinctively, but it whispered past with no more interest in him than a mechanical rabbit.

'Mike? Are you still there?'

'I'm here, I'm here.'

'Are you all right? We found a hell of a lot of blood inside the house.' There was sudden concern in Reddesdale's voice. 'Is the girl all right?'

'She's all right. I took a graze, that's all. My father always said we had Romanov blood in us, it comes out so fast.'

Reddesdale began to curse, fluently and evenly. If Malchek ever doubted that the commissioner had walked a footbeat, he doubted it no longer. Every phrase was pure slum precinct.

'I'm impressed,' Malchek observed wryly. 'Even I didn't know a few of those.'

'Ha. Well, are you ready to come back?'

Malchek sighed. 'No.'

There was a silence. 'Mike . . .'

'Look, it's simple. If it wasn't Gonzo, OK it was somebody else. I'm not coming back until you find that leak and plug it, or until you've nailed Edison. I can't give him to you on a platter.'

'What do you mean?'

'I hope you're sitting down. Clare not only knew what Edison looked like when he was with Dondero in the park, she knew who he *was.* Is. Only she didn't realize it until a few hours ago.

He *wanted* her to know, that why he set it up the way he did this time. He wanted an audience who could really appreciate him, for just a few minutes.'

'What the hell are you talking about?'

'Do you remember that Clare said he looked almost familiar because he had such an even-featured, handsome face?'

'Yes.'

'Well, it was more than that. He was familiar because she'd seen him before. In New York, in her agency, around the bars and clubs where advertising people hang out. Seen him but never seen him, because back there he was a nobody. Dressed like a country plumber in glasses, slouched, quiet, a hack. His name is Tom Alva, he's a small-time freelance layout artist who does the scut work on dull accounts.'

'Alva?'

Tiredly, Malchek spelled it.

'But why didn't he just— ?' Reddesdale began.

'Because of me,' Malchek told him. 'Because of *me* getting involved and baiting him. It just got his goat. Somebody else laughing at him, I guess, somebody putting him down. He's very uptight about his reputation as a killer. She was doubly dangerous because if she ever saw him in New York, and put it together, he would be blown from both sides. But me . . . that was something else.'

'Christ.'

'Yeah, I know. *Mea culpa*, I should have left her in Halliwell's big red hands. Anyway, give it to the papers, will you? That will let her off the hook completely, there won't be anything she can do to him after that. As for me, put me down for dead. That should take the pressure off us completely. When you've got him, we'll come back and she can testify on the Dondero thing, if you need her. Somehow I think they'll have bigger things to lay on him. God knows, it shouldn't take you long to find him with what you've got now.'

'I guess not. How will I . . . ?'

'I'll keep in touch. Just say . . . just say Clare is somewhere safe, and leave it at that.'

'Mike . . .'

He suddenly wanted to get back to the room, to see if she

was awake, to be sure she was there at all. He hung up the phone with one quick movement and stared at the coiled plastic cord snaking and turning in the shadow, winding itself tighter and tighter. Outside the booth an owl warbled, and a sudden tiny shriek ended under a flutter of wings.

What if Edison had come back to Spider Meadows in time to see them both leave the house? What if he was out there now?

He slid the door of the booth back fast and crunched his way along the stony edge of the blacktop, then left it for the grass. He circled the motel and checked out the perimeter. There were no Cougars in the parking slots, and there wouldn't have been much time for Edison on the move since then, and he was sure no cars had followed them. Clare had given a false name at the desk, and their car was out of sight of the road. The main highway was six miles away, and there'd been no more reason for them to turn in where they had than anywhere else. They were OK for the moment, he felt sure of it.

When he turned the key in the lock and slipped silently through the door, she was awake and waiting, curled in the single easy chair, her eyes wide and empty. He pushed the door shut behind him and clicked the lock.

'I had to tell them about Alva. I didn't want to wake you.'

She just kept staring at him.

'We're OK for the moment. I checked. It's only a matter of time until they have him. It will all be over then.' He couldn't say the words. 'We ... you and I ...' After a moment he stopped trying, and just looked at her.

Clare felt as if she were drowning in the dark. She'd been terrified when she awoke and found him gone. It seemed as if she'd crouched in that chair for hours, waiting to see him there in the doorway at last. Alive, real, come back to stand there wordlessly. The tape gleamed on his cheekbone. The planes of his face were lit with an intermittent glow from outside. The whole shape of him was as straight and safe as a sword held between her and everyone else.

'Oh, Mike ...'

She came to him then, in a rush that would not be, could not be, halted. His mouth found hers, and her lips parted under his impatience. He could not control his hands any longer, touch her often enough, everywhere enough, soon enough Finally, after all the days and nights of pretence, his arms were really round her. She sank into him, strained into him, felt the sharp bones of his pelvis, the tense muscles of his thighs against hers, the demand of his body, rising.

He began to talk to her, unable to stop. The silent man, the locked and barred man suddenly opened wide. And she gave him all the soft and loving silence he needed, letting her body alone speak to him, and be heard.

He carried her to the bed and unwrapped her like an unexpected gift. His mouth drifted over her breasts, his tongue searched her neck and belly, his hands finally slipped between her thighs, long narrow fingers searching deep into the flooding warmth. She was like a flower opening, her legs and mouth widespread petals. Her own hands moved insistently, eager to possess and discover him in turn. The shifting sinews of his shoulders, his spine, the heavy satin of his stomach and the hard heat of him that pushed past her moving palms like an impatient, blind animal, fevered, hungry for home, and omnipotent with its promise.

She guided his body into her own, and wrapped him within her, lifting her hips to meet his thrust with a thrust in parry, and then again, until surrender. He ran wild inside her, a velvet hammer pounding, a sleek fish darting in a silver sea, diving, rising, up and up.

At last they both cried out into the darkness, a long open sigh of release from themselves. The neon from outside painted them as they finally lay silent, almost afraid to believe the doors were open between them for ever.

Before dawn, while Clare slept softly against his shoulder, the pain of his wound reawakened Malchek. He lay motionless, enduring it, not wanting to disturb her.

Suddenly life gets simple, he decided. All those other roads. All those other ways to go, and this is where I was headed all along. I couldn't have turned aside. I shouldn't have tried.

He watched the loose-wire flicker of the motel sign patterning the ceiling above the bed. It would be nice to suppose it meant something. Perhaps the chattering light was sending a message in a code he could not read.

White, orange, white, white, orange, white.

Codes my father taught me.

Suddenly exhaustion let down the last barrier. Now, after all the stifled years, he accepted that this last emptiness remained and would never be filled. The tears were hot and slow, and he wept silently for the death of his father. Gone before he could ask forgiveness. Dead even as he killed in Nam.

Another road that had ended, long ago.

Another junction missed.

They left the motel shortly after dawn, having paid in advance the night before. There were strands of mist between the pines, and the branches hung motionless in the half-light, with only an occasional drip from a needle's tip. There were three other cars in front of the motel, their windows shrouded in condensation, and all the blinds in the rooms were drawn.

The suitcases went in, the doors closed, the engine throbbed briefly, and Malchek let the car roll down the slight incline to the road with the clutch in, as silent as the woods around them. He didn't gun the engine until they were some way down the road towards the highway, and then only gently. Still they didn't speak, but held themselves in a kind of pact with the morning, as morning animals move, quiet, slow.

When they reached the highway it was empty, black with dew in either direction, and trackless. He paused at the intersection, weighing the possibilities.

There was no knowing how badly Edison had been hit, and how much it would affect his movements and intentions, if at all. He turned the car north.

As soon as the papers came out, Edison would know he couldn't go home again, ever. He was out in the cold, and so were they until he was nailed.

'How much money have you got left?' he asked Clare.

She turned, startled out of her silence. 'I don't know.'

'Look.'

She got out her purse and counted. 'About three hundred dollars. Why?'

'Get out the map and tell me the closest big town.'

After a moment's rustling she said, 'Redding. You have to take the next right.'

He took the next right.

When Malchek called Reddesdale that night from yet another motel room, the line was bad. The commissioner's voice sounded strained but triumphant. The Alva story had broken in the late afternoon editions.

'Paydirt, Mike. The FBI searched Alva's place. Everything was there, neat and tidy. Arsenal in the basement, explosives, everything. Files, records, neat as a pin.'

'He's a businessman,' Malchek said wryly. He watched Clare moving softly from suitcase to bureau, her hands full of his socks. He hadn't told her they'd be moving again in the morning.

'And then some. Trouble is, all his files are in some kind of code. There are quite a few interesting names in clear, but all the relevant information is coded – it's driving the Feds wild. They've got a computer on it, but one of them told me it's probably what they call a book-code. Unless they know the book, it's unbreakable.'

'I wouldn't bother trying the Bible.'

There was a silence. 'How are you?'

'Tired. What else have you got?'

'Fingerprints, of course. He was in the army, sniper in Korea.'

'Tell me something I *don't* know.'

'All right. It was a busy day for the banks in Redding.'

Malchek drew in his breath. 'Yeah, I've got me a rich fiancée. Always knew I was cut out for the good life.' Clare turned and made a face at him.

'I'd say congratulations if that was all.' Malchek heard a rattle of paper from the other end. 'At nine-thirty the main office of the Bank of America in Redding transacted some business for Miss Clare Randell with the Bank of America here in San Francisco. She spoke personally with one of the vice-presidents at the BA, and they cleared her savings account for her. She walked out with seventeen thousand in cash, much to the dismay of the Redding officials, who couldn't talk her out of it.'

'Her boyfriend doesn't believe in credit cards.'

'Uh-huh. At two-thirty the main office of the First Federal Bank in Redding transacted some business for a Thomas Prentiss Alva with the First Federal in New York. He walked out with nine thousand in cash, much to the dismay of the officials who couldn't convince him travellers' cheques would be safer.'

Malchek went hot, then cold. The two main banks had been in the same block in downtown Redding. Only the time difference between coasts and a couple of hundred yards had separated them. Clare saw the look on his face and came to sit beside him on the bed.

'Any other reports on him?'

'None,' said Reddesdale mournfully. 'We've got APBs out to airports, bus and train stations, shipping, both borders, passport number, description, for what it's worth.'

'He can buy a new passport, whatever he needs.'

'I suppose so. The FBI is coming in very heavy on this, Mike. Apparently some of those names gave them a hell of a jolt. Big business, unions, politics.'

'It's getting cheaper to kill your opponent than run a campaign.'

'Apparently. What's he going to do?'

'Take the money and run, what else? He must have plenty stashed outside the country. I would, in his place. What have you said about Clare and me?'

'Not a damn thing. They think I'm some kind of genius detective down here, pulling this out of the hat.'

Malchek smiled, but it hurt, so he stopped. 'Anything from the street? He'll have to get help somehow, although with the publicity I imagine he'll find prices have gone up.'

'Nothing so far. It's only a matter of time.'

He hung up, leaving his hand on the receiver and staring at it blankly. Only a matter of time, yes. But how much? If they *didn't* pick Edison up, how would they know when they were safe? When could they be sure he was gone?

*

They had two days of uneasy peace. They kept moving, kept waiting. The changes of location were beginning to weary them both, all the motels looked the same, the roads hummed at them, they had only each other to hold on to. But it wouldn't be much longer. It couldn't be much longer.

And then, over breakfast in a little diner in Weed, it ended. The story of Edison/Alva was still front-page news, the pictures and interviews with former colleagues must be giving the bastard quite a feed-back if he was still around to enjoy it, Malchek grudged. Fame and appreciation at last, although at a price.

He turned the page and froze. His expression was so fixed, so horrified, that Clare spilled her coffee putting it down.

'What is it, Mike? Have they got him?'

Slowly, carefully, he lowered the paper on to the table between them and exposed what was there. An entire page, blank, except for five black words in the centre.

After a moment Clare spoke in an almost detached voice. 'Knossos Bold. He uses it a lot, it's his favourite typeface. It was a joke they used to call it Tom's Trumpet.'

Malchek's hand shook, briefly, and then he clenched the edge of the paper, wrinkling it. The message, however, was still clear enough.

MALCHEK: YOU'RE A DEAD MAN

sixteen

Reddesdale was going round in circles, and Gonzales took his coffee cup away from him to fill it. No sooner had the Commissioner put down the phone to the FBI than Dempster brought in another report from the task force they'd put on to the hunt. Reddesdale took the steaming cup in one hand and the sheaf of typed flimsies in the other, telling Dempster to get another bottle of those pills from the doctor downstairs. The older man looked disapproving as usual, but went out on his errand without comment. It made a change. Maybe even Dempster was running out of his supply of Old Maid's Exasperation.

The phone went again. The white one this time, and Reddesdale raised an eyebrow at Gonzales.

'He's seen it.' He picked up the receiver and Gonzales heard Mike's angry tones clear across the desk. The Commissioner nodded and nodded, waiting for a chance to speak.

'Mike, for God's sake shut up and listen, will you? We've got the guy from the newspaper, we've turned him inside out, but it's no good. Yesterday a messenger came in from one of the publicity outlets for Daystar Industries – you know, one of those entertainment conglomerates. He handed over a piece of artwork, said it was a rush job, a teaser campaign for some new picture. The guy didn't think another thing about it, the layout was OK, the messenger gave the right account number, what the hell, business as usual. He put it straight through. What?'

Gonzo watched the Commissioner's face go through a series of changes. 'No, the messenger was a little guy, the usual one they always use. Of course we followed it back. Somehow the layout was pushed into channels at the publicity office, nobody knows who did it, nobody will accept the responsibility. The higher up we go, the more bland everything gets. What the hell does it matter? We *know* who did it. What we don't know is what he means by it.'

There were more angry, wild words from the phone, then silence. Reddesdale dropped it into the cradle and looked bleakly at Gonzales.

'He's cutting away from us. He says only this office knew he was still alive. The leak is here, right here, wide-open. He doesn't want anything more to do with us. Nothing. He says we can stop the border surveillance, it's a waste of time. Edison isn't going anywhere until he's killed Malchek. That's what it means. Or that's what he says it means.'

'I guess he ought to know,' Gonzales said thickly.

Reddesdale nodded, turned his chair away, and looked out

of the window. Behind him he heard Gonzales drop into one of the leather chairs. A fly was buzzing somewhere in the room, circling round and round the two men who were afraid to exchange either a look or a thought.

Just in case.

While he was waiting the big man changed the bandage carefully, easing the gauze away from the long, clotted gouge across his ribs. Thin streaks of blood and serum oozed out in a few places, but it was clean and gradually closing. He washed around the wound, packed in the antiseptic, and re-taped clean gauze over the whole painful mess.

That done, he flushed the soiled dressings down the toilet and shaved. His eyes were clear and he knew there'd be no trouble with infection now. He'd slept well the night before.

When Morrie finally called him back from a payphone, he sensed panic in the first few words.

'Can it, Morrie, I don't want to hear about that. I told you what I wanted, and I told you what would happen if I didn't get it.'

'Tom, please ... they've been all over me. How much longer are you going to hang around, for God's sake? They'll close on you, they're bound to, you can't dodge for ever.'

'I'll dodge as long as I have to. They don't know half the ways there are.'

'But it's so *dumb*, Tom. What the hell does it *matter*? I can get someone to take him out after you've gone, and the girl too.'

'No. *I* have to do it. He's the reason I'm having to leave what was a very good life, and I want it paid for. I won't leave it like that. Nobody beats me. Nobody.'

'You're crazy,' Wallack breathed.

Edison laughed briefly. 'No, not c ... crazy. Goddamn angry, but *not* c ... crazy. I'm not going out looking like a loser, Morrie. I intend setting up a new stand somewhere else. Being driven out of my own game by some scat-assed c ... cop would look *very* bad to my new customers. I can't afford that kind of publicity. *I* have to finish it. Now – did you get me the number?'

'I got it, but it won't do you a damn bit of good. The car

Malchek signed out of the department was found abandoned in Weed yesterday afternoon. Luggage was gone, nothing inside at all.'

'Shit.' His mind started working. 'How big is Weed?'

'Not very big. Why?'

'Get me a c ... car and some pictures of both of them. Also some FBI identification, doesn't have to be too good. Is the passport ready?'

'No ... it's ...'

'You're getting me angry, Morrie. All it takes is a word to my lawyer, I told you that. The records of what I've done for all your c ... customers are down in black and white, and he's got the keys. Now, I'll ask you just once more. Is the passport ready?'

'I'll have it for you this afternoon. Where do you want it?'

Edison gave him an address in Salinas. 'Park it in the drive facing out, keys in a hole behind the rear tyre. By two sharp. Put the stuff in the glove compartment. I'll be in touch.'

'Tom ...'

'*Ciao*, Morrie.'

By noon the next day he had them in a blue '71 VW moving north out of Weed. He called the number to Morrie and told him to use his communications contact in the SFPD to put it on the state hot sheet. He ate a good dinner and slept like a baby in the best hotel in Weed.

The VW turned up two days later on another used-car lot in Redding. No new buy there. But the lot owner said they'd put their luggage into a cab, and by chance he knew the driver, a regular on the street where the lot was located. The driver said he'd taken them to the airport. He looked at Edison's badge, and at the pictures, and picked out the one of Malchek with the drawn-on moustache. But the girl with him was blonde, he said. And heavily pregnant.

A pretty girl at the third airline counter he tried had booked them on to a connecting flight to Crescent City, with a change at Arcata. She agreed with the moustache on Malchek, but said the girl with him was *not* pregnant. She remembered them because it looked like they'd been having an argument. The man was very pale, and they'd looked tired. Like they were ending a trip, not starting out on one.

Rather than take the time to drive over the mountains, he booked a seat on the next connection to Arcata, and left the car in the airport parking lot.

Once the plane was airborne, he got out the pictures and looked through them again. He'd drawn various modifications – a beard or a moustache on Malchek, glasses, different hairstyles and colours – on each. It was obvious that Malchek knew the secret of successful disguise as well as he himself did.

What you *didn't* do was put on a fright wig, a strong Hungarian accent, full beard and moustache, dark glasses and a cane.

What you *did* do was keep it simple. Cops went crazy trying to get a reliable description from witnesses. Most people will notice and retain only one or at best two features in passing. Few ever agreed completely on anything, but if they *did* agree, it was usually on one outstanding feature.

So you don't go for a limp – you go all the way to beat-up walking cast with lots of reassuring autographs on it. Very heavy eyebrows. Or an ugly wart that no one could take their eyes away from in order to notice whether you were short or tall. Glasses – but with odd frames, wire grannies or Buddy Hollies. A *big* moustache. Very curly hair, or bald – bald was good. Make it strong and dominating, but simple.

And then you move into the middle. The big, faceless middle class – the nice people who don't bother anyone so long as they look clean, dress OK, smile, and say the same banal things.

Hi, guys.

He smiled and put the pictures away.

But by midnight in Arcata he had to accept that the little bastard knew the game, all right. Too well. They'd left the plane at Arcata, but had never picked up the flight to Crescent City. He'd tried the other airlines, rent-a-car companies, used-car lots, cabs, the bus lines, even some charter-boat skippers in the goose-necked harbour. He finally decided they'd probably hitched a ride south or east instead of north. He'd be willing to bet they'd stood next to some car Malchek had scouted in the airport parking lot, putting the hood up and feigning a breakdown. It was the hectic end of the summer and the town was overflowing with tourist traffic and strangers. They'd picked the right spot. Big highways converging, movement, heat, and the silly season. It was either go on busting his ass, wasting his money, and staying out in the open, or go back to his Department informant again. Risky, but there was now no alternative. Time was getting tight. In the end, they had more of it than he did.

He stood staring at the map in the bus depot. Blurry behind smeared plastic, it showed him what he was up against. The whole goddamned State of California, and everybody out for a good time. A million people on the move.

He wiped the sweat off his face with his sleeve, and then stood tapping his newspaper against his thigh, watching a wasp dance lazily across the discoloured plexiglass of the map-cover. It touched, hummed away, touched again, and away. Like Malchek, moving, moving.

Suddenly his anger swept over him, and he swung the newspaper against the wall, smashing the wasp to a pulp. An old man looked up at the sound, then shuffled away, mumbling. The wasp was a sticky streak spread from Burnt Branch to Weaverville. He was so absorbed in his satisfaction at destroying the surrogate Malchek that he didn't notice the light touch on the back of his hand until it was too late. As he turned, the second wasp stung and stung again.

Cursing, he brushed the thing away and looked at the damage. Already a hump was rising between his knuckles, and he sucked at the stabbing pain automatically. Maybe that's a lesson we both should keep in mind, Malchek, he said silently, walking towards the bus under the San Francisco sign.

Don't lose your cool, and watch your back.

seventeen

The noise bothered Malchek.

Eventually he got out of bed again to have another look at the empty street. The room felt cold, and he wondered why he still couldn't get used to pyjamas. Outside there was nothing but the pavement and the street-light and an empty cigarette pack on the edge of the grass.

Had it been there before?

He rubbed his eyes, and went into the bathroom to take an aspirin. The water ran over the edge of the glass before he noticed, and he dried his hand before tipping the white tablets out of the nearly empty plastic box. As he did so he caught sight of himself in the mirror and grimaced. It was probably the moustache that made him look so white, the contrast of the dark against the light. And the dark under the eyes.

On his way back to bed he looked out of the window again. He was sure the cigarette pack hadn't been there before. Maybe the noise had been someone walking by. Maybe whoever it was had tossed away the empty pack.

Who had it been?

'Mike?' Clare's voice was soft. She had learned to keep it soft, rather than risk his quick move towards the gun or the door.

'It's OK, babe, go back to sleep.'

'Easy to say, but you can't expect me to if you're going to stand there naked against the light. Sleep isn't exactly the thing that occurs to me when you do that.'

He smiled and came back to the bed, kneeling to kiss her lightly and then lying down beside her. She could tell by the way he put his arms round her that he was too weary to have the point made again. She snuggled into the hollow of his shoulder, and felt the sharp bones press against her throat.

'Have you slept at all?' she asked after a moment.

'Yes, sure . . . I only had to go to the john. Go to sleep.'

But her eyes stayed open, and she looked past the curve of

his body to the window. What had he been looking at this time? She had learned not to ask questions, either.

'Nothing,' was all he would say. 'Nothing.'

Eventually his breathing grew shallow, and she knew he was asleep. For how long this time? An hour? Two? Not more than that, it was never more that that. All during the night, every night, she would waken to see him standing at the window. Different windows, different motels, different towns, but his attitude was always the same. Ready to move, ready to push her off the bed, ready to take the gun and face the door. He had actually done it once, and then waited with the gun held out in front of him in both hands while the motel owner dropped the garbage into the garbage-can, put the lid back on, and returned to the office, whistling.

The days were no better. He never took the wheel. He trusted her driving, but it was more that that. He wanted his hands free. Whether they stopped at drive-ins or small restaurants where there was only one entrance, he ate very little. She moved her hand against his chest, and felt again the ribs and the hollow stomach. Even the light touch of her fingertips was enough to make him turn and move restlessly in his sleep.

And now this apartment. To break the pattern, he told her. They'd paid for three months, but they'd leave after a few days or so and go back to the endless motels.

They'd stocked up quickly at a supermarket, and she'd made a big pot of soup that stayed hot on the back of the stove, and that worked a little better. He seemed to be regressing to the patterns of an animal existence. He slept and ate at random, like a cat. He napped during the day, but only when he was sure she was absorbed in a book or TV programme and would not move out of the room.

They would go to bed suddenly, and the lovemaking would be deep and wild, and then he would be away from her before she had a chance to say soft words, the after words. Away, to stand at the window, to stand at the door, to listen, to be ready.

He had developed an obsessive need for order. He couldn't abide anything out of place or out of line. Everything had to be put away as soon as it was used. He had to know where everything was, always. They bought six papers a day, and he went over them inch by inch, looking for any small item that would tell him something, then folded them carefully and threw them away.

His .38 was always near, on his hip or in his hand. He was constantly breaking it down, mixing cleaning solvent in a coffee cup; working with a wire brush and rags to clean non-existent bits of rust and dirt from the snub barrel and trigger guard. It even lay on the bedside table when they made love. She had only to turn her head to see it glittering there, blue-black and efficient. The rifle he had bought two days ago got the same treatment.

He had come into the bedroom earlier that evening and found her touching it, kneeling down in the closet where she had been lining up the shoes for him. Her fingers had been exploring the chasing on the stock.

'You can pick it up if you like,' he'd said, a strange smile in the corners of his mouth. 'It's not loaded.'

'Why do they bother to try and make it look pretty?' she asked bitterly. 'It's only meant to kill, isn't it? Why pretend, with all these curlicues and scrolls? It's ridiculous.'

'Yeah, I agree. We didn't have curlicues in the army.'

'Just notches?'

It was a joke, but as soon as she'd said it she was sorry. She'd jumped up and gone to him, but the whiteness around his mouth said more than she could.

She knew what was happening, but she didn't know why. Again and again she asked him, why couldn't they go back? Why didn't he leave it to the department to protect them? He'd needed six others before, how could he possibly hope to manage on his own?

'You're still alive, aren't you?' he told her, and wouldn't talk about it any more. She knew he still kept in touch with Reddesdale, but it was only at night now. Late at night, and his brief, monosyllabic conversations told her nothing. He spoke to no one else.

All she knew was that they were waiting, that he was afraid, that he was getting thinner and paler and more exhausted with every hour and day that passed.

142

And she wondered when he would begin to hate her for it.

When he woke her it was still dark.

'Get dressed, honey. Put on warm clothes. Hurry up.'

'Are we leaving? I haven't packed . . . I haven't—'

'No, we're not leaving. But there's something we have to do. Come on, babe, move.'

She did as he asked, and went out with him to the car. He was carrying the rifle-case under a blanket, and they drove down the quiet, sleeping streets under the lights. A dog barked at the sound of their engine, but nothing else stirred.

He drove for about twenty minutes, past the dark shops and supermarkets of Crescent City, past the lines of frame houses, round the bay and down the highway. Over the hills and into the woods.

They left the red VW at the edge of a gravel road, a few miles past Mill Creek. Just another beetle in the forest. After a quick glance around he simply waded into the underbrush and started looking for what he wanted. Watching him carrying the rifle high in one hand, Clare wondered if he felt at war again. Another question to bite back.

The sky was growing light, and she looked around her in awe.

The redwoods they had seen before should have prepared her for the forest they were entering. But these northern parklands were virgin stands of the taller, leaner, coast redwoods, without a pedicure. The heavier rainfall had encouraged a thick, ferny undergrowth that rustled between the feet of the giants, and morning mist hung in slow-moving ribbons over the valley groves and streams. The trunks of the fallen lay massively between still-standing brethren, their scaly, lichen-stained bark filled with dusty leaf-mould and the insect highways of centuries. A thick incense of moisture and time hung in this cathedral, and they sometimes waded chest-high through greenery, showered sporadically with the rain of their own passage. It was a strangely silent place, but occasionally small things moved under the ferns in an invisible scuttle and twitch as they approached, squeaks of warning and alarm came ankle-high and sudden.

They struggled and walked for twenty minutes until he found a clearing that suited him. While she spread the blanket he loaded the rifle and fired some test rounds into an ancient trunk that lay on the far side of the open space. Apart from the short basement range in the gunshop, he hadn't had a chance to get the feel of the unfamiliar Ruger carbine.

The rifle had a flat, mean smack that startled Clare. She had expected a bigger, louder sound. More explosion and less whip-crack. Malchek fired five more shots, then lowered the gun and walked over to where she sat on the blanket watching him. He pulled the .38 from its holster and held it out towards her.

'I want you to learn to use these guns.' He gestured with the snub-nosed .38. 'This is a Smith & Wesson thirty-eight revolver, five shots in the cylinder. I've had it three years and it tends to pull to the left.' He touched the stock of the rifle. 'This is a new Ruger Mini-Fourteen carbine. It's a gas-powered semi-automatic weapon, and there are ten rounds in each magazine.' Quickly he showed her how to shove in the grooved metal magazine and control the firing mode. 'The effective range of the revolver for you will be a maximum of twenty-five yards. The Ruger can kill easily up to three hundred yards – after that it's up to the skill of the person doing the killing.'

'I don't want to kill anyone, Mike,' she protested.

'You shot at Edison. Didn't you shoot to kill?'

'Yes ... but I thought he'd killed *you*. I didn't care about anything then. I just wanted to ... to ...'

'Say it.'

'I wanted to hurt him. I wanted him to scream and hurt.' Her voice was a shamed, husky whisper in the rustle of the forest.

He almost faltered then, but swallowed it. 'I want you to *remember* how that felt, honey. Taste it. Face it. It's in all of us.'

'But ...'

'*All* of us. Some can just be pushed further than others before they hit their break-point. Man is a predator, OK? He's got ten fingers, ten toes, no tail, and he tells himself he's better that the other predators. But he's not. Man is just a wolf with a bigger brain. Maybe that will save your life, so *don't* push it away. Load the gun.'

'Why?'

'Because you're right. Because I can't do it all alone. Because I need to know you can back me up. Because you're all I've got now, babe. Load the gun.'

So she took her instruction; her hours of inexorably detailed instruction from her expert. Hated it. Began to be interested. Then was interested. Began to be tired. Was tired. Began to be bored. Was bored. Was short-tempered. Was angry. Was resentful. And, at last, was allowed to rest.

Her head swam with trigger pressures, magazine loads, mirage and running leads, pulse jerks, and all the rest of it. He still didn't seem satisfied, but she didn't care. Unable to feign even civility, she dropped down on to the blanket and, resting her forehead on her knees, resolutely shut out the forest, the sound of the shots, and him.

He said nothing, but busied himself cleaning the weapons and stacking the remaining targets carefully by the edge of the blanket. When he spoke his voice had the tone of somebody ready for the next attack.

'Come on, Clare. I don't want to stay out here any longer than we have to. We're wide-open, he could come from anywhere.'

'Then why ... ?' She spoke dully into the darkness of her inverted body, her breath rising warm back to her face.

'Sometimes you have to chance the balances, babe. You knowing the guns so that you could back me up was more important than the risk we're taking. But the longer we stay here, the worse the balance becomes. I want to move out before it changes over. Come on.'

So she rose, arthritically slow, and took the rifle in a wary embrace. 'Maybe we could put all this to good use.'

'What?'

'Maybe Bonnie and Clyde started out just like this.'

He stared at her. 'I don't think that's funny.'

'You don't think much of anything is funny these days.'

'Can you blame me?'

'No, you're too busy blaming me.'

He sighed. 'That's not true, Clare.'

She sighed back in mockery. 'Oh, yes it is. Weary days, Mike, weary days and you're getting sick of them, aren't you? You're trained as a hunter, but you're being hunted instead. You want to go after Edison instead of waiting for him to find you, but you can't. Because of me.' As her voice rose her grip on the rifle tightened. His eyes went from her face to her hands, and he felt the hamstrings tighten behind his knees.

'Clare, I love you.'

'Oh yes. *Yes.* But you can't kill with me hanging around your neck, can you?'

He looked at her for a long time. Spit had gathered in the corners of her mouth, tears in her eyes. The edges of an ocean.

'Clare—'

'You know, *I* could just shoot you right now, couldn't I? I know how, you've taught me all about killing and guns.'

'Not very well. I thought I told you never to lift a loaded weapon above knee level unless you intended to fire.'

She glanced down. The rifle was pointed straight at his belt, with no more than twenty inches between muzzle and buckle. Although every muscle in his body was straining to drop or run, he kept his voice casual. 'On the other hand, maybe you're right. Why wait for Edison to kill us when we can do it so easily ourselves and save him the effort?'

He saw her resentment give way as she realized what she had unconsciously done. What a moment's angry carelessness could have become. She stared at him, and when her shock hit eye level, she let go.

The rifle never hit the ground. His outstretched hand caught it behind the trigger guard just six inches above the blanket. Clare fell beside it, crouching like a sick child, crying, apologizing, reaching blindly for his forgiveness. His head throbbed and his mouth was dry. He took her in his arms and wished for a magic word to make them both better.

When the worst was over he spoke into her hair, his eyes scanning the trees around them, listening for any sound above her last, wretched, shuddering breaths.

'OK?' He pulled away slightly and looked down at her.

She shook her head miserably. 'How much longer, Mike?'

'Until you get it *right*,' he smiled

'I didn't mean the guns.'

'No, I know you didn't.' He glanced uneasily at the forest around them. 'Never mind. We've done enough ... we'll go back to the apartment now. We'll be all right.'

But later that afternoon, when they were making love and he drove himself deeply into her again and again, she felt his locked arms tremble with the strain.

And they had never done that before.

By ten that night she found out just how much trouble he was in. They were curled together watching an old Kirk Douglas movie, soothed by the inevitable triumph of the good sheriff over the bad gunslinger. He got up during a commercial and came back wearing a heavy pullover, stopping to turn up the thermostat as he passed.

'This place is getting cold,' he commented, wrapping himself around her once again.

'You're joking. It's hot in here.'

But twenty minutes later he had begun to shake.

'You're not kidding, are you? You really *are* cold,' she said, turning to look at him in amazement. His skin looked almost blue, and the shivering was broken by intermittent sharp movements, almost convulsive. 'What is it? You must have caught a chill out there ...'

'It's not just a chill, honey. It's stupidity. I'm a goddamn jackass, in case you hadn't guessed that already.' Another tremor shook him, and he wrapped his arms around his body, bending over as if his stomach ached.

She watched him, afraid. 'Mike ... you're not ... you're not addicted to anything, are you? That medicine bottle ... the empty one ...'

He glanced at her in disgust. 'Don't be a fool, Clare, of course I'm not. Jesus.' For an instant she thought he was going to pass right out, his eyes rolled back and he stiffened violently. The shaking began again after a moment.

147

'This is stupid, sitting here. Come on, get into bed and I'll turn on the electric blanket. I was right, wasn't I? It wasn't a silly thing to buy.'

'In the normal course of events, I am quite capable of keeping you warm in bed.' The pompous tone of his pronouncement was somewhat marred by his chattering teeth. 'I just happen to have this problem at the moment.'

He trailed after her into the bedroom, suffered her to take off his shoes, and crawled under the covers without undressing. She switched on the thermostat control, and looked at him in dismay. She'd loved the dark-brown sheets that had come with the little luxury apartment, but now against the pillowslip his face shone blue-white and ghastly. He clenched his jaw to stop it vibrating.

'When does this wonderblanket start warming up, next Christmas?' he ground out between his teeth.

She slid her hand under the edge ... the blanket was already quite hot. She sat down on the side of the bed. 'You said a minute ago that this was stupidity. What is it, really?'

'Would you buy malaria?' Another violent rigor convulsed him.

'I'd buy blackwater fever from the Upper Zambezi if that's what you say it is.'

'No, just ordinary, old, everyday malaria. A lot of us caught it but good in Nam. They had a "cure" all right ... but it turned you a nice bright yellow. Most of us never finished taking the pills once we started to feel better. Nobody wanted to look like a gook – a guy could get shot that way. And it was OK, we stayed healthy. Then, a few years ago, I got overworked and blam! – back it came. My doctor offered me that same old cure, but I said cops got called enough names already, "yellow" I didn't need. He gave me something else in the end ... and I got better.'

'You look it.'

'OK, he never said it was a cure. And he warned me if I didn't watch myself, keep in condition ... it could come back.' Another chill started. 'Boy, did *he* know what he was talking about. But anyway, I brought the pills along, didn't I? No problem.'

'I'll get them.' She went to the bathroom and came back with the little brown bottle, unscrewing the cap as she reached the bed. Tilting it over her palm, she tried to shake the pills out. She could hear them rattling ... maybe one was blocking the narrow neck. Poking an exploratory finger inside she extracted the offending object – one packet of silica gel for keeping the tablets dry. A frantic shake produced nothing else. No tablets.

The bottle was empty.

She showed him, and his face went even more bleak. 'I heard the rattle ... I just assumed ...'

Clare turned, suddenly distraught at the growing violence of the chills and the look on his face. 'I'll call a doctor ...'

'*No!* There's no need for that. Look, I've been through it before, Clare, there's nothing to worry about. I know *exactly* what will happen, so calm down. It's simple. The chills will go on for a while, and then I'll start running a fever. Maybe quite a high one. I'll be pretty sick, but only for a few hours, then it will break and the sweats will start.'

'My God, you can't—'

'*Don't* go all twittery on me, for crying out loud. If *I* can stand it, you sure as hell ought to be able to. Just leave me alone. In a little while I won't care much one way or another, anyway.'

'What if I went out and just bought some ordinary quinine? Wouldn't that help?'

'No point now. Once it starts, it goes right on until it finishes. Quinine might help to stop the next attack ... but we'll talk about that later. *Don't* you go out alone.'

'The *next* attack?' It was sounding worse and worse.

'It goes in cycles. That's what it's all about. They come every two days.' He closed his eyes and surrendered to the rigors, clutching the blankets around his shaking body until the control box on the bedside table began to click on and off in a mechanical frenzy of overheating.

She watched him for a little while, stunned by the complete and total domination of the attack. His face was pinched, and his fingernails were blue, actually blue with cold. Finally, not knowing what else to do, she climbed into bed beside him, trying to add the warmth of her body to the blanket. She began to perspire within seconds, but his flesh remained cold.

'Bet you never had this effect on anyone in bed before,' he muttered, turning to lock his arms around her, grateful for her softness and her heat.

'Oh, I'm famous for reducing men to a quivering jelly,' she whispered into his shoulder, wishing there was something, anything, she could do.

'I don't think I want to hear about that.'

'Chicken.'

'Oh baby, hold me, will you? Make me warm, please.'

His soft whisper was as startling as a scream. It was so unlike him to plead for anything. He was the strong one, he was the controller. Now, for the first time, he needed her, and she was useless to him.

She could not even warm him when he grew cold.

By three that morning he was delirious.

The last reading on the thermometer she'd found in the first aid kit from the car had been 104.4° before he accidentally knocked it to the floor. Initially the fever had brought sickness and pain, but now he was past that point, twisting and thrashing wildly until she could only manage a random swipe at his body with the wet towels she kept soaking in a bowl of ice water. His skin burned yellow-white and taut across his bones as he lay naked on the dark sheets, giving off more heat than the electric blanket ever had. No sooner had she sponged him down than his skin was dry again, baking the moisture away.

Clare was terrified. To her, any fever over 103° demanded a hospital. Frantically she soaked and applied the towels again and again, until the sheets on either side of him were drenched, and yet under his burning body they stayed dry.

It was deathly quiet in the building and outside. No traffic passed. The street-lights shone down on empty pavements. A dog suddenly barked in the distance, the staccato message coming in through the open window. The chill night breeze wasn't helping any more than the ice water to bring his fever down.

At first he only moaned with the pain, but this changed after a while to mutterings, and then raving shouts. Some of the things he said sickened and confused her. His life had been filled with enough violence to stain a hundred minds. Vietnam, the city streets, the alleys, the slums, all of it was there in his mouth.

Eventually it got simpler. Much simpler.

'Help me, Clare. Help me, Clare. Help me, Clare.'

But she could do nothing.

By five o'clock she was utterly convinced he was going to die. Surely even a healthy body would be savagely disrupted by this, and his was far from healthy. Not enough food, not enough sleep, he had been burning himself away before the fever even came. Now he seemed to be diminishing before her eyes.

The raving had stopped. He lay there unmoving, in a blaze of heat, his eyes closed and sunken, his lips pulled back from a panting mouth, his breathing as frantic and shallow as a running deer's.

The first doctor in the book was named Aarons, and after a sleepy initial exchange of facts his voice became firm and clear.

'Your husband told you the simple truth, Mrs Michaels. You're doing all anyone can do now. I know it looks bad, but believe me, the fever will break soon. As soon as it does, try to get some fluids into him, as much as he'll take. I'll come over in the morning before I go to the office and start on some medication.'

'You mean take two aspirin and call me tomorrow?'

He had a dry laugh and she hated him, clenching the phone so hard it made her hand ache.

'Maybe it does sound like that, but believe me, *please* believe me, if there was anything practical I could do I'd be over there in ten minutes.' He paused, sighed. 'Look, I know how scared you must be. Malaria is one of those things from the late show, isn't it? Digging the canal and men dying like flies? But malaria is as common as mumps in a lot of the world, even today. Some cases can be damn stubborn, even in this day of so-called medical miracles. But he won't die, I promise you. He'll be feeling much better long before I arrive. Strangers couldn't nurse him any better than you can, and you sound like a level-headed girl. I'll see you in a few hours.'

She sat staring at the phone after he'd hung up.

It was over, anyway. Tomorrow Mike would be weak, drained, unable to do the things necessary to keep them both safe. It was over, the running had to come to a stop. Surely even he must admit defeat now? They couldn't stay out alone any more. Love was more important than honour, whatever that was. Edison could blow up the entire state as far as she was concerned, as long as Mike stayed alive. It was almost a relief to have the decision virtually made for her. For them both.

There only remained the problem of how to do it. Call Gonzales? But Mike had been keeping in touch with Reddesdale, and *only* Reddesdale. There had to be a reason for that. Was Gonzales still a suspect? She went into the bedroom and leaned over Mike, begging him for the Commissioner's private number, but he was either past hearing her or the lock in his head was so strong it survived even his delirium.

She dialled Information, but was told Reddesdale's home number was unlisted. After a moment she asked for the office number. Someone would surely be there – didn't the police work day and night?

But after two rings a machine answered, and she realized that, while cops work all the time, administrative staff do not. Well, what difference did it make in the end, it was Reddesdale's own office phone, wasn't it? Mike trusted him, so she could. To wait until morning was intolerable, she wanted it over and done with. And she didn't want to be talked out of it.

'Commissioner, this is Clare Randell. Mike and I are in Crescent City, and Mike is very, very ill. We're in Apartment 4B, 312 Blaine Street. Please send someone to bring us home.'

She dropped the phone back in place and looked at it. Now their salvation lay in Reddesdale's hands. How long would it take him?

eighteen

Edison wiped the moisture from his face with the back of his sleeve, then pulled the seaman's knitted cap back into place. If The Man had what he'd been waiting for, then it might be finished soon. He might be on his way to Rio tomorrow.

He didn't like the idea of a personal meet, but that had been part of the deal. 'Face to face or nothing,' said the voice on the phone at the rooming house where he'd been posing as a long-shoreman. They were looking for a mover, not a stayer. Who suspects a guy trying to earn a day's bread of being a fugitive? Getting the work papers had been duck soup for Morrie – the unions wanted their secrets kept too.

Early-morning fog still shrouded the Embarcadero, but the tops of the towers on the bridge were becoming more visible every minute as the thick bank of mist poured back out to sea with the tide.

He watched the little man come towards him down the long dock. Camelhair coat, shiny shoes, very nice. Wonderful what a difference money could make.

'You're kind of small for a c . . . cop,' he said to him.

'They weren't so fussy when I joined,' was the brief answer. 'What have you got?'

'What you wanted – their location. Apparently Malchek is sick – the girl called in. Fortunately I got in early, and it was right there on the answering machine.'

'Where are they?' he prodded.

The little man looked up at him, and Edison was genuinely startled to see such animosity in the bland face. All in the eyes, he decided. He doesn't let it out, but it's all there. He waited.

'You're going to kill them, and then you're getting out of the country, isn't that right? Going for good?'

'That's it. Where are they?'

The little man gave him an address. 'Once it's done, I'm off the hook with Wallack, is that clear? He gets no more help from me, ever. I've got too much to lose now, and I'm not risking it for anyone.'

Edison shrugged. 'C . . . Clear that with Wallack, not me.'

'But you're the one who got the evidence from the old Commissioner. Not Wallack.'

'True. But having a lock on you here in San Francisco won't do me much good in Brazil.'

'What about your files, all those things in code? What if they break your code?'

'Not my problem. But they'll have a tough time, it's not the kind of thing they're apt to have on hand. Anyway, I'll keep you in mind, you've been a big help. Maybe I'll want to come home sometime. If you're still around, I'll be in touch.' Edison grinned amiably. 'I hate to let go of things. Even little things. Everyone has a use to someone like me. I've only begun to c . . . climb.'

'No,' came the horrified whisper. 'No, you can't *do* that. I've given it all to you, right down the line. Done whatever you asked, lied, misled, betrayed them all. You smug bastard, you can't promise to let go one minute and keep hold the next.'

Edison shrugged. 'Why not? Who's to stop me? *You?*'

The movement was slow, and he'd been expecting it all along. That, or an ambush. The address had come out too easily, it had to be false. But he had seen the abortive half-reach towards the inside pocket just before, and he saw the half-reach towards the overcoat pocket now. It was almost laughable the way ordinary people thought they could beat him.

He had the knife out and travelling up under the little man's breastbone before the gun even cleared the camelhair coat pocket. The blue eyes bulged, and he grasped the upper arm of his victim before he began to crumple. To anyone watching it was a friendly gesture. There was a liquid gurgle when he twisted the knife left then right, and a thin dribble of blood ran down the pointed chin before the eyes rolled back for good.

Gently, Edison helped the corpse to a bench facing the bay, and lowered it into a sitting position, staring out at the water. He used his thumbs to close the eyelids. Anyone passing would think the little man had dozed off, and leave him alone. For a while, anyway.

Sitting down next to the dead man, he pulled out the knife

and slid it back into the sheath strapped to his forearm under the thick, blue sweater. Then he reached across, pulled out the wallet, and went through it. Yes, here it was, methodical as ever: and address – Apt. 4B, 312 Blaine Street, Crescent City. The initials M and R were written faintly at the top.

Idly, he flipped through the credit cards while he decided what had to be done first. Jesus, what a name. Calhoun Farley Dempster. It would be enough to make anybody turn queer.

nineteen

The fever had finally broken at six-fifteen. Dr Aarons arrived just after eight o'clock.

Startled by the knock on the door, and Clare's sudden movement as she got up to answer it, Mike's eyes widened apprehensively.

'Who the hell is that?'

She paused in the doorway. 'Probably Dr Aarons. I called him during the night, when I thought you were going to die.'

'You *what*?' He struggled weakly on to his elbows but was unable to stay there, and half-rolled over on to his side, reaching for the .38 on the bedside table.

'I thought you were going to die . . .' she said defensively.

'But I *told* you . . .'

'Yes, you told me. But if it was Edison on the other side of that door right now, what could you do about it?'

He regarded her bleakly. 'I'll be OK in a few hours . . . the attacks put you down fast, but you come back fast too.'

'And after the next attack? What then? And what about during the attack, what if something happens then? What do I do?' The knock was repeated, more insistently. 'I love you, Mike, but you're *wrong*. It's time we let six or seven men take over the job you've been trying to handle on your own.'

She turned and went out before he could answer, flooded

with a nagging sense of betrayal, unable to look at him lying there with no defence. She didn't *want* to be right.

After the doctor had left she turned the handle of the bedroom door as quietly as possible and looked in. Mike was asleep, his face shadowed but less pale against the dark pillowcase. She closed the door again and stood motionless for a moment, thinking about some of the things the doctor had said before he left. About stubborn men and the problems they caused themselves and those who loved them. He more or less warned her that with Mike she had a man who wouldn't give in to his own weaknesses, and she'd have to live with it.

She knew that.

It isn't done in this day and age to talk about 'You were meant for me' except in a song. Stand up and say it, then wait for the laugh. But if your breath jams in your chest whenever you look at someone, and if you'd die for him and be dead without him, and if nothing else mattered *but* him, what else *was* it? And is a washed dish or an ironed shirt any less the language of love than 'Oh, baby' or 'Your burning lips pressed to mine?'

Probably, she concluded wryly. Probably there's some deep, feminist chasm I'm leaping lightly. But in all this running and killing, where is the sign saying 'Average people line up here?' How does an ordinary girl like me who occasionally burns the toast and fixes her hems with safety-pins face up to the extraordinary anger and purpose in the eyes of a man like Mike?

Worse, how does she face up to the accusation that will replace them when he finds out she called for someone else's help?

She doesn't. She runs away and washes the dishes. Hoping the help will arrive before she has to admit she's denied her man the right to make his own decisions.

At nine forty-five the phone rang.

She was so startled that she stared at if for a minute before picking it up. As she did so the bedroom door flew back and Mike stood propping himself in the opening.

'Hello?' she said cautiously.

'Is that Clare?' came a voice she didn't recognize.

'I'm sorry, you must have—'

'This is Clyde Reddesdale, Clare. It's all right, you don't have to be afraid ... unless ... are you alone?'

'No ... no ... Mike is here.'

Mike was certainly there. Blazing with more anger than she could ever imagine in a man's face. Even his hands looked angry, clenching the door jamb on either side. 'What ... have ... you ... done?' he stabbed at her.

The voice in her ear continued. 'Now, Clare, I want you to listen carefully to me. If I know Mike, he'll want proof that it's ...'

Mike was beside her, snatching the phone away. He held it and listened for a minute, then spoke.

'Did she call you?' He listened for another moment, then sank down on to the couch beside her, limp and defeated. 'Dempster? *Dempster?*'

She could hear Reddesdale's voice going on and on, and she reached out to touch Mike for reassurance. He didn't respond, didn't even seem to notice her hand on his thigh. She felt the tears welling up, overflowing. What had she done to them?

He was still listening, nodding, eyes closed. 'All right, Clyde, all right, I think it's pretty obvious that he got what he was after. What other reason would there be for killing him?' He opened his eyes to look at his watch. 'No, even by plane he couldn't make it this quick. Who? Brand. OK, OK, whatever you say. Yeah, thanks.' He replaced the phone, then dropped his face into his hands, elbows resting on his naked knees. When he spoke the words were muffled and slow.

'I've been calling Reddesdale at home because there was obviously a leak on his staff. He was trying to find out. It might have been a number of people who were on a need-to-know basis, including Gonzo, Dempster, and several secretaries. Now we know it was Dempster. Old self-effacing, sharpen-the-pencils Dempster, the guy you never notice.'

'Like Tom Alva.'

'Yeah, I guess. Dempster is famous for being first in and last out, and today was no exception. He played the answering machine, got our location, and took it to Edison.'

'Oh God . . .'

'Maybe he intended to kill Edison and cover his own betrayal. Maybe not. His old standard-issue revolver was in his coat pocket when they found his body down by the Bay half an hour ago. And Edison wouldn't have killed him unless he'd finally got what he wanted.' Still his hands stayed in front of his face.

Clare stood up and walked stiffly across the room, cold and leaden. Her whole body felt as if some kind of magnet was trying to drag it through the floor. 'I'm sorry, Mike,' she said with a cardboard mouth.

He dropped his hands and took a long breath, watching her standing rigidly next to the small dining-table.

'Oh, I guess it's all right. They've been in touch with the local sheriff and he'll be along any minute to take us somewhere else, somewhere safe. There's no way Edison could get up here before noon, unless he's on the crew of the starship Enterprise. No real harm done.'

'You must be joking.'

He stood up and went unsteadily towards her, putting his hands under her elbows and turning her round. She kept her eyes down.

'If you mean that I might be angry at you because you did what you did, sure, I might be. In the old days I would have simply taken you out into the shed and horsewhipped you. But here we are, all up to date, stuck with what we call equality. With me lying in there the way I was . . . you were head of the family, and you made a decision. Right or wrong, you acted on it. Big deal. If it's any consolation, I happen to think it was the right decision. I *do* need help, Clare. I can't pretend I'm superman anymore, can I? I mean, hell, *look* at me.'

But she wouldn't.

'Come on, hard-nose,' he said softly. '*Look* at me.'

She took a breath and spoke earnestly to his collarbone. 'If I'm very good from now on, and only take the car out on Wednesdays, and bake your favourite cookies, and always laugh at your jokes, will you do something for me?'

'Like what?' He wiped a tear from her cheek with his thumb.

'When you've got your strength back, will you take me out into the shed and horsewhip me ... just a little?'

His arms closed around her. 'All right. Just a little.'

twenty

Sheriff Brand was a tall, thin man with a sharp eye and a short manner. They sat almost knee to knee in his kitchen, the older man in sharply creased tans, and Malchek in faded jeans and a sweatshirt that Clare had bought him. It had a pig on the front to which repeated rotations in launderette dryers had given a rather sat expression, but it still amused him.

'I got the bones from your commissioner, but maybe you ought to fill in the rest. You usually work with the brass down there?' Brand opened.

'No, I'm just a detective,' Malchek said quietly.

'Lieutenant, though, detective lieutenant?'

'Yeah.'

'Haven't been acting much like a lieutenant lately, seems to me.' There was no animosity in the older man's tone. Just curiosity; this is an interview with an alien, it seemed to say.

'No, but this isn't what I'd call my usual kind of case.'

'Me neither, lieutenant. Fishing disputes, drunk fights, some minor drug running into the coves, that more my line these days. Not many folks up here draw the attention of a professional killer. We live pretty quiet.'

'I heard you deploy your men. Didn't sound smalltown to me.'

Brand grinned suddenly, his face creasing like an accordion with a day's growth of beard. 'Twenty years in San Diego, retired a lieutenant, like you. Only older. About a hundred years older, I'd say.

Malchek nodded, obviously relieved to be dealing with a

professional rather than an easy-going appointee or a hotshot young cowboy out to make a name. He gave Brand an account of the problem, leaving little out except feelings for Clare. He supposed they were self-evident. While they talked two deputies sidled in with negative expressions and took seats by door and window respectively, sitting easy but alert.

'Well, you got a simple choice, seems to me,' Brand concluded. 'I mean, you got to get back, that's plain. But tonight or tomorrow?'

'Can you spare men for a watch tonight?'

'Sure.'

'Then tomorrow. We'll get a chopper down tomorrow morning. I'll be a good enough hand by then, once I've slept off this attack.'

But in the morning it was obvious no helicopter was going to take off from Macnamara Field. A big storm had started churning up from the south-west around midnight. By morning the trees outside the Sheriff's house were thrashing wildly in the the wind, their leaves showing silver bellies against rain that spat sporadically at the window like buckshot.

'I guess we better put you on the regular ten o'clock flight after all,' Brand said.

'No, sorry. The whole reason I took Clare and ran was because Edison doesn't give a damn *who* dies as long as we do. I'm not going down with fifty other people screaming in my ears. No way.'

'Sit it out, then.'

Malchek turned from the window and walked across to where Clare sat in a chair, pretending to read. He put his hands on her shoulders, his thumbs absently stroking her neck while he thought.

The boy in the dark-blue sweater was nearly asleep when the two unmarked cars pulled up across the street in the afternoon. The wind and rain on the roof of the abandoned treehouse had synthesized a lullaby he found hard to resist. He'd been lucky to find it in the yard of the house across from Brand's. He could just see between the trees on the corner when they all emerged; the girl and the man flanked by deputies from the local sheriff's office, and the new arrivals in plainclothes. He wrote the details on a crumpled brown-paper bag that had held his sandwiches. Once the two cars had pulled away, the boy climbed down and pushed head down through the gusts of wind to the telephone booth halfway down the block. He dialled the Klamath Glen number he'd been given.

'Driving, just like you figured. And two cars, like you said. Both Fords. The girl in a white Falcon, the guy up front in a yellow Galaxie. They each got two with 'em, that makes six. No, all right, forget the girl. Yeah, I got them.' He read out the plate numbers he'd jotted down. 'I didn't see anything about that, except the thin guy was carrying a rifle-case. No they didn't load no real luggage. Just a couple of shopping bags is all. Yeah.' His face darkened. 'Who would I tell, for crying out loud? I know what Eddie told me.' The voice at the other end of the line whipped into his ear. 'No ... I won't forget.' He hung up. Suddenly he needed to find a toilet someplace. There was a Texaco station on the next block. He hurried to his car, rolling up his sleeves as he went.

Clare sat in the back with Gambini. He had a shotgun on his knees, holding it lightly across stock and barrel, the muzzle towards the door. Terson was driving.

Ahead, the yellow car wove through the late-afternoon traffic, keeping a steady pace past whipping awnings and empty tin cans skittering across sidewalks. When they rounded the bay Clare could see waves spewing high beyond the breakwater, and the lighthouse was lost in the murk. Between low cloud and sea-spray, the horizon seemed close enough to touch. The car rocked briefly whenever they left the protection of buildings and caught the full gust of wind that channelled up the streets from the waterfront.

'Don't blame them for keeping choppers down in this,' Terson said, righting the wheel again as they gained the bulwark of a Woolworth and a Safeway. 'Must be gusting at ten knots at least, and worse to come, they say. They're re-routing commercial flights around the mountains already.'

Mike wouldn't have taken a commercial flight anyway, Clare wanted to say. She watched a woman battle a baby-buggy into a doorway and turn to stare accusingly out of the downpour that was lashing her infant into hysteria.

If only we had taken the plane, she mourned. We'd be safe home by now. But Mike simply could not accept being looked after like a parcel. She could just discern the shape of his head through the rear window of the yellow car ahead. His profile was outlined against the windscreen whenever he spoke to Van Schaaten. Every few minutes he would turn round to check that their car was still behind his, but she couldn't see his face. It was furthest apart they'd been in weeks and she hated it.

There were more guns in each car than people, but without him she felt as if she'd come out into the storm without her coat.

There was a jam blocking the turn to 101, and Terson put the Falcon bumper to bumper with the yellow Galaxie. Clare could see Mike more clearly through the half-steamed rear window. He smiled at her.

They made the turn on to 101 at just five-thirty, but already darkness was in charge. The false, stormy twilight gave everything around them a strange, two-dimensional definition as street-lights and shop-lights were turned on early. Rain gleamed like a thousand snakes down the curved backs of the cars. Colours were cartoon-bright against the heavy, even grey of the sky. Car windows were a steamed mystery, and only an occasional flare of a match put features on the blurred figures within.

Tired people going home to a tired Friday night in front of the box. They'd turn to one another during the commercials and say, 'Listen to that wind.'

Guns would fire and tyres would scream inside the mahogany and glass, and actors would yell, 'Hold it right there, buddy,' to other actors running down a carefully sordid alley. But real cops weren't like that, she knew now. They were Terson and Gambini sitting with their guns close, watching the cars and the streets around them. They were soft-spoken, uneasy, fussy about details, and smelled of aftershave.

'How is he, Miss Randell?' Gambini asked.

'He was pretty sick.'

'Seems OK now.'

'Yes.'

'I'm surprised they let him on to the force with that medical history.'

'They took the army's word that he was cured.'

'Oh.' He lit a cigarette. 'But he wasn't.'

'No. They were wrong.'

'Happens, I guess.'

'Yes.' She turned to look out at the last few houses.

'One thing and another, he'd better start looking for another job,' Terson observed laconically.

'Not him.' Clare turned to Gambini in surprise, and he grinned. 'He'll talk them out of it, you'll see.'

'Silver-tongued devil?' Clare smiled, warming to Gambini's evident faith.

'Oh no. Goddamn stubborn bastard, that's all. And a good cop. They'll buy it, in the end. You'll see.'

The two men exchanged a glance in the mirror, and Terson almost smiled. She wondered how much they knew about Mike's flight with her, what version or half-version they'd been given. To ask would be admitting doubt into the car, and they didn't need another passenger.

Once the highway entered the forest it was as if someone had closed the last window in a house. The car was quiet, stable, smooth.

'That's better,' Terson said, passing a shimmying old pick-up. Headlights were beginning to glitter the raindrops on the windscreen now, whenever another car passed. Darkness was complete under the trees. After a while Clare began to feel drowsy. The only noise in the car was the swish of the windscreen-wipers, the occasional chink of the passing indicators, and Terson humming between his teeth. The figures in the yellow car ahead were only silhouettes in the occasional flare of approaching headlights. Davis's head barely topped the rear seat, and Van Schaaten and Mike had apparently finished their earlier conversation. She drifted away.

An hour later the sound of Mike's voice in the car jerked her awake. For a moment she was confused, because she could see only Terson and Gambini. Then the radio crackled again. She hadn't even noticed it when she got into the car.

'We'll pick up some coffee at the drive-in up on the left.'

The freeway stopped a couple of miles from Klamath, and the road was ordinary highway again, bracketed with neon. Outskirts of the town began to build up, supermarkets open later for weekend shoppers, drugstores, dry-cleaners, restaurants and motels. 'Big Tree Burgers – eat with Giants', read the sign at the drive-in. A solitary redwood spiking up from the cement forecourt necessitated a round-about approach, and it seemed to tower over them in lone dismay far from the forest. A different undergrowth glittered below its whipping branches, metal insects and rain-coated moles ran between puddles of colour reflecting the neon.

Instead of waiting for car-service, Terson and Davis went in and came out with big containers of coffee and a stack of paper cups each. They were under way in less than ten minutes, eating sandwiches that Mrs Brand had packed for them.

Once through Klamath the road spread to expressway again, curving away under the lights. The few cars they passed threw up rooster-tails of spray, and Terson had to drop back fifty yards to avoid the Galaxie's wake. The gradual turns and banked lifts of the beautifully engineered road had Clare almost drowsy again. When the car slowed she paid no attention, until Gambini spoke.

'When we came through here this afternoon in the daylight it was fantastic. Like driving through a church gone to seed.' He rolled down a window and the sudden blast of cold air brought Clare fully awake. 'Listen,' he said.

'I don't hear anything,' she said after a moment. 'Just the car.'

'That's it. They're virgin stands through here, so thick not even that wind can get through. This part of the road is only a couple of miles from the coast, but you'd never know it.' He helped himself to another apple.

The rain-washed air filled the car with a scent of pine and wet earth, and the rising splatter from their front wheels hissed just below the level of the window. In the black-glare of their headlights she could see the bulk of the forest starting beyond the margin of the road, a wall of bark rising out of sight above them. Gambini rolled up the window slowly, leaving a gap at the top. 'You mind? Trees smell better than tuna fish.'

Terson cursed suddenly from the front seat. 'That goddamn semi has been hogging the centreline for the past ten miles. He knows we're here, but will he get his ass over? He will not. Every time Van Schaaten tries to pass him, he slides out a little more.'

Mike's voice was suddenly in the car again. 'I don't like the guy in the semi up front. He's doing this block job deliberately. We'd better drop—' The sentence chopped off as the big red trailer-truck suddenly slewed across the road in front of the yellow Galaxie, jack-knifing itself into a V-shape that blocked both lanes.

The Galaxie, travelling close behind it in order to pass, didn't have a chance, but Van Schaaten did his best. He swerved with the truck and the front end of the Galaxie skidded into the bulk of the inside fender below the high cab, wheel and tyre taking most of the impact. Clare screamed as the front end of the Galaxie rode up the truck, its hood flying back to strike its own roof.

'Jesus, it's a set-up,' Terson yelled, hitting the brakes and turning into his own skid before the Galaxie had stopped moving. The smaller car went into a spin immediately, but he utilized the motion to do what he had in mind, which was to turn back and get the hell out of there, as instructed. Gambini had the shotgun up in both hands, the apple still clenched between his teeth. As they went round he bit through it, and the core fell unheeded into his lap. He looked back as the wheels gained traction on the slimy road, and shouted.

'There's another one coming up, Jake. They're boxing us, dammit.'

As the Falcon came to a near-stop and Terson dropped it into low, Clare pushed open the rear door on her side and jumped out, falling over on the wet road and trying to scramble to her feet on its slippery surface of dead pine-needles and old oil scum. She could see the big red semi more clearly now as the headlights of the second truck approached from behind. The yellow car was a smear at the front, like a dead wasp under a brick.

'Mike!' she screamed above the roar of the two engines behind her. Gambini's wild shout of fury was thrown after her like a lariat. As she lurched towards the yellow car she saw men piling out of the double-doors at the back of the trailer, four of them. The driver was stepping down on to the rear deck of the Galaxie which had come to rest beneath the cab door. He was carrying a shotgun like Gambini's, and she knew instantly that it was Edison.

The scream died in her throat, but he had picked up the thin wail above the noise of the approaching truck. His head came up. So did the double muzzle of the shotgun. She thought she saw white teeth in a smile, but then the passenger door of the Ford burst open and Malchek was precipitated on to the pavement. He rolled limply, then suddenly started firing at Edison who towered above him with one foot on the roof of the Galaxie. Edison had no leverage, one hand was still on the cab door, and the other was levelling the shotgun towards Clare. Malchek's shots jerked the door out of Edison's hand, and the tall man threw himself back into the cab. Malchek had not seen Clare, and he was screaming something to Van Schaaten and Davis who were still in the car. Davis must have been hurt but still alive, because she saw his arm lift the rifle case and sling it weakly towards the ditch. Mike went down as it slid across the wet asphalt, and at the same moment the blast of Edison's shotgun shattered the windscreen of the truck cab above, and a waterfall of glass cascaded over everything.

Clare went down, too, sprawling awkwardly into the shallow ditch that separated the road and the trees. Her face splashed into the stream of cold rainwater that ran along the bottom, and she lifted it out to shout again when a low, dull 'whump' came from in front of her and the Galaxie burst into flames.

A curly gout of fire ran up the cap of the truck, and the door on the opposite side was thrown open. The men who had been circling around from the trailer fell back at the lick of heat, and from inside the car she could hear Davis screaming. It made her feel sick as she crawled through the mud towards Mike. He was crouched some ten yards in front of her, one hand lifted to shield his eyes from the glare. She could see him tensing himself to run back for Davis, but he caught sight of her out of the corner of his eye, and hesitated.

She couldn't have said which emotion was strongest in his face as he turned towards her, terror or anger. All she wanted or cared about was to be next to him again, to feel him beside her. She saw rather than heard his groan of despair, and then he was shouting.

'Go back, for Christ's sake. Go back, Clare.' But she kept moving towards him, remembering what Gambini had shouted about the other truck boxing them in. If it was a trap, it was *their* trap.

In another few seconds she was with him, listening to the whining crackle of the flames above the twang and groan of superheated metal. Davis had stopped screaming.

A broadsword of headlights fell across them as the second truck came up, airbrakes hissing as it glanced off the Falcon. They could hear Gambini's shotgun and Terson's revolver as they abandoned any attempt to drive out, and opened fire instead.

'My God, he got his army after all,' Malchek breathed into her hair as his arm went round her. She huddled into him, shivering. The ditch was slightly deeper at this point, and the water gushed across her ankles and knees as she knelt with bowed head, afraid to watch. The wood rose clear behind them, and though the rain was filtered through the heavy branches overhead it still penetrated. She'd put on a raincoat for warmth when Gambini had opened the window, but Mike was only wearing a denim jacket over a thin pullover. They both would soon be soaked through.

The glare from the flames was lessening slightly, and she was losing the edges of his face in the shadows. He risked a look over the weed-grown edge of the ditch, ducking back to put his lips next to her ear.

'Edison's army seems reluctant to join in, they're just huddling there behind the truck. We've got to get into the trees, babe, it's our only chance.'

. 'All you townspeople get torches and meet in the woods,' she hiccuped hysterically through chattering teeth.

'Shut up and listen. I'm giving you two minutes. Take the rifle. When I say go, run into the trees. Run low.' He thrust the rifle into her arms. 'You loaded it with your eyes closed the other day, babe, do it again. The clips are in the outside pocket of the case. When you've got it loaded, start firing as wide and wild as possible. If you hit something, it's a bonus. Just don't hit me, for God's sake, I'll be the damn fool with the white face, running towards you.'

'But—'

'Go on, damnit . . .' He pushed her roughly, and she found herself scuttling towards the shelter of the trees that stretched up into the pitch-blackness overhead. She heard his .38 cracking sporadically behind her as she ran, and then the first low creepers grabbed her ankles with slippery fingers.

At last she was there, panting and gasping for air beside a six-foot-thick trunk. She crawled behind it, pushing into ferns that showered her with extra rain. There was still enough light from the burning car for her to locate the clips in the leather-buckled pocket of the case. She extracted the rifle itself and fumbled in the dark for a moment before she realized she was trying to force the magazine in upside down. Eventually it was home and secure, and she put as many of the spares into her raincoat pocket as she could. Peering round the tree cautiously, she locked the bolt and lifted the rifle to her shoulder. It was hard to hold, and her wet hands slipped on the stock. Taking aim at the men behind the truck, she fired and nearly dropped it. The metal of the truck above their heads suddenly showed a bright silver streak. They scattered. Nobody fell. She kept on firing but everything was high. When she overcompensated, she managed to rupture the front tyre of the Falcon, trapping Gambini and Terson once and for all. They were still firing from inside, and nobody had got out of the second truck yet.

She finished the magazine, extracted it, pushed another in and started again. So intent was she on her assignment that she almost screamed when Mike came round the other side of the tree. He fumbled for the rifle-case in the darkness, and dumped the rest of the clips into the pocket of his jacket, along with a box of extra .38 ammunition he had stuffed in before leaving the apartment.

'Look, Gambini and Terson have got enough trouble without *you* hitting them – what happened?' She told him, and he nodded. 'Rain always makes a high shot, I should have warned you.' Suddenly he grabbed the rifle from her and fired to the right of the first truck cab. The men in the back, who had been peering tentatively around during the break in firing, disappeared again. Clare caught a flash of movement near the front.

'Drop, you bastard,' Malchek growled. 'Let's finish it.' But after a moment he stopped firing. 'The hell with it. Come on, babe, into the trees. All we have to buy is time. This is the main highway. Somebody has probably reported this mess already, or they will any minute. We can wait out the night and then circle round to pick up help in the morning. Let's go.'

It was like running into the open mouth of a black bag.

Within minutes they'd lost all light from the sullenly burning car, and were feeling their way through the tangle of ferns and roots, hands linked desperately tight.

'Whatever you do, don't let go,' he said.

Clare was too terrified to answer. The redwood forest had awed her in the daylight, but in the dark it was stupefying. They could feel the massive trees around them, pressing down. Overhead there was the howl of wind and the thrashing of interlocking branches, but here below it was like the bottom of a midnight sea. She blindly sensed the alien size of the trees. Each colossal trunk they brushed past seemed to loom above them in an invisible and oppressive threat, as if poised to fall any moment. It was the reverse of looking over the edge of a tall building, the inverted vertigo of ants at a picnic of giants. Because there was virtually no taper to the trunks, they repeatedly walked into them without warning. Some had twisted roots like tumbled rocks around the base, but others rose sheer. The density and height of the trees meant that the only things that would grow on the floor of the forest were ferns, and these, in the diffuse twilight of the days, had grown straight up to each tree. One minute they would be in thick undergrowth, the next nose to bark. The trees were widely spaced, but even so they seemed to encounter them with depressing regularity. Mike would crash first, as he was leading, and she would come up against both his back and the tree at once. He kept muttering something she couldn't catch.

'What?'

'Nothing.'

'But you keep saying the same thing.'

'So would you, if you'd had a Russian grandfather.'

Whatever the phrase meant, it sounded terrible.

The darkness had a substance of its own, thicker only where the redwoods stood oblivious to their headlong flight below.

'They pay people to build mazes like this, you know,' she gasped as they leaned against another ancient wooden shin.

'So I hear. Don't stop, keep going.' He pulled her away from the tree, but almost immediately encountered something else. 'There's a fallen one here.'

She reached out, touching first the soaked denim of his jacket, and then the horizontal ridges of shaggy bark that ran away on either side. 'Can we get round it, then take a rest?'

'OK.' He didn't sound too enthusiastic about her suggestion, but began to move to the right, keeping the tree against his shoulders. She could tell it wasn't as big as the one they had used as a target the other day. Air was flowing over the top and brushing against her face, a gentle zephyr compared with the tumult and howl of the wind high in the night above. Suddenly Malchek lurched to the left and she lost her grip on his hand. There was a bit of thrashing, then silence.

'Mike!'

'It's OK. The trunk has rotted, made a kind of hollow at the base. Just edge along, you'll find me.'

Almost immediately her searching fingers found the gap in the broken trunk, and she followed the inner surface until she nearly fell over Mike, who had sunk down on to the thick, soft floor of dead ferns and rotted wood-pulp. He caught and held her close for a moment before settling her against the trunk next to him.

High, high overhead the wind raged through the branches like some wild thing running another impenetrable maze. Air was moving through the forest below in a sibilant whisper and the rain was no more than a mist there. Everywhere around them the ferns moved and whispered in faint echo of the tumult above.

'Do you think he'll come after us?' Every movement of the ferns seemed to hide someone or something that menaced.

'Not yet. Maybe not at all. Or maybe he has. I don't know.'

It seemed an oddly equivocal reply, and she shivered against him, seeking reassurance. There was none. Only an answering shiver that shuddered into a convulsive spasm. His hands were even colder than when she had first taken them.

The chills had started again.

He held his arm up, his watch a pale, greenish beacon in the darkness. 'Right on schedule ... ten past ten.'

'Oh Mike, no.' She clung more tightly to him, seeking now to warm rather than gain warmth. The chills shook him spasmodically, and his teeth chattered in the damp air.

'It's not so bad as it was before. I'm not saying it's *great*, mind you ...' His voice trailed off.

But it was not impossible.

He wondered if the following fever would be similarly diminished. If so, it might make the difference between survival and death. He knew the ideal treatment for a malaria relapse was not running for your life through cold rain in light clothing. Well, they had a *cure* for pneumonia.

There was a sudden rustling in the ferns round the tree. A stronger movement than before. He felt it more than heard it. Something – or someone – was walking on the other side of the fallen tree. And coming closer. Any hope that it might be Gambini and Terson, or an elk made restless by the storm and the commotion on the near-by highway, was lost in the sound of the first curse.

'Goddamn you, pig, I'm going to take you.'

For an instant Malchek thought they had actually been discovered, but the voice continued its monotonous litany, and his initial alarm receded. He remained as still as the hunted thing he was, Clare small and unbreathing beside him. Another chill came, and it took all his strength to keep the tremor from communicating itself through the ferns to Edison, who had stopped beyond the trunk of the fallen tree. They could hear him panting, and felt the slight jar as he dropped against the trunk to rest. There could be only a few feet of wood between them. Edison's voice lifted in a shout, distorted by the trees and the wind overhead.

'I'm not going home without your scalp, you little bastard. Run, go on, run, I'm right behind you.'

There was another jar through the trunk as Edison pushed himself away and moved off through the brush. A sudden gleam of light swept over their heads and on through the glistening mass of ferns. Bright raindrop eyes flashed in the dark green, their after-image clear even when the finger of Edison's flashlight was pointing away, moving away. They could hear his voice muttering like a distant broadcast of bad news, and then there was only the overhead roar of the wind and the drip and swish of the ferns around them. He would have liked to have taken Edison then, but the chills meant he had no control, no certainty of aim, and if he missed ... Too risky, better to wait.

He took his hand away from Clare's face. Another chill shook him, but it was bearable, controllable. She wrapped her arms round him more tightly, her breath flowing warm down the front of his sweater. He buried his face in her wet hair, tasting the rain.

'We'll be OK, babe. We'll get through it.'

'Oh Mike, I love you.'

'No matter what? No matter what I ... what I was?' The question he had firmly intended never to ask was torn from him in the midst of another irresistible chill.

'Or ever could be. I can't stop it, it's part of me. *You're* part of me, don't you see that? And I'm part of you.' She chuckled, giggled, hysteria edging the breath that grazed his cheek. 'So how bad can you be if I'm part of you. I *never* join any outfit that's not one hundred per cent—'

His mouth silenced hers, and he kissed her again and again. This was where real warmth came from. For a wild moment he felt like a vampire sucking heat instead of blood, and then he knew that it was not desire. The chills were becoming fever.

The next phase had begun.

He insisted that they start moving again, and they resumed

their staggering, blind, painfully slow progress, cannoning from one gigantic trunk to the next, soaked by the rain and chilled by the wind. He intended to move in the opposite direction to that taken by Edison, then circle back to the highway, where rescue trucks and HP units must have been swarming by now. He wanted to get as far as possible from Edison while he could. But even the storm could not defeat the steady rise of his temperature. Things began to blur. The damp, echoing roar of the storm overhead gradually began to resemble the insect buzzing of the tropic jungles where he had killed and killed again. He knew he was losing his grip on reality. When he gave Clare a command and she did not react correctly, he raised a hand to hit her. Then he realized he had spoken in gook pidgin. His vision was distorting, what there was of it, and his sense of direction was swarming with message and counter-message until his head felt like a beehive.

Eventually they half-stumbled, half-slid into some kind of narrow canyon or gully that meandered along with a stream down the centre. On either side fronds of fern covered the walls completely, and to their outstretched hands it felt like a fur-lined tunnel. Although they were still protected, the wind was much stronger there, and it occurred to him that the gully might lead directly to the sea. Unfiltered by the trees the rain slashed down with its full force and they were entirely soaked in a few minutes.

Every time a frond of fern touched his burning face, it reminded him, made it seem then and now, all at once.

Clare tripped over a root and lurched against him. He steadied her instinctively, not quite sure who she was but loving her.

His bare feet had walked paths in that distant jungle. His heavy cotton peasant's jacket and knee-high pants were loose and comfortable, the dark stain on his skin hiding the paleness of his fear.

'Mike, we've got to stop soon, you're burning up. Mike?'

He'd stood at the edge of the grove of bamboo, thin, silvery leaves quaking gently around him.

'As soon as we come to the end of this, we're stopping,' Clare said firmly. 'We'll find a shelter, something.' Was that the girl, or the old man? He stopped, his hand sunk wrist-deep into the ferns, his chest heaving painfully. Cold air in, hot air out. He was a match-flame in the darkness, he could almost see his breath burning on the air, a pale, flickering heat.

He had been grateful for the darkness, the lack of moonlight, the soft, fitful breeze. So many leaves conversing together in the shadows that his own breathing was lost. The rifle had been heavy in his hand. Heavier and heavier. But he had raised it, and seen through the sight that old man in the garden suddenly become all the old men in the world. Even as the bullet left the gun he was looking at his father, at his grandfather, at everyone he'd ever loved, grown old and defenceless. Ten horrifying seconds later he was looking at another empty husk dropped into the centre of a spreading stain. Looking at all his victims. And it was wrong. He automatically killed the guards who stumbled out of the house, but it was wrong. He kept crying all the time, because it was wrong. He apologized every time he fired, because it was wrong. He walked away still carrying the rifle, but he knew he wouldn't use it again. Not like that. No matter how they threatened him. No matter what they said.

'Look, here's a little hollow in the wall, look, Mike. A cave. Well – almost a cave … and it's dry. It's dry …' She was pulling his arm, urging him to move.

It wasn't his rifle, was it? It was another rifle, wasn't it? No scrolls? No decoration?

Why was he here in this cold, windy slit in the earth? Someone was tugging and pulling him along a wall alive with moving ferns. Above them the wind tore through giant trees, whining, whistling, roaring.

Or was it more than the wind that still screamed in his head? Clare. Clare was telling him to stop. To hide.

But they *had* to keep moving. They were still too far behind enemy lines to hole up. When she tugged him towards the cave he resisted, pulled her to him, held on. He was going to protect her, no matter what. He was going to look after her. He loved her. God, he loved her so. And she needed his protection badly.

Some bastard named Malchek was trying to kill her.

twenty-one

Gonzales shakily opened his door and stepped out. Not since he'd ridden with a gung-ho sergeant on a chase through the Tenderloin had he been so terrified in a car. The entire journey from San Francisco, with Reddesdale behind the wheel and the quite illegal but effective siren and light miraculously clearing the highway before them, had been a nightmare. No, worst than that. When things got tight in a nightmare, you generally woke up. Try as he might, he had not been able to do that. Not the time they had run the red light and narrowly missed the lumber truck, not the time the women had screamed and jumped back, not the time Reddesdale had threatened to get out and punch a Highway Patrol cop in the mouth.

When word of the blockade on 101 had come through Gonzales had made some remark about wishing he could get up there, and the next thing he knew, they were on their way.

Too late, he'd recognized the glint in Reddesdale's eyes. Everybody mount up, we'll head 'em off at the pass. It didn't strike Gonzales as incongruous that a Commissioner of Police in one of the country's major cities should want to get into action. Just crazy. But they were there and, looking around, he felt insanity recede and a heavy weight of depression take its place.

A two-truck had dragged the big semi to the edge of the highway, the remains of the yellow Galaxie still self-welded to its cab. Rain was washing down the wreckage, but as he passed close by he could still catch the stench of burned flesh rising from the blackened metal. Ambulances had taken the bodies away.

Further back along the shoulder stood a second semi, drawn up behind a white Falcon with a flat tyre. Two Highway Patrol cars were bracketing them, and a Crescent City Sheriff's Department car stood last in the line. There were also two yellow Parks Service jeeps on the opposite shoulder. Several wet and weary men were trying to keep their cigarettes alight in the downpour.

Gambini and Terson were among them, Gambini with a bandage round his left hand and Terson with a black eye. They aproached their superiors with an air of combined apology and anger.

'Sorry,' Gambini said. 'They're gone. All of them.'

'Gone where?' Reddesdale demanded.

Terson sighed. 'Davis and Van Schaaten to the nearest morgue, Edison's "troops" to the nearest jail, and the driver of the second semi to the hospital. Shock.'

'He wasn't part of it?' Gonzales asked.

'Damnedest thing. All he knows is, he passed a semi about three miles back pulled over with engine trouble, a lot of guys standing around it looking scared. Figured it's none of his business keeps going. Next thing, he sees that *other* semi jack-knifed ahead of him, some car plastered up against it burning like hell – and another car, us, trying to turn round. Says he hit the brakes, and didn't see much more because he was too busy trying to keep it out of a skid. Then we opened up on him. When he stopped he just hit the floor and prayed. Thought it was a hijack, I guess. What the hell, we were unmarked cars, what else would he think? He's a nervous wreck.'

'And Mike and the girl? Edison?'

Terson nodded towards the woods. 'In there, somewhere.'

'All of them?'

'All of them.'

They stared at one another for a while. There didn't seem much left to say. Then two other men approached the group. Gambini introduced them as a Captain Moore of the HP, and Sheriff Brand from Crescent City. Moore was the ranking officer, and Reddesdale spoke directly to him.

'We know we're right out of jurisdiction here, Captain. We just came to help if we can – Malchek is a personal friend.'

This apparently displeased the captain, who seemed to feel Commissioners of Police simply did not mix with the hired hands. His careful military bearing was defeated somewhat by a too-large yellow slicker that drooped heavily from his squared shoulders. Rain dripped past his face from the gutter of his wide-brimmed hat.

'These officers have given me to understand that they were transporting an endangered witness to the city. Why wasn't I notified? We could have supplied extra protection and avoided this entire fiasco.'

Reddesdale peered up at him. 'It's a little more complex than that, captain.' He began to move away from the group and the HP officer was forced to follow. Brand turned to Gonzales with a grin.

'Hope you brought plenty of pens. He likes things in triplicate.'

'Oh, yeah?' Gonzales watched the HP officers for a minute. 'He's sent some men in after them, has he?'

'Oh, sure. The best the HP school can produce. Trouble is, they only produced them last month. They're about as familiar with the area as they are with a ladies' john. Still, they might get lucky, you never know. As long as he keeps his rule-book out of it. All spit and shit, you know the type. Posted from behind an instructor's desk after twenty years on his ass. Got theories to test. Keeps trying to find the page.' Brand looked like a man who wanted to spit but didn't chew.

'You saw Malchek. How was he? Bad?'

Brand, Gambini and Terson exchanged a look. Brand answered. 'Hell, no. Thin as a pole and white as a sheet, but he had his act together, I guess. Wouldn't you say?'

Gambini nodded.

Terson looked sceptical. 'He was run out, lieutenant,' he said brusquely. 'He was bone tired.'

Brand offered his cigarettes around. Rain had spattered the pack, the cellophane was puckered.

'He *really* your Commissioner of Police?' Brand asked, staring at Reddesdale.

'That's what it says on his door. Personally, I think he's just a natural-born street cop they keep tied to the chair.'

'He's busted loose now.' They all glanced covertly at the jerky, agitated movements of Reddesdale's hands as he talked to Moore. The HP captain was looking a little less amiable, suddenly.

Gambini gave a disgusted look towards the woods. 'A ten-year-old kid could get through those dopes. Look at them.' He dropped his cigarette into a puddle and stepped on it savagely. Reddesdale left the HP captain and came over to them.

'Captain Moore feels that sufficient men are already in the woods, looking. He feels very strongly that we would only hamper the search.' His voice was expressionless.

Brand snorted. After a moment he spoke. 'Well, seeing as the Captain feels that way, Commissioner, I don't figure we'll do much good standing here in the rain like a bunch of hat-racks. Why don't you come on back to Klamath with me and we'll get a coffee or something.' His eyes didn't match his words, and they all caught it. Five minutes later they were following Brand's car up the highway, Gambini and Terson silent in the back seat.

After rounding a curve a mile or so down the road, Brand's rear signal started to flash, and he made a sudden left across the ditch into the blackness of the forest. Reddesdale followed, the car lurching and skidding on mud and pine-needles, their headlights sweeping erratic patterns across the incredible trees. About twenty or thirty yards into the forest itself, Brand stopped and got out of his car to come back and lean in through the window.

'Old logging road here. I think one of the Rangers knew about it, but Moore didn't let him get his mouth open.' Brand blew his nose expressively into a dark-blue handkerchief. 'Thing is, we can't take the cars more'n halfway down. Need a jeep, really. But the road curves round to the cliffs the other side of this stand, and we might catch them coming out. What do you think?'

'I think I should have worn my galoshes,' Gonzales said grimly.

twenty-two

The storm was lessening slightly. The wind did not have the same shrill note of hysteria that had marked it in the beginning. It still raged and tore at the trees high above them, but Malchek sensed a moving away, something backing off, going inland.

He'd been forced to halt twice, leaning against a tree and throwing up breakfast, lunch, dinner, and maybe last weeks meals as well. Clare had stopped protesting at their headlong pace, reserving her breath to stay alive. She followed dumbly on, her icy hand locked in his blazing fingers, praying he would faint. He did not.

He held his head back and let the rain wash some of the sourness out of his mouth. The icy fingers thrust into his eyes, his hair, his ears, but did not cool him. Twice he had tried to take off his sodden jacket, but Clare had nearly gone berserk, so he left it on. The fever had to break soon. It had to. It was not so high as the previous one, nor so wide, but it sufficed. The problem was, things kept drifting on him. One minute the whole stupid mess was perfectly clear, the next he was trying to remember what it was he was trying to remember. Or forget. Or whatever. The only consistent thing was *away. Get away.*

The end of it was nearer all the time. His legs were shaking under him, and the fever had burned him hollow. He felt like and empty envelope of skin pushing through the branches and leaves, and wondered why something didn't puncture him and let all the air out. The only thing that reminded him of his muscles was the pain.

'We'll find a place to stop soon.'

'I *found* a place a long time ago,' Clare complained. 'But you wouldn't get into it.'

'What place was that?'

'A little cave, back there in that gully. Behind the ferns. I *told* you.'

'Did you? Sorry. What did I say?'

'You said you could hear a bell ringing. It was the Angelus, you said.'

'Jesus. If you'll pardon the expression.' Why couldn't he hear the sea yet?

'Mike ... next year can we go to the desert for our vacation instead?'

'Sure, babe. Sure.'

He arbitrarily picked a direction and moved. What they needed was a boy scout. Just one boy scout, even a small one. He'd *forgotten* so damn much. And Nam had not been like this. Except for the rain. Rain he knew about.

The rest of that night, walking. The next day crouched in a deserted chicken-coop the size of a match-box. The next night, walking. And the next. The rifle went, and the survival kit he'd stashed outside the city. Everything got sucked away in that river, under the wide, oily water. It looked so quiet, until he was up to his thighs and the undercurrent pulled his ankles off the mud bottom and he went down. Fast, so fast, the banks went by like the Santa Fé express, he almost sprained a wrist on that branch, snatching at anything. There'd been a forest on top of that bank, but not like this. Whiplash bamboo and creepers, a stink of rot everywhere, and the whirring of paper wings until the air seemed filled with the buzz of one gigantic insect watching, hovering, waiting. Rain then, and more rain. Walking, walking, every mile like the last, every hour like the last, until it seemed he was standing still and the jungle was moving. Then a tree. More bamboo. Then another tree. Little trees, you could see their tops. And finally a place to sit that wasn't just scum over thick, black-tar mud. The chills had started then. And later, the fever.

'Do you hear something?'

The voices of the peasants who'd finally found him? The voices of the Army doctors? The doctors said he would be all right. As good as new. But he wasn't. Nothing was.

'Is it thunder ... or ... Mike, is that surf?'

'What?'

'That rumbling, thudding sound. Is it the sea?'

'We're two hundred miles from the sea.' Stupid woman.

'What? But ... oh, never mind. I think it's the sea, over that way. Mike ... there ... it is. It *is*.'

He stopped her headlong forward rush with a steel arm and she snapped round like the last child in a crack-the-whip chain.

'It *is* the sea,' he said, startled, wary.

'Yes,' she stammered. 'I *said* that.'

'Yes.'

She stood helplessly, staring at him. There were fewer trees here. Other pines, and some softwoods mixed in, and more light, even if it was only a paler shade of black. His face was a white oval, his eyes glittered as he looked around.

He went down on his knees, suddenly, straight down and hard. She half-fell, half-sat beside him, expecting any move but that one. At first she thought he'd collapsed. Then, when he began crawling, she followed, mud and leaves squidging up between her fingers.

Dropping flat on to his stomach, he wriggled into a low, roundish bush. In the centre there was a hollow space where some animal had patiently trampled down a sleeping area. Too much one way or the other brought them up against inch-long thorns, but there was room enough for both of them to sit.

'I knew the minute I met you, you were the kind of guy who'd take me to all the best places,' she confided as she dragged herself in after him, the thorns catching in her hair.

'I am known for having a certain style,' he admitted wearily. He rested his face in his hands for a moment, then put an arm round her. 'End of the line for me, honey. No further.'

'About time.'

'I guess.'

At first sitting didn't seem much different from running, for his heart still pounded and breath was expensive. And sitting quiet took effort too when you wanted to whoop in the oxygen and rub your aching calves.

She had asked him, that century ago in the woods, whether he didn't think it ludicrous to be teaching her to shoot in the middle of all that beauty. He had denied it then, but now he saw her point. Other people went to drive-ins and parties. *They* were sitting in the middle of a thornbush trying to avoid being slaughtered. Some love affair.

When all this idiocy ended, if it ended with them still alive, would they be able to face the stunning trauma of a simple electricity bill? And would ordinary electricity bills and a mortgage be enough?

Because, while he wrote out that cheque to Pacific Gas and Electric, inside him the animal would be sleeping, the animal he had been. Curled up as tight as they were now in this thornbush. He could only hope it would sleep quietly behind the thorns of smiles and kids and Clare and routine. It would never die. Never ... never ...

'How can you sleep sitting up like that?' Clare whispered indignantly.

He blinked and opened his eyes wide. 'You get the knack on stake-outs. In case the captain decides on a spot-check.'

She touched his cheek lightly. 'You're still burning up. Lie down. I'll keep watch.'

It was just a matter of where to fall. Against the thorns, or against her.

He awoke suddenly, completely. There was a little more light, or perhaps just a little less darkness. It's difficult to tell when your head is about to blow off its stem.

The rain had stopped, and the wind had died to a fitful breeze without a voice. He tried a deep breath and couldn't get it. Terrific, somebody had strapped his chest with steel wire. He couldn't decide whether the fever had broken or not. His clothes were still soaked from the rain, but he didn't feel at all cold. Another terrific.

When he sat up, slowly, every muscle and bone in his body protested, and the slight effort left him nauseated. Here is our bold, intrepid hero about to throw up his guts in the bushes again, he sneered.

There weren't any birds conversing near them. Why? After a moment he heard the answer. A rhythmic movement through the underbrush, steps, hesitation, another rustle and crackle. It was a man all right. Elks rarely mutter to themselves. Known fact. He let his breath out slowly, suddenly realizing he had been holding it against the tightness in his chest. Another few minutes passed, and then another sound came. He felt like muttering a little too. Edison was relieving himself, he heard the hiss followed by a grunt of relief and the brief snarl of a zip. Damn. Unless Edison was a kidney case it would be hours before that need came again, and he could have used it. A little more light and he might have located the wisp of steam as the hot urine hit cold air. The sound seemed to come from the left, however. He tried to focus on the shadows, but the size of the trees outside their ring of thorns could have concealed a ten-ton truck without the bumpers showing either side. No hope.

Now he was moving. Moving on. He wasn't even trying to be quiet about it.

He'd wondered about that before.

Edison had learned to kill as he had. But not in the same way. Any man who was that noisy was used to moving with a group around him. Navy, flyboy, infantry ... his stealth was greater than a normal man's, but not as great as it could have been. Compared with Malchek, he moved like a hippopotamus, and that was good. That was very, very good.

Gradually the sounds of Edison's progress diminished. Quietly, Malchek began to empty his pockets on to the bed of dried ferns and dead twigs. Four clips left for the rifle, over half a box of .38 cartridges. It would only take one.

Clare was watching him. He could feel her attention riveted on the little heap of death he was building between them. He reached into his inside pocket, pulled out his pocket-knife, and transferred it to the inside of his right boot, just behind the ankle bone. He took out his handkerchief, which was nearly dry, and wiped down the rifle. He found a good, fist-sized rock and knotted it into the square of cloth, slipping the ends down on a belt-loop and letting the rock ride his waistband, behind the .38 holster. He glanced around. The thorns looked interesting although he didn't have the time or materials to employ them usefully. It only took a minute to break off a pocketful.

She didn't ask him. She knew. Maybe she had always known, so words weren't any use, anyway. Words were her business, but Edison was his.

'Stay until I come back for you,' he whispered, emptying the loose change out of his pockets. He tore off the tail of his shirt and wrapped the .38 bullets tightly in it, flattening the result into a pad that fitted into the back pocket of his jeans. The clips he divided between the jacket pockets. Tearing off another strip of cloth, he tied his hair back from his face with a band across his forehead. 'If I don't come back for you, wait another night and then start moving away from the sea. Don't come out until then, and take a good look at anyone you ask for help before you show yourself. Even if he's wearing a uniform.' He reached out under the thorn bush until his fingers encountered mud, and he grabbed a fistful. Spreading it between his palms, he smeared it over his hands, face, ears and back of the neck, even where the hair hid it. As he wiped the dirt on to his eyelids he wondered if they'd perfected that eyeball dye they'd been messing about with in Nam. And what was the other thing? Oh, yeah. Black toothpaste.

('If you're planning to pick off a gook in the dark, *try* not to smile. He'll plug you right between the teeth.')

To Clare he was a terrifying sight. Covered in dirt, soaked, his hair tangled and matted, his darkened face split only by the flash of teeth and eyes. His scowl turned him into a nightmare mask that hung before her in the gloom, like some carving in a jungle hut. His clothes were plastered to him like skins, and only the dull gleam of the guns put him into this century. In his eyes was the heat of the fever, and something else. Something feral and hungry. He's exhausted, she told herself. Sick, exhausted, every nerve raw, stripped down to this, his essential core.

This is what they sent out to do their dirty work, those things he cried about in his delirium the other night.

This is an animal.

Thinking only to reassure her, he smiled, not realizing that his grin was even more terrifying than his scowl. It threw the contrast even higher between what she knew of him and what she had been told. It presented her with a problem.

Animals don't smile.

'Boo!' he whispered suddenly, and she jumped. He whispered something else. 'Charley will love all this.'

'Who ... who's Charley?' she stammered, thinking his mind had finally gone.

'Our oldest kid, Charley. Envy of all the other kids on the block, right? For playing cops and robbers he'll have a real cop. For playing soldiers he'll have a real commando, all his own. We'll have to make sure he doesn't start charging admission, though. Commercialism he gets from *you*.' He leaned forward suddenly and kissed her, hard, then turned and skinned underneath the thorns on his belly, and was gone.

She could taste mud on her lips, and it took a while for the tears to wash it away. Oh Charley, your father is a crackpot, your father is a madman, your father is ... was ... Oh Charley.

After thirty seconds the trees began to dissolve round him. He had to hold on to stay vertical. Pushing from tree to tree like an oarless boater, he drifted in a rough circle round the thornbush until he came to the damp streak he was looking for. He supposed any psychology professor could tell him the reason most men prefer to pee *against* something. Territory, maybe. But he was glad of it. Always informative, these little details. Of course, he already knew Edison was tall, and it didn't matter a damn whether he was gook or white. Anyway, he wasn't sure if he could remember the different smells of urine after all this time. You are what you eat, hey baby?

His head was awash with a hundred signals, broken, intermittent, flashes that made sense, and others that did not. Edison was right-handed, so he'd drift in that direction no matter how hard he fought it. Especially since he was moving at random, on the prowl. Yes, there was the first sign. Branches backlocked together where they'd been pushed aside. Branches don't grow in line. He began the track.

Little by little it came back. All he had to worry about was his own noise, and that was easy. Especially now that the faint dawn light was helping him, revealing the betraying places to avoid – twigs that would snap, little pockets of leaves that could hide a hole, mud that would skid him where he didn't want to go, startle him into an instinctive and noisy grab for support. And the wind was an ally. You could move with the wind.

Flat on his face at the edge of a clearing, he could see Edison's footsteps across a thick mat of needles, as clear as in tidal sand. Water drains from the surface of pine-needles, and a walking foot leaves dark puddles across the surface. He'd stood for a long time before risking the clearing, though. Long enough for his feet to sink deep here at the edge, next to the tree. Malchek smiled. So Edison *was* worried.

It took him twenty very careful minutes before he heard Edison breathing up ahead. Malchek halted, his fingers gripping the ridged surface of a redwood while he forced his own breathing to stay shallow and slow. Edison was panting with the effort of fighting the underbrush which was thicker here near the edge of the woods. Malchek yearned to do the same, but dared not risk it, even under the cover of Edison's own choking gasps.

He raised his head to judge the cover. Too good. The trees were closer here, new pines and softwoods growing up between the giants. It must have been logged at one time, redwoods are jealous trees, they keep it all to themselves if they can. The sound of the sea was more distinct, but it sounded as if it were beneath him. Cliffs? It was getting easier to breathe, and Edison was silent. Alarm stiffened Malchek and he looked behind him. Nobody. OK. Blood thrummed in his ears, temples, wrists. Even now he wasn't sweating. New way to stay warm without thermal underwear; catch pneumonia and ride the fever.

He eased his fingers from the bark, the imprint still pressed into the flesh as he moved forward and then dropped, settling the rifle over his hip bone. Time to risk a look.

He was almost disappointed.

He supposed he and Clare looked like Edison did at that moment. Clothes torn and flapping wetly round a scraped and bruised body, mud up the legs and white-faced. Edison wasn't playing Sambo.

It was a clear shot, no more than forty yards with nothing in the way. All these goddamn trees, and that jackass decided to play 'Stag at Bay' at the edge of a clearing. He thinks that bush is hiding him, but there's a perfect frame between two forks. I want the throat, but I'd better go for the shoulder. I'm getting out of this. I'll have a family to support. I need my job. OK, Reddesdale, you've got it your way. He pressed his eye into the sight. Black cross-hairs bisected Edison's collar-bone, and he could see the weave of the jacket where it had frayed away from a three-cornered tear in the lapel.

He knelt, poised flawlessly for the hit, his balance perfect, his gun steady. And he could not pull the trigger.

Taking a breath, he lifted his head back from the sight, blinked twice, then pressed into it once more, the plastic ring-ing deep round his eye. Edison had not moved. The hairs were still centred on the hollow below the padding of the jacket shoulder, and still his finger would not move.

Well, butcher, here we are, back in business at the same old stand. Let's go, let's go. That's the enemy, right? He's been trying to kill your woman, right? Kill!

He shot. He missed.

Edison went down, but down without a sound. He was un-touched and Malchek knew it. He also knew he should have aimed low to allow for the upjerk of wet ammunition. He hoped God was watching. You horse's ass, he told himself.

'One hundred per cent for style, zip for brains, little man,' came Edison's voice from beyond the trees. 'But it's nice to know you're still out there. I was beginning to feel a little lonely.'

Malchek smiled but gave no answer, just watched the tops of the ferns bowing and dancing in the breeze from the sea. Edison was moving left. I wonder how many loads he's carry-ing for that goddamn over-and-under? He'll need me well in the open to use it effectively, and that's a no-chancer. Let's see if we can lower his stockpile.

He chose a low hummock between two trees, one a redwood and the other a sugar-pine about a quarter the size. If he stood and ran he'd be exposed for approximately a second and a half from the waist up, and then he'd be back in brushwood again. He took a short, tight breath and made the break, expecting the gun-ripping boom of the shotgun and not getting it. Instead, as he was exposed, a searing chatter of shots went close behind him, the echoes telling him far more than he wanted to know.

With his face in the dirt Malchek went back to his grandfather's language. The shotgun had been visible back at the highway. The machine-pistol had not. Stupid to assume Edison would come underarmed. He'd probably had it in his belt, with the spare, extra-long muzzle strapped to his leg to be jacked in when necessary. And I just made it necessary. The shotgun was for making a big, newsy mess. The machine-pistol was for making sure. Edison is nuts, all right, but it doesn't leave him stupid. Worthy adversaries, my ass. We're just a couple of one-horned bucks pawing the ground. Me with malaria, and him with half a mind and his hands in his pants. Sorry, Clare, but I couldn't take him out like that. It's *me* coming back to you, not the animal I was. Call me honourable and try not to laugh.

The ferns were still moving. That made the next move unavoidable. When in doubt, run like hell. Malchek eased back and started his own belly-crawl. He found a small animal track, patiently worn and narrow. Perfectly safe, unless you were being tracked by a squirrel from above, and Edison didn't seem to be interested in climbing trees at the moment. No ferns to bow over me, baby, peasants take the low road.

He decided to make for a ravine he'd noticed on his approach, a narrow groove that started shallowly enough, but then dropped sharply and curved round in a question mark. With any luck it might carry him behind Edison. He's not taking chances, he knows I'm here. Slowly, baby.

His belt-buckle caught on a projecting twig concealed by a drift of leaves, and the dry wood snapped with a sharp, clear crack. The leaves had kept the rain off. Shit, he thought briefly, and rose on to all fours to scuttle towards the cleft. The shotgun cleared its throat and spat pellets into the trees above him. A few clattered down in the distance like spent gravel but he was into the deep part of the ravine by then and shaking, trying to stifle a cough that threatened to turn into a spew of acid from his empty and protesting stomach.

'Why don't we find a good clearing, Malchek, and face off

ten paces back to back? Nice and clean?' Edison's voice taunted from the woods over his head.

'Stick it up your ass,' Malchek muttered, and began to slide cat-footed along the mushy bottom of the ravine, wet leaves clumping his boots into snowshoes. 'And while it's up there, pull the trigger,' he added quietly.

The ravine was a fake promise. It was running out, shallowing at the other end before it gained him the advantage he wanted. Can't go down, how about up? He lifted his head and tipped it back and back, his eyes climbing trees that had no tops. Forget it. The trunks of the redwoods ran straight up with no taper, rough enough for a foothold but too broad for a grip. What I need is a baby one, maybe only five hundred years old. There were other trees mixing in here, too, where a logged-out gap had left enough light to give them a chance. And a gap would give Edison a chance too.

What's that bastard going to do? What's he doing *now*?

It was very quiet overhead. He's sure as hell doing *something*, Malchek decided. Where's my trusty Indian sidekick? Down at the trading post getting drunk on firewater, probably. All I have is this urban attitude to get me by. I could use a nice fire-escape, or a third-storey window. The butcher is out of practice. I haven't been keeping my knives sharp.

He began to move again, his back against the side of the ravine, feeling the bottom rising to meet the lip until the overhanging fronds grazed his hair with damp, tentative fingers. A fresh shower of moisture scattered over his face. End of basement. First floor: animal droppings, dead leaves, fallen branches, ladies' lingerie, step to the rear of the elevator, please. Was Edison waiting at the top here, or back there where he'd heard the twig snap? And which way was he facing? The light still wasn't good, five-thirty by his watch and the trees adding their own gloom. It had to be a long dawn here at the bottom of the pond.

He pulled the handkerchief-wrapped rock from his belt and, leaning slightly forward, pitched it side-arm as far and as hard as he could back down the ravine. It fell softly on the mat of leaves, sounding successfully like a football. Edison's shotgun roared, deafeningly close.

Jesus Christ, he's right over my head, Malchek realized, and went up over the edge, pressing his briefly bought advantage. He had a glimpse of Edison braced behind a redwood with the shotgun pointing away, before his own crashing progress announced the rush. The muzzle of the shotgun swivelled with incredible speed towards him, and Edison let fly.

Cunning bastard, he was waiting for that, Malchek grudged as the edge of the load caught his shoulder. He threw himself into the bush and began to move low and fast, while blood spread from the holes in his upper sleeve. The damage was superficial and he ignored it, letting the pain slide out of the other side of his mind. I can still run like shit. Watch me. At least it's light enough to avoid the goddamn trees. What the hell is *that*?

It was a sign. Civilized, green metal with white lettering, and an arrow. 'Fern Canyon' it said, and there was a path running directly underneath it, wide enough for two to walk side by side, and worn clean by a thousand tourist steps.

'Gee, Hazel, will you look at these goddamned trees?' he grunted, pelting down the path and hearing the crash of Edison coming on behind. 'Ain't you glad we come up here and seen it for ourselves? They'll never believe it unless I take a snap, you stand over there by that big one and smile.'

He passed the imaginary Hazel, smiling blindly into the imaginary camera, and found himself sliding down a very real set of rock steps that the kindly Park Service had placed for Hazel's patent-leather slingbacks. Unfortunately the steps proved more of an obstacle than an aid. Rain had licked their surface clean and treacherous. He nearly lost the rifle and skidded halfway across the stream at the foot of the little canyon before he could regain his balance and turn to run back against the inner wall, pressing himself into the mass of ferns that hung there in a swaying green curtain.

Watch that first step, Hazel, he warned silently, it's a bitch. He waited for Edison to slam into view.

Nothing.

Maybe he'd stopped to have his picture taken too.

The hell with Reddesdale. I catch one glimpse of Edison and I'm going to shoot both his eyes out. Come on. Come on.

Still nothing.

Shit, shit, double shit, triple shit with raisins. Come *on*.

Fake out. OK. He wasn't coming. Yet. So let's us elves find a mushroom to hide under.

He began to sidle along the wall, the bitter smell of the crushed ferns making him want to sneeze. Was this the place we were in last night? She saw more than I did, I was back in Nam about then. But she did say cave, didn't she? How long is this thing? Long enough to have a name and a sign all its own, wide enough for the ever-helpful Park Service to put stepping-stones over the deeper reaches of the stream, big enough to get plenty of tourist traffic in the summer. He hunched along, his eyes working into every crevice, every shadow that looked a little darker, a little deeper than the one next to it. There? Was that it? On the opposite side of the stream, of course. It would be. What do you want for free, a tank and bazooka battalion? Yes. OK, do it. Do it *now*.

He tried to leap across the stream and crashed painfully against the far side of the ravine. His fingers scrabbled at the ferns, then ripped at them until he fell through the opening Clare had felt the night before. Dry dead ferns smoked up around him in a dusty billow and blended into the haze of his own exhaustion.

Still no sound from Edison, but he was out there all right.

Malchek had avoided splashing into the stream, and he had not been exposed for more than a moment while scrambling into the cave, so maybe it would be all right. He turned himself round like a dog, in a circle, manoeuvring the rifle vertically in the confined space. It couldn't really be called a cave, it was more a split in the rock, but he was completely hidden by the ferns that had dropped back over the triangular opening. Would Edison be looking for a break like that? He'd disturbed the ferns more than he should have in his panic to find the place, but with any luck the shadows and the profusion of fronds would cover most of the damage.

He settled down to wait, and instantly his fever tried to take over. Sitting still, he could gradually get breath back, but the bands were still tightening round his chest, and periodically his vision swam with strange distortions. The stream seemed to swell and subside. The far wall advanced and retreated like a moving curtain. He felt in his pocket for the thorns.

At first Clare thought the footsteps were Malchek's. But as they drew closer she realized there were too many. Edison's men from the back of the semi? They were breathing hard, and she heard a low curse in Spanish. She huddled into as tight a ball as she could, afraid to peer out, afraid not to. In the gloom it was so difficult to ...

She didn't recognize the first one, the little one. But the rest were like coming home. Brand, Tetson, Gambini and Gonzales. 'Stay low, they'll come to you,' Mike had said. Oh Mike, you were right. You were right.

What should she do? Stand up? Shout? What if they thought she was Edison and fired at her before ... no, they wouldn't do that. They knew she and Mike were here, didn't they? But they were moving past, moving away. Suddenly she saw the heap of loose change Mike had left on the ground. Scooping up the mixture of dimes and quarters, she threw them with all her might at the backs of the men. The noise was not great, but it was totally unexpected in that semi-silent forest. So was the result, so far as Clare was concerned. All the men turned, practically as one, and she was looking into five guns, ten eyes, and a lot of ragged nerve-ends.

'Mike?' It was Gonzales's voice.

'No, only Clare,' she whispered, and began to slide out belly-flat the way Mike had done. She'd just got to her feet when they heard the crack of a rifle followed a moment later by what sounded like a machine-gun. They stared at each other.

Nobody knew what to say.

Then Clare snatched Brand's rifle from his startled grasp and began to run towards the sound.

It was ten minutes before Edison came, and Malchek nearly missed seeing him because he was dividing his attention between watching the floor of the canyon and pushing the thorns inside his boots. Only an impression of something moving too fast against the rest of the forest brought his eyes up to the top of the ravine and so to Edison. He was sidling along about two feet back from the edge of the gap, the shotgun tilted down and ready. He was going as quickly as he could, his eyes flicking back down the cut, watching.

Malchek nodded approval and put his boot back on. Trying to get ahead of me, very good, very good. His approval did not interfere with his aim, but a rolling rock under Edison's foot did. The rifle bullet caught him not in the knee, as Malchek had intended, but along the ribs and past the lower lobe of the left lung.

Edison yelled and this time went back under the force of the shot. Malchek released the trigger and squeezed again, but the second bullet went over Edison's head as he dragged himself into the thick brush. Malchek lowered the sight and fired blindly into the moving, threshing branches.

Not knowing whether he'd made a hit or not, he burst out of the cave and splashed back across the stream, coming to rest under the overhang, listening to the sounds from above. He thought he could count on a few minutes' respite while Edison got over the first shock of being hit. No, the big bastard was still moving away, crawling and cursing.

OK, baby, I've slowed you down, that's something. Malchek's mind raced as he looked left and right, trying to decide which was the shortest way to gain the top again. No telling, it all stretched away equally, no change in level to give a clue. One thing's certain, I'm *not* going straight up. Edison might not expect the obvious, but he adjusts to it fast enough. Anyway, I couldn't make it.

He began to run back the way he had come, staggering and lurching with the renewed effort. The stay in the cave had weakened rather than rested him, his muscles had relaxed past the point of easy return, and keeping his breath was a fight all its own. Twice he had to stop or faint, the world going round in time to a major organ recital swelling in his ears. Finally he regained the stone steps, and half crawled up them, using the rifle as a crutch. Against regulations, of course.

The imaginary Hazel was still saying 'Cheese', there against the redwood. The shadows gave an almost oriental slant to her eyes and cheekbones. Keep smiling, Hazel, something to tell your grandchildren about. He supposed, like the tree falling alone in the forest, that she was gone when he looked away. But every time he looked back she was still there, still smiling, still watching him.

Up, that was the answer. The classic sniper placement.

Edison would take a little while to get over that hit. He'd kept moving to get away from Malchek's immediate threat, but once he had adequate cover he'd stop to assess things. Five minutes, maybe three, for shock and reorientation. But the rate at which he'd been able to move away said the wound wasn't serious.

The path was working for him this time, curving back to parallel Fern Canyon, and he prayed Edison had not dragged himself this far before stopping. At last he found his position, a young fir, about thirty feet high, bracketing the path with a stunted oak. He hoped he could make the leap to the lowest branches, but his chest and head were getting bad.

He leaned down, fished the pocket-knife out of his boot, and opened it. Driving it into the tree as high as he could reach, he pulled himself up to it, held on, then repeated the process.

The thorns in his boots were keeping him awake all right, but by comparison with the rest they were mosquitoes. He was running out of everything. Please, God, get me up this god-damn tree. I am climbing Jacob's ladder, only I don't want to go *all* the way, OK? The rifle had lost its sling, and he had to keep pushing it up ahead of him. The needles of the tree penetrated his sweater and pants with infuriating pricks and stabs. Good, it all helps.

He could not get as high up as he wanted, there was just no way. Accepting his limitations, he settled himself astride a fairly thick branch and struggled to find support for the rifle. It took all his concentration just to keep from pitching down through the branches to the path below. When it felt as secure as he could make it, but not good enough, not nearly, he forced himself to stillness. He had a firing swing of about sixty degrees, and he could pull the rifle free and relocate if he had to. He hoped he wouldn't have to.

He couldn't believe it when Edison's first shot rang out, shattering the branch above him and sending splinters of wood showering down over his shoulders. He'd gone back to the machine-pistol.

'Possum up a gum tree,' said Edison from somewhere to the right. Too late, realization hit Malchek. The encroaching shadows of his own fever had deceived him. It was not dark in the woods any more. The sun had been rising steadily, and the young fir was not nearly dense enough. Moreover, it stood against the bare trunks of the redwoods, not other firs. There was no confusion in the background. The growing light must be silhouetting me, and Edison lucked on to just the right place at just the right time. Listen, God, you're playing dirty tricks on me again, Malchek complained silently, and began firing into the brush at his right, steadily and inexorably covering the area where Edison's voice had originated. No good. When he finished the clip, Edison would finish him off easily. He had to get down. Fast. And there was only one way.

When the clip was finished, he just let go. Slowly at first, then gathering momentum, he slid from branch to branch, jarring the tree and himself, holding the rifle close to his chest and tucking in his head, trying desperately to control the attitude of his body as it cracked from branch to branch. The ground came up like a fist and connected.

He was flat out on the path, no breath, no cover, and no way out.

Which would it be, the shotgun or the pistol? Remembering Edison's face at Spider Meadows, he reckoned the shotgun. In the head, if he was lucky. But he hadn't been lucky for a long time now.

The air was coming back at last, he had half a breath to go on. With agonizing slowness he began to flex his legs, trying to get leverage, trying, trying. The rifle slid from his grasp. There was something very wrong with his left shoulder. Whether it was the impact of the fall or the earlier grazes of the shotgun pellets, or just the betrayal of a body with nothing left in it, he didn't know. All he knew was that the rifle had to stay behind, and he had to go.

Close before his eyes, the ferns had tremendous clarity. He could see every separate, delicate scale, the dark spores on the backs, the pale stems and the wisps of grass and other plants between. The ground was a mountain range, and an ant busily crossed in front of him as he crawled painfully and desperately into the green bank. Beneath the oak. Beneath the redwoods. Beneath the impossible pale-pink sky. His mind spun.

Remember, remember. You're the hunter, not the quarry. Never think like the victim, only like the hunter. Turn it around, turn it around, you jackass. If Edison has a clear view of you, what's the probable alternative?

I have a clear view of Edison.

I'm not lying here to die, I'm lying here to kill.

The noises were close now. Very close, but, slow, and he knew that Edison was in trouble too. There was a chance.

His fingers groped along his body towards the .38 on his hip. He knew it was there, the holster was digging into his belly, twisted around by his fall but still holding its deadly load. And maybe *that* was why he had never gone over to a clip-on. He liked to thread the belt through, he liked the gun tight against him, the way it was now.

Too tight.

There wouldn't be time to pull it free. If he wanted to stop Edison he had only seconds now. And that meant only one alternative. He'd have to shoot past his own body, maybe even through it, to reach the target.

'It was a good game, wasn't it, Malchek?' Edison's voice had a sing-song lilt, he was happy, he was so happy. 'Wasn't it? I move, you move, we move. Can you stand up? Stand up, then, and take it facing me. It's beautiful, we're beautiful, don't you see it? None of the others will ever know what we know, or have the power to *decide* who lives and who dies. It's a kind of purity. Maybe a kind of holiness. We're golden hunters, you and I.'

Edison was coming along the path. Even though Edison's words were wild with triumph and exhaustion, Malchek knew his gun would be rock-hard and steady.

He wished he could say the same about his own.

'But now the end has come, hasn't it?' Edison went on sadly. Regret was in his throat like a toad in a hollow log. '*My* decision, finally. As it had to be. You knew that, didn't you?'

Edison was a massive shape on the path, as big as the redwoods, as big as yesterday's thunderheads, towering, threatening, smiling, coming on.

Praying that what his fingers told him about the position of the .38 was true, Malchek fired.

Searing flame crossed his belly and the shock of the explosion under his ribs pushed an involuntary scream from his throat. He'd missed.

Edison was still smiling, still coming. And then, from somewhere behind him, Malchek heard one sharp, sudden shot. A rifle. Blood gouted from Edison's left thigh as he screamed once and then collapsed on the path, twisting and curling his body foetus-like around the pain.

Malchek, too, lay sobbing and gasping in the ferns. If only the .38 had been canted two degrees higher he would have hit the big man in the gut and finished him. But that would have meant two degrees deeper into his own body, and he'd never have known whether he'd won or lost. Now someone had given him his chance. Gambini? Terson? Some nameless park ranger? Somebody had put Edison at his mercy at last. But he had to make sure now. *He* had to end it.

Things were blurring, whirring, he could hear the ant's feet thudding in the distance, monstrous ant, monstrous wood. The pain surging through him was like someone else trying to get inside his body, trying to take up the space inside his skin with acid and ice, squirming and sliding, trying to take over.

He could not stand, so he crawled. Closer and closer to Edison who still rolled and moaned out there on the path, spreading blood in wider and wider arcs around himself.

Sensing Malchek's approach, Edison turned his head and his eyes rolled wildly, his mouth spitting out a stream of curses.

Malchek reached for the lichen-streaked bark of a tree beside the path, his fingers grazing then grasping the rough surface, his hand finding the living bark and clinging to it. He pulled and pushed himself up, towering in his turn over the sprawled man whose madness still spun in his eyes.

Leaning his numbed shoulder against the tree, Malchek reached across his charred sweater and pulled the .38 out of the split holster. It was not fever or delusion that racked him now. It was simple anger. A pure, burning anger beyond anything he'd ever known in his life. Neither obsession, nor hate, nor guilt, nor any other complexity. He was just so goddamn fucking *fed up* with the whole thing.

Flight, pursuit, waste. Stupid waste, all of it. People afraid, people dead, all because of this moaning, dirty thing on the ground.

'A kind of holiness, you said? Like gods? Well, maybe you fly high on that kind of religion, freak, but I don't. I never did.' He lifted the small, blue-black menace of the .38 higher so that Edison could have a good look.

Edison tried to grab his feet, but Malchek kicked out at his face and laid him back against the path. Taking a breath and a step together, he brought his foot down heavily on Edison's right arm just above the elbow and shifted his weight inexorably forward. He heard the bone crack and Edison screamed again, trying to grab at him with his free hand, the fingers snatching helplessly at the bottom of Malchek's jeans.

Taking careful aim, Malcheck emptied the remaining bullets of the .38 load into Edison's arm, starting next to his own foot and working methodically towards the hand which shattered under the impact of the fourth and final shot. Edison screamed and then, suddenly and convulsively, was still.

'There you are, "god",' Malchek murmured conversationally. 'Afraid you won't be doing any golden hunting anymore. And you'll have to learn to wipe your ass from the left.'

He dropped his empty gun on to the path. The thudding footsteps of the ant were still in his head, its many ant feet pounding closer, closer. Louder. Too loud.

He turned and accepted without question the apparition that came towards him. Reddesdale, Terson, Gambini and Gonzales running down the path. Trailing behind them, far behind, came Brand and Clare. She was crying, leaning dazedly against the sheriff, who was carrying a rifle. Why was she crying? It was all over now.

Other men appeared. It was like the scene of some accident, faces and eyes staring. Perhaps the trees had spawned them. They had all stopped. They were all watching him. Expecting something more. What?

Reddesdale decided, in that frozen moment, to return to his desk and stay there. Something had passed him by in this forest, something moving fast, and he could no longer call it back.

Edison lay silent in a sprawl of blood. Malchek was a gaunt, mud-smeared scarecrow swaying above him, clothes torn and blood-soaked, long hair wild, eyes glaring hot above a twisted smile.

'Maybe they can teach him to knit one-handed,' he suggested helpfully, taking a step back and then a step forward.

Gonzales caught him as he fell.

twenty-three

He was late. He hurried down the hall, fumbling for the gleam of new brass on his keyring. He unlocked the apartment door, but had a hard time getting it open. The wing of an armchair projected beyond the edge, and he shoved it against the carpet until he could slide it through the narrow gap.

'Hey,' he called. 'We don't have to build blockades anymore, remember?' He dragged the armchair to approximately where it belonged and looked around. She'd been painting since she came back from the office. Again. And there was something else . . .

Clare emerged from the bedroom warily. 'Do you like it?'

'Any time. Especially in the shower . . .'

'I meant the new lamp,' she smiled, coming over and lifting her face for his kiss. He kept one eye open and located the lamp on the corner table.

'I'm crazy about it,' he finally said into her neck.

'Mmmmmmmm . . . especially when you put the soap . . .'

'I meant the lamp.'

'Oh.'

He chuckled, kissed her ear, then turned away to sink into

the armchair with a grunt. When he had loosened his collar and accepted the drink she made him, Clare nudged him over so she could perch on the arm of the chair.

'How was it?'

'You smell like turpentine.'

'Seventy-five dollars an ounce. Did they give you a hard time?'

'No more than I expected. Between Halliwell's obligatory lecture on insubordination and half the guys in the duty room crabbing because we didn't invite them to the wedding, it was above average to lousy.'

'How do you feel?'

'Average to lousy.'

She ran a finger down the side of his face and underneath his collar, loosened it a little more, and began to rub the back of his neck. He let his head drop forward. 'That's nice. That's good.'

'Maybe you went back too soon. Another couple of days . . .'

'No, I feel OK. I just wanted you to feel sorry for me. You're very willing when you feel sorry for me. I've been considering hypochondria as a hobby.'

'I'll bet.' She got up and went into the kitchen.

He twisted in the chair to get out of his jacket and tossed it towards the sofa. It missed. Dropping an arm down, he picked up his drink from the floor and took a slow swallow, savouring it.

'How was Gonzo?' she asked above the clatter of plates and pans.

'Same as always. A certain air of reproach hung around the place until I told him I was sorry about . . . all of it. He was so stunned he bought my lunch.'

'I thought you were against apologies on moral principles.'

Malchek smiled down into the ice-cubes. 'So did he.' The condensation was running down the outside of the glass, dripping on to his knee and making damp circles. 'I may get free lunch all week at this rate.'

She clattered a little while longer, then came to stand in the doorway, blowing on to a wooden spoon. 'Did they put you on assignment yet?'

'Oh, sure. Nothing fancy, just an eight-hour watch.'

'Daytime?'

'To start with, yeah. Protective custody case.'

There was a silence. 'If she's pretty I'll make a scene.'

'It's a he. Don't worry about it.'

'OK.' She went back into the kitchen.

'It's Edison,' he said after a moment, moving the glass to make more intersecting rings.

She reappeared without the spoon, and came slowly into the room towards him.

'But why?'

'Why does Edison need protection? Because he's in a position to buy himself treatment by talking, and he knows it. So do all the people who've employed him in the past. Jail's too chancy, obviously, so it's protective custody. A safe house. I'm the resident expert on that they tell me.'

'But why *you*?'

'It's Reddesdale's order.'

'But that's terrible. It doesn't make sense. I mean ... Edison hates you ... you hate him ...'

'No, I don't hate him. Not now. When Brand dropped him he became everybody's property, not ours.'

Clare opened her mouth to correct him, watched him lifting the glass and drinking, the taut throat both vulnerable and strong. It didn't matter. She bent down and picked up his jacket as he went on reflectively.

'And ... I don't suppose he hates me. They've got him calmed down, he's in a wheelchair, it's all over so far as he's concerned. If he can't fly, he's not an eagle. I guess it's a test for me. Or maybe a penance. Anyway, it's Reddesdale's going price for my hanging on to a gold shield. And I *want* to hang on to it, Clare. It means a lot to me.'

'Oh, Mike ...'

'Honey, I could have been out on my ass in a flash for any one of the dumb things I did. Or busted to black and whites with no explanation necessary. This way, I learn a lesson. Maybe I need it. I think I probably do.' He reached up and pulled her on to his lap. 'Forget your righteous indignation, babe. It's my mountain, not yours.'

After a few minutes she looked up into his face. 'OK.'

He grinned, appreciating her effort, and ruffled her hair. 'How does the glamorous copy group head feel about going to bed with a tired cop?'

'She'd have to turn the stove off first.'

'Then why don't you go do that?'

She smiled and slid off his lap. As he stood up and stretched, he noticed the pile of letters on the mantelpiece. He looked through them and found it. 'What's this from Pacific Gas and Electric – twenty-three dollars eighty-eight? We've only been in this place three weeks.'

'It says connection costs, stuff like that,' she called from the kitchen, then came in and turned the light out behind her.

He ran his eye down the lines of computer typing. 'Oh, yeah, I see.' She came up behind him and reached round to start unfastening his belt-buckle.

'You aren't going to let a little thing like an electricity bill get you down, are you?' she murmured into his shoulder-blade.

'Not while I've got a little thing like you to get me up, no.' He allowed her to finish with the buckle, then turned and started pushing her gently towards the bedroom. 'Remind me to write out a cheque for them before I go in tomorrow.'

She glanced over her shoulder and slowed. 'You're a quick payer, aren't you?'

He considered, nodded his head, reached out.

'I've decided it's easier, in the long run.'

Wilbur Smith
Hungry as the Sea £1.20

His latest bestseller.

Through shipwreck and hurricane, through the ice-world of
the Antarctic and the thundering surf of the African coast,
in the arms of the lovely Samantha and on the bridge of his
powerful *Warlock*, Berg is a man in his element. Deposed as
top man in a huge shipping consortium, he's running a debt-
ridden ocean-going salvage outfit – fighting back against the
ruthless ambition of the arch-rival who stole his wife and son and
robbed him of an empire – hell-bent on retribution . . .

'Surges forward with a bone in its teeth'
TIMES LITERARY SUPPLEMENT

Douglas Fairbairn
Street 8 80p

Street 8 is on the wild side of Miami. Here the sleepy Florida
resort becomes a violent Latin metropolis run by the anti-Castro
gunmen fighting for '*La Causa*'. Bobby Mead, used autombile
dealer, has a wayward teenage daughter who has friends in this
dangerous community, and other problems of his own . . .

'A thunderous *tour de force*' OBSERVER

'Taut, tight, gripping . . . one expects no less from the
author of *Shoot*' NEW YORK TIMES

Piers Paul Read
The Upstart 95p

Son of a poor Yorkshire parson, Hilary Fletcher grows to manhood
with a deep loathing of the smug and privileged upper
classes, intensified by his humiliation by the wealthy Metherall
family. In his revenge, he breaks legs and ruins marriages, drives
a childhood friend to bankruptcy and seduces the friend's teenage
sister. Hilary becomes a burglar, a pimp, a murderer – a
self-made monster steeped in evil and debauchery . . .

Raymond Chandler
The Long Good-Bye 90p

'Alcohol is like love. The first kiss is magic, the second is
intimate, the third is routine. After that you take the girl's clothes
off . . .'

The first time Marlowe met Terry Lennox, the man was drunk —
the second time, even drunker. Marlowe meant to ask why he'd
had his face reconstructed, and the rest of his life story. He
didn't ask him, but if he had it just might have saved a couple
of lives . . . Then there was Captain Gregorius, the sort of cop
who solved crimes with a night-stick to the base of the spine . . .

'Grips the mind from the first sentence . . . tense as a tiger
springing into action' DAILY TELEGRAPH

The Little Sister 90p

When she walked into Marlowe's office she looked just the part,
a pathetic but appealing small-town girl from Manhattan,
Kansas. Marlowe sensed something phoney about her — then all of
a sudden his telephone came alive with the sultry voices of
movie stars, the slurred tones of gangsters, the clipped phrases of
the police. Every call led him into something deeper than the last . . .
maybe he'd be better off without clients from Manhattan, Kansas . . .

The High Window 90p

'Mrs Elizabeth Bright Murdock and family wanted to hire a
nice clean private detective who wouldn't drop cigar ashes on
the floor and never carried more than one gun . . .'

Marlowe met Mrs Murdock on a hot afternoon in her palatial
residence. She had jet buttons in her ears and a bottle of port on
the sidetable. She also had a secretary. Pretty girl. Quiet sort —
scared three parts out of her wits . . .

Dick Francis
Risk 85p

His new bestseller.

'An amateur jockey who won the Cheltenham Gold Cup is kidnapped, beaten up, bamboozled and its almost the last page before you find out why' DAILY MIRROR

'Dick Francis holds his form like a top-class chaser . . . a joy to see him back in the field' TIMES LITERARY SUPPLEMENT

Dorothy Uhnak
The Ledger 80p

Enzio Giardino is big-time Mafia – the boss of a million dollar narcotics outfit, with the Special Investigation Squad on his track. The way in to the kill is through Elena Vargas, one-time mistress to Giardino and hard-as-nails hooker . . . which makes a drugs case into a woman's-angle job, and Christie Opara takes up the assignment. Soon the lady detective and the Puerto Rican prostitute have more than a little in common . . .

'Detective Opara is going to become one of fiction's most popular police people' SUNDAY MIRROR

The Witness 80p

Billy Everett was a black civil rights leader – one gunshot later he was a crumpled corpse. The man with the still smoking gun was a cop. Detective Christie Opara had seen the real killer thrust the gun into the cop's hand. Now she had to stalk that killer through the city's longest, hottest, deadliest summer . . .

'Continuously lively and absorbing' SUNDAY TIMES

Ed McBain
Jigsaw 70p

There's nothing like a little homicide to give the 87th Precinct a shot in the arm. Or the chest, as the case may be ... Detectives Brown and Carella had themselves a puzzle with six missing pieces. Put it together and there's $750,000 for the taking.

In this case bodies were easy to find — clues came a little harder ...

'McBain's so far ahead of police-procedural writers that its virtually a one-horse race ... Hyper-readable, witty, credible' SCOTSMAN

Fuzz 80p

With the temperature 12 below zero there was nothing good happening in the 87th Precinct — but for the usual quota of muggings, rapes, knifings and burglaries.
And then the city officials began to get killed off one by one ...

'The best of today's procedural school of police stories — lively, inventive, convincing, suspenseful and wholly satisfactory' NEW YORK TIMES

Long Time No See 80p

Usually it's cold and bleak enough on the Precinct in November to keep the crazies off the streets. Then someone does a knife number on a blind, black beggar. A second killing takes out his blind, white wife, and a third puts one more blind victim in the Precinct morgue. If only, just this once, Detectives Carella and Meyer could get a corpse to talk ...

'The best 87th Precinct, as well as the longest, for several years' SUNDAY TIMES

Agatha Christie
The ABC Murders 70p

'Let us see, Mr Clever Poirot, just how clever you can be . . .
Look out for Andover on the 21st of the month . . .' The
letter disturbed Poirot greatly. It was written by a killer – and in
deadly earnest. Sure enough, a Mrs Ascher was murdered at
Andover on that date. A second letter announced a second murder
at Bexhill, then a third, followed by a fourth at Doncaster . . .
Beside each corpse lay a copy of the *ABC Railway Guide* . . .

Francis Iles
Malice Aforethought 80p

'It was not until several weeks after he decided to murder his
wife that Dr Bickleigh took any active steps in the matter . . .

'*Malice Aforethought* has become a landmark of crime, a
classic of murder and retribution . . . Iles commands understanding,
even sympathy, for this henpecked, paltry little man with his
daydreams of self-assertion . . . his way of escape
. . . his blunders . . . struggles . . . and his emotions when
tried for his life' TIMES LITERARY SUPPLEMENT

George Fox
Amok 95p

He lives like a wild beast – kills like a professional executioner:
they call him the Amok . . .

When the Japanese forces evacuated the Philippines in the
last bloody months of the war, one man was left behind – a
renegade giant capable of nightmare violence and terrifying
brutality, armed with a razor-edged Samurai blade, and ordered
to delay the enemy advance as long as possible. Three decades
later, he is still killing – a murderous spectre haunting the lives
of every man, woman and child in an isolated island community.
He's the reason that two men have returned to the Philippines –
one has come to kill him, the other to save him.

Sidney Sheldon
Bloodline 95p

The day her father died in a climbing accident, Elizabeth
Roffe inherited his empire – a giant pharmaceutical industry
operating across the globe. But soon it's clear that someone,
somewhere wants her dead. There's one person she can turn to –
Rhys Williams, her father's second in command and the man she's
always loved – but is he too a suspect?

'Sheldon is a writer working at the height of his power'
NEW YORK TIMES

Alan Scholefield
Venom 80p

A house in fashionable Eaton Square – and a policeman dead
of shotgun wounds. The hostage, a sickly boy, only son of a
wealthy family; the demand, a small fortune; and the kidnapper is
a former OAS gunman – already wanted for murder. Inside the
the house there's another factor – one of the boy's pets is loose,
and it happens to be a black mamba – the deadliest serpent
known to man...